MURDER AT ARCHLY MANOR

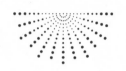

MURDER AT ARCHLY MANOR

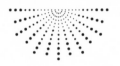

SARA ROSETT

MURDER AT ARCHLY MANOR

Book One in the High Society Lady Detective series

Published by McGuffin Ink

ISBN: 978-0-9988431-6-2

Copyright © 2018 by Sara Rosett

Cover Design: Alchemy Book Covers

Editing: Historical Editorial

Map Illustration by Hanna Sandvig: bookcoverbakery.com

Newsletter sign-up for exclusive content: SaraRosett.com/signup

❀ Created with Vellum

ACKNOWLEDGMENTS

Thank you to my wonderful Patreon supporters,
Margaret Hulse and Connie Hartquist Jacobs.

The definition of supporter is "an adherent, follower, backer, or advocate." You've been all those things to me and it means so much to me!

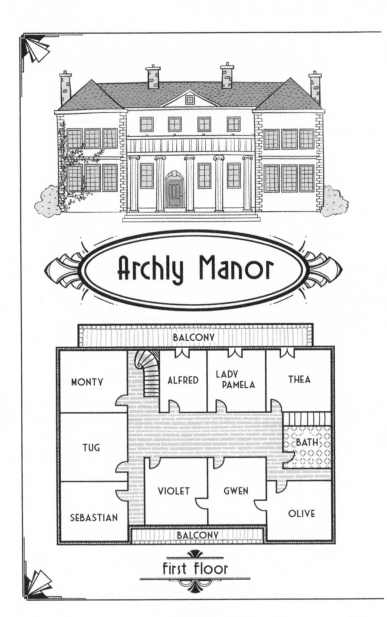

Archly Manor

BALCONY

| MONTY | ALFRED | LADY PAMELA | THEA |

TUG

BATH

SEBASTIAN | VIOLET | GWEN | OLIVE

BALCONY

First Floor

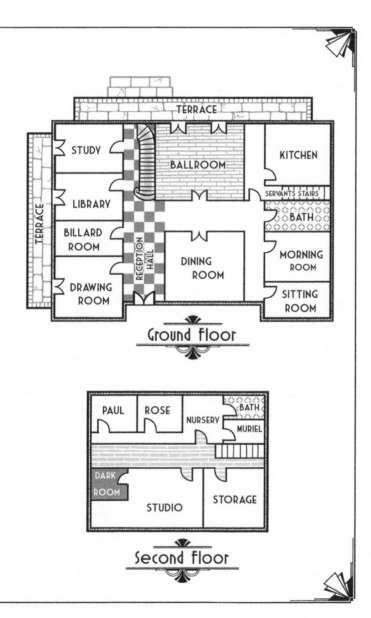

Ground Floor

TERRACE

STUDY

LIBRARY

BILLARD ROOM

DRAWING ROOM

TERRACE

BALLROOM

RECEPTION HALL

DINING ROOM

KITCHEN

SERVANTS STAIRS

BATH

MORNING ROOM

SITTING ROOM

Second Floor

PAUL

ROSE

NURSERY

BATH

MURIEL

DARK ROOM

STUDIO

STORAGE

CHAPTER ONE

I didn't intend to become a lady detective, but when one's relative is swept into a police investigation and the outcome looks rather grim—well, one can't stand aside. One must do something.

The tragic death at Archly Manor was widely reported in the newspapers. The coverage wasn't surprising. A murder in high society always draws attention. Unfortunately, the articles were a combination of exaggeration and innuendo, which is why I felt I must set down the facts . . .

London, Summer 1923

*O*ne might suppose a well-bred young woman with a good education wouldn't have any difficulties finding employment. At least, that's what I'd supposed, but I discovered those assumptions were wrong—*quite* wrong.

On an overcast morning in late July, I had stepped off the train from my little village of Nether Woodsmoor into the bustle and busyness of London, confident that within a few days I would be one of that fascinating breed, the working girl, striding off to put in a day's work, knowing a paycheck was not long off.

My view of the situation had been quickly brought into line. It had been a rather abrupt descent from the heights of my expectations to the depths of reality. I had become familiar with the shallow veneer of apology that accompanied the words, "Sorry, but we don't have anything for you."

But today would be different. I was seated on the other side of the desk from a newspaper editor as he looked over my article. His closed office door barely muted the clacking typewriters and the loud conversations from the newsroom. I realized I was twisting my handbag in my lap, causing the decorative beads to strain against the threads that held them in place. I released my grip and pressed my gloved hands against the folds of my skirt.

Mr. Clark, editor of *The Express,* hadn't even bothered to perch his pince-nez on his nose to read the sample article I'd labored over the night before. Holding his glasses in the air a few inches in front of his eyes, he skimmed down my handwritten story that described the Duchess of Seton's ball. The fact that his lips didn't twitch meant he didn't even get to the incident involving Barbara Clairmore's sash, Kippy Higgenbotham's nearsightedness, and the melting ice sculpture.

He raised his head and extended the paper across the desk. "I'm sorry—"

I scooted forward to the edge of the chair. "I'll work for you for a week for free."

He rattled the paper. "The last thing I need is another society girl reporter."

Despite the mugginess of the day that made the room stuffy, a chill twisted through me. The newspaper was my last resort. I hadn't contacted Mr. Clark at *The Express* when I first arrived in London. I'd applied for other jobs. Father would not be too pleased if I became a reporter. And Sonia—I could hear her strident voice. "So unladylike! So unseemly. So *beneath* one of our class." Yet, it was work I could do. I could write. If Essie Matthews, who never wrote one of her own essays at boarding school, could write a society column for *The Hullabaloo*, then I should be able to land a job at *The Express*.

Mr. Clark shook the paper at me again. "You'll only clutter my desk."

I kept my hands in my lap and leaned forward. "A fortnight. Give me two weeks to prove I can do it. You won't regret it."

He swept his pince-nez over his desk, nearly toppling a pile of papers several inches high. "Do I look like I need more articles?" His tone became more severe. "I did a favor for Sir Leo. I spoke with you. Now I need to get on with my work." He tossed down the paper.

I stood. He remained seated, his attention already fixed on a typewritten page from one of the stacks. I was tempted to snatch up my article and tell him exactly what *The Express* would miss out on, but Mum's words rang in my ears. "Good breeding always shows."

I picked up the article and resisted the urge to crunch it into a ball. I folded it neatly. "Thank you for seeing me. I'll tell Uncle Leo what a pleasure it was to meet you."

I don't know whether or not he picked up on the sarcasm in my voice. I didn't wait to see his reaction. I swept through the racket of the newsroom but slowed when I reached the quiet of the wide staircase. Disappointment weighed down my shoulders and worry gnawed at my insides. I could put on a good show for Mr. Clark for a few moments, but the reality was rather bleak.

What was I going to do? Even with careful management, I could only stretch my funds for a little over another week. Soon I'd have nothing to pay Mrs. Gutler, and she'd been clear—she didn't provide charity. "That's for the church, not working women," she'd said when I'd taken her poky little attic room.

Two men hurried up the stairs to the newsroom, their faces intent. They both raised their hats, and I managed a brief nod as I continued down the stairs. Until I'd seen Mr. Clark's disinterested face, I hadn't realized how much I had been counting on working as a reporter. I had canvassed every relative, friend, and acquaintance I could think of who might be able to help me find a job. Since Mr. Clark of *The Express* hadn't come up to snuff, I had no other options. No one had inquired about the Position Wanted advertisement I'd been running since I'd realized finding a job wouldn't be easy. I could only buy a newspaper and scour the Positions Vacant section again, something I'd done without fail for more days than I could count.

As I rounded the landing and continued to the ground floor, I realized I still clutched my sample article in my hand. *You could always go home.* The thought whispered through my mind. It would be so easy to go back to Nether Woodsmoor. I considered it for two steps, then I stuffed the article into my bag. The beads swayed, and I shook off the thought of returning to Derbyshire.

I wasn't going home. It wasn't home. Not anymore, not with Sonia pushing her way in and trying to erase every trace of Mum's existence at Tate House. I would just have to keep at it. I squared my shoulders and marched across the lobby, my heels clicking over the mosaic of a sunrise. I'd keep at it until my last shilling was gone, at least.

I pushed through the heavy glass door into the stuffy afternoon. A thick layer of dark clouds trapped the heat like a lid on a jar, sealing the humid air around the city. I trotted down the shallow steps and turned in the direction of the tube station, wishing that it would rain even though I'd forgotten my umbrella. A shower would clear the air.

My steps checked as I passed a tea room. A hunger pang twisted in my stomach as I looked through the window at a table spread with scones, clotted cream, little cakes, and delicate sandwiches. I forced my feet to move. Threepenny worth of buns would have to do until the morning, when Mrs. Gutler would serve breakfast and helpfully remind me how many days were left until rent was due.

I bought a newspaper from the boy at the corner, then continued down the street toward the tube entrance, which was several blocks away. A few fat drops of rain plopped onto the sidewalk. Within a few steps, they increased to a patter, and a crack of thunder split the air. The drops became an all-out deluge, and I scurried toward a fruit stand awning, using the newspaper to shield the bit of ribbon and two ostrich feathers on my side-rolled hat. Rain splashed onto the back of my neck, and the white ties on my bow collar fluttered as I ran.

Other pedestrians were also scurrying to cover, and I bumped into a dark-suited chest in the crush as I rushed under the edge of the awning.

"Pardon me."

"Excuse—" I looked up into familiar gray eyes under hooded lids. "Jasper! I didn't know you were in London. I thought you were in . . . somewhere foreign. I can't remember where. Africa? Or was it South America? Don't you recognize me? It's me—Olive Belgrave."

His face cleared. "Olive! I haven't seen you in an age. You look so different with your hair chopped off."

We shook hands, and I said, "It's so good to see you. You're looking well."

"And you."

As more people joined the crowd, I was pushed up next to Jasper with my nose nearly in his chest. I hadn't seen him for years—not since before the war. When my cousin Peter came home to spend the holidays at Parkview Hall, he'd always brought Jasper along. Jasper's parents were in India, and Jasper said he preferred Parkview to shuttling between his "various dotty aunts" as long as Aunt Caroline and Uncle Leo didn't mind him visiting, which they didn't. When I was fourteen, I'd had a tiny and short-lived crush on him, but he'd treated me exactly like he treated my other cousins, Gwen and Violet.

He'd never given me the easy win when we played croquet on the lawn. He'd never hesitated to cut me out at the tea tray either, snatching the last bit of cake or sandwich just before I reached for it. Worse, he'd mastered the ability to instantly look as innocent as a cherub in a Renaissance painting after swiping it. His wavy fair hair and clear gray eyes had helped create the illusion of blameless innocence, but it was his innate charm that sealed the deal—especially with the women. Everyone from Aunt Caroline down through Cook to the lowliest scullery maid would do anything for him.

But he was different now. Physically, he'd come through the war unscathed. He had rotten eyesight and had been refused each time he tried to join up. He had spent the war working in the depths of some government building for the Admiralty. In one of Peter's rare bursts of conversation a few years ago, he'd said he'd had a letter from Jasper. Jasper had been demobbed and was now the gent about town.

Even if Jasper hadn't spent time on the battlefield, he'd changed—not as much as Peter, but lines marked his face around his eyes and mouth, replacing that cherub-like quality with something colder and more distant. From the occasional tidbits of gossip I'd heard, Jasper seemed to be living a bit recklessly, running with the crowd of Bright Young People whose names often turned up in the society pages—and not in a good way either. The papers were all too happy to chronicle their excessive drinking and flamboyant displays of wealth.

A man dashed under the awning and bumped Jasper's shoulder. We shifted an inch closer to the piles of apples. "Last I heard, you were off in foreign places yourself," Jasper said. "Your mum's alma mater in America, wasn't it?"

"I was. I'm back now." Mum had been American. She'd attended a women's college before she visited England and met my father. Her short visit extended to months and eventually a wedding. She returned to the States for visits, but she'd insisted I should have a "real" education after attending finishing school with my cousin Gwen and coming out. Mum was adamant that there was no better place for that education than her old university. I'd always thought it was just a fond idea of hers, so I'd been surprised when Father had told me that she'd set money aside for my education before her death. It had been tucked away for years gaining interest and would be more than sufficient to fund my travel, tuition, and lodging.

The familiar simmer of anger burned in my chest at the thought of that fund. It had been so securely watched over for so many years, and then to have it all gone, whisked away in a foolish "investment." Despite all the chatter about dividends, potential, and interest, Father might as well have tossed it on a bonfire.

"Didn't enjoy it?"

Jasper's words snapped me back to the present. "Oh, yes. I quite liked collegiate life. Suited me down to the ground, but I had to return."

Rain drummed on the canvas overhead, running in rivulets off the edges and splattering to the pavement. I shifted closer to a stack of cabbages to keep the splashes from soaking my beige stockings and panel skirt.

"Yes, I was sorry to hear about your father's illness," Jasper said. "How is he?"

"Quite well, thank you," I said, glad Jasper thought I was in England because of my father's health, not because I couldn't return to America. The truth about my financial situation was out in the little village of Nether Woodsmoor, but apparently the news hadn't traveled all the way to London. "Father's still weak and has to take it slowly, but he's recovering."

"I'm glad to hear it. And I understand congratulations are in order?" The rain abruptly shifted to a light patter, and a few people darted out from under the shelter of the awning.

I swallowed my true thoughts about my father's new wife and forced out the appropriate words. "Yes, thank you. I'll pass your felicitations along."

The thought of Sonia always caused me to grimace, and I must not have completely succeeded in hiding it. The corners of Jasper's mouth turned up and the skin around his eyes crinkled as he smiled, which took away some of the new severity of his face, making him look younger and more relaxed. He tilted his head closer to mine. "You don't have to pretend with me. Familial discord is a subject I have a long acquaintance with."

"I didn't hide that well. Must work on that." I looked around, but no one was paying attention to our conversation.

He saw my glance, and added, "I'm rather good at keeping secrets, too."

"As I well know," I said, thinking of a warm summer afternoon, the drone of bees, and the unexpected slap of cold water when I fell into the river.

"I'll add this one to the list," he said in a confidential tone, and a familiar twinge of warmth glowed in my chest.

Perhaps I wasn't completely over that crush. But that was silly. I was a grown woman, not a moony schoolgirl. "It's not exactly a secret, at least not at Tate House."

"Ah, I see. Thus, London," he said. "The grand city called to you, did she?"

"With an incredibly loud voice."

His eyes, which could be so lazy and reserved, took on a piercing quality as he ran his gaze over me. I was very aware of my mended cuffs and that my Cuban heels had definitely seen better days. I took in the excellent cut of his suit and the quality of his gloves. Compared to his sartorial splendor, I must have looked down-at-the-heels. "I'm just on my way to tea," he said. "Will you join me?"

"That would be lovely."

He offered his arm, and we set off down the street. "I passed a tea shop not too far back," I said.

"Oh, I don't think so. Far too plebeian."

"Not your style?"

He looked at me out of the corner of his eye. "I do have a reputation to maintain." He smiled. "No, that's not it at all. Reestablishing an old friendship calls for something a bit grander. The Savoy, I think."

CHAPTER TWO

$\mathcal{I}$ savored the last bite of peach Melba and sighed with contentment. Once the food began to arrive at our table at the Savoy, the music and tea dancers and the hum of conversation faded out of my awareness. I didn't pay nearly as much attention to Jasper as I did to the scrumptious scones and the delicate cakes and sandwiches. I put down my spoon. "That was delicious. So delicious, I'm afraid I haven't been a good companion."

Jasper took a sip of his tea. "It's perfectly fine. It's good to see a woman actually eat. I don't see how you society girls survive. Most exist on tea, champagne, and an occasional cucumber sandwich. And then they dance all night. It's astounding, really."

"It's these fashions." I gestured at my narrow dress. "Everyone is reducing now. Of course, when one is hunting for employment, traipsing all over the city and scraping to make every shilling last, it's easy to fit into a frock like this." There was no point in trying to hide anything from Jasper now. Even though he lolled in his chair and his hooded gaze roamed over the restaurant lazily, he was astute. After my unladylike consumption of every morsel placed in front of me during tea, he was perceptive enough to deduce my circumstances.

He asked, "Financial difficulties?"

"Haven't got a bean, not really. I thought it would be easy to find a position as a governess, but it was the same every time. When I sent my references and explained my background, it always seemed so promising. But once I actually met the families, everything changed. No one was interested."

"I daresay not."

"Why do you say that?"

"I doubt there are many mistresses who like the idea of inviting a young woman like you into their homes."

I lifted my chin. "What do you mean? That I'm not qualified?"

"No, I meant you're far too attractive."

A blush heated my cheeks, and I toyed with my spoon. "I'm sure that wasn't it."

Jasper laughed. "Oh, I'm sure it was, old thing. Perhaps if you hadn't cut your hair and were able to scrape it back in a tight bun, and if you wore some dowdy clothes . . ." He tilted his head as he studied me. "No, you'd never be able to disguise those eyes."

I raised my eyebrows, surprised. He wasn't speaking in his usual disinterested tone. He settled back in his chair, and his voice shifted to a lighter note. "That's where you went wrong, obviously. You should have mentioned it all up front. 'Attractive female with arresting navy blue eyes seeks governess position.' It would have saved you hours of bother."

"I shudder to think what sort of replies I would get to an advertisement like that."

He grinned. "Yes, of course. Totally inappropriate."

"Yes. In so many ways."

"I'm sorry. I shouldn't make light of it." He sobered. "You've tried other avenues?"

I shifted straighter in my chair. "Clerk, shop attendant, cashier. But no one sees a young woman with a classical education and extensive training in how to be a lady as a good candidate for those positions. My eyes are no help to me there either. I even applied to work as a domestic, but I was told it wouldn't do—that I would cause problems in the servants' hall."

"Indeed, you would." Jasper leaned over the table. "You'd be wasted polishing silver and answering the door. What you need is something that will let you use that first-class brain of yours. You always ran rings around me and Peter when your father tutored us."

"Unfortunately, no one else seems to think my brain is appropriate for their vacancies. If only I had trained to be a typist or secretary. I would enroll in a class to learn Pitman's shorthand, but that will take longer than I have."

"That desperate, is it? Surely you can return to Tate House?"

"No, I'm not going back there. It's awfully grim. Sonia—my stepmother—doesn't want me in the house. She's decided the local curate will do nicely for me."

"Not a good specimen?"

"He has a huge Adam's apple that bobs up and down in such a distracting manner that I can hardly think of anything else when I speak to him. And then he's nervous and—well, to be perfectly honest, he perspires awfully. He's a nice fellow but not for me."

Jasper took a cigarette case from his pocket. "Yes, you need someone other than a sweaty curate." He held out the cigarette case to me.

"No, thank you."

He snapped it closed. "I'd forgotten your asthma." He pocketed the case.

"No, it's fine. It's gotten so much better in the last few years. Don't skip on my account." Cigarette smoke did sometimes trigger a tightness in my chest. And occasionally being under a strain brought on a feeling of shortness of breath, but I'd had fewer incidents as I'd grown older.

Jasper shrugged. "I'll wait until later. So you're determined to avoid Tate House?"

"Sonia is such a managing female—she was a nurse. You know how bossy they are. I'm sure that if I returned to Tate House, she'd maneuver it so that the banns—with the curate or anyone else—would be read in a fortnight. And I won't have that. I won't be managed."

I realized my voice was too strident and a few people had looked my way. I relaxed my shoulders and leaned back in my chair. "I may have to sell the Morris." My birthday fell a few days after Gwen's, and for as long as I could remember, Uncle Leo had given us both the same gift. Last year it had been motors, Morris Cowleys. Mint green for Gwen and forget-me-not blue for me. It was far too extravagant. When I'd protested, he'd said gruffly, "Caroline and I feel like you're one of our own. Let's not hear anything else about it." The motor was one of the few things of significant value that I owned. Well, other than Mum's pearls, but I wasn't selling those no matter what.

"You have it in London?"

"The Morris? No, it's in Nether Woodsmoor. In dry-dock, so to speak. It's not running, and I don't have the funds to fix it." Father was stony, and I wasn't about to ask Uncle Leo for the money. It was one thing to give a gift; it was quite another to have to maintain that gift. It was probably fortunate it had broken down shortly before I decided to set off for London. I wouldn't have had the money to garage it in town.

"Have you thought of—"

A shriek sounded behind my right ear, and a thin woman in yellow chiffon swept into view. She pulled up short beside Jasper's chair. A matching turban covered her head except for a few perfectly formed golden curls that curved against each cheek, framing her aquiline nose. Kohl lined her close-set green eyes, and her lips were bright red. "Jasper, darling. What a treat to find you here."

Jasper stood. "It's a pleasure to see you as well. Lady Pamela, this is a good friend, Olive Belgrave. Olive, Lady Pamela Withers."

Lady Pamela barely bothered to turn her head. "Delighted." She tapped Jasper's arm. "Now, do tell me you will be at Sebastian's Silver and Gold party." She pointed a red lacquered finger at his chest. "And don't tell me that you didn't receive an invitation, because I specifically told Sebastian to send you one."

"Commanded it, did you?" Jasper asked.

"Of course. And Sebastian always does what I want. Most men do," she said in an aside to me.

"Not I, I'm afraid," Jasper said. "I have a previous engagement."

Lady Pamela's red lips puckered into a pout. "Break it off. You know Sebastian's parties are divine. You can't miss it, darling. You'll regret it forever if you do. Oh, there's Thea. I must fly." She took a half step away, then looked back over her shoulder. "So nice to meet you . . . Olivia."

"Olive. Olive Belgrave," I said, but Lady Pamela was already sailing away, her chiffon rippling.

I raised my eyebrows at Jasper as he sat down.

"I have no excuse or explanation," he said. "That is the infamous Lady Pamela."

"I have heard of her."

"And probably not in a good way," Jasper said. "She runs with a fast set."

"About your speed, isn't it?"

"You ask too many questions, Olive."

"On the contrary. We've talked about me the whole time. Terribly rude of me. Tell me what you've been doing since I saw you last."

"Nothing of significance. I totter down to the club then totter home most days. Occasionally I exert myself and go to a frivolous party. I'm frightfully useless. When the Communists take over, I'm sure I'll be one of the first sent to the gallows."

"I don't believe that for a moment—that you don't do anything useful. I've known you for years. You might look as if you're lazing around, but your mind is always busy—planning and plotting. Now, tell. I know you must do more than read the newspapers and play cards at your club."

His manner changed, and the easy rapport between us evaporated. Even though he didn't move an inch, it felt as if he'd physically shifted his chair away from me. His voice was light, though. "I assure you I'm a boring old sod now."

"I still refuse to believe that. Now, the truth."

His eyes narrowed. "All right . . . let me think. You mean something useful, I suppose? Hmm, thought so." He tapped the table. "Here's something—I dabble in the arts."

"You always were excellent at caricatures."

He looked shocked. "Not me, my dear girl. I sponsor artists." He looked at his watch, which was in the new style, a strap on his wrist. "I'm afraid I must be going."

"Have to get to your club for your afternoon snooze?"

"Wicked girl," he said. "I should have known you'd make fun of an old man. Have you no respect for your elders?"

"I do, but you're far from elderly."

As we departed the Savoy a few moments later, Jasper said in a serious tone, "I'm sorry about your . . . difficulties. I will keep an ear to the ground."

"For someone looking for a well-read and well-bred young woman with no typing or shorthand skills. Good grief, when I say it aloud like that, it's a wonder anyone would want to hire me."

"Don't sell yourself short."

"Right. I have a first-class brain. I'll be sure to put that in my Situation Wanted advertisement, right under the line about my eyes."

He adjusted his hat. "I can see now that you're not going to let me forget that, are you?"

"Never."

"Very well. I'll let it be a reminder not to give unsolicited advice. It rarely goes down well—giving advice, I mean, solicited or unsolicited," he said, but I didn't take him seriously because he had a definite twinkle in his eye.

He walked as far as the tube station with me where we said goodbye. I rode home in a blissfully sated state. It had been weeks since I'd had a proper tea. When I arrived at the boarding house,

Mrs. Gutler handed me a small envelope. "I hope it's not bad news."

A cold wash of fear hit me. All I could think of was the telegram I'd received in America from Uncle Leo with the news that Father was seriously ill and I should return to England as soon as possible.

We had all lived in dread of these little envelopes during the war. The words inside could change the course of one's life. Thankfully, the one that had arrived about Peter had informed us he'd been injured, not killed. But my cousin Gwen had received one from the family of her fiancé with the news that he was missing. I ripped the envelope open before my thoughts could get carried away.

It was from Gwen.

Need your help. Urgent. Return to Parkview soonest.

CHAPTER THREE

$\mathcal{R}$oss, the chauffeur from Parkview, opened the door of the estate's saloon motor. "Are you quite sure you don't want me to wait?"

I stepped onto the drive of Tate House. "Yes, go on to Parkview with my bags."

He closed the door and scratched his hairline. "Are you sure?" Since Parkview's chauffeur hadn't returned from the Battle of Loos, Ross had taken on the additional duty of driving the estate's saloon motor. He'd changed out of his gardening clothes into a pair of faded slacks and a jacket to meet me at the station in Upper Benning, but he hadn't been able to scrub the dirt from under his fingernails. "I'm happy to wait." He looked up at the clear blue sky.

"No, you go on. I'll enjoy the walk to Parkview after this," I said, my gaze going to the gabled house, which stood in the shade of the towering trees that surrounded it.

"All right, miss." Ross touched his cap, then opened the driver's door, his tone indicating he thought I was stepping out of bounds. In his mind, guests arriving at Parkview should be driven from the train station in the motor. They shouldn't traipse through the countryside on their own. His attitude wasn't the old-fash-

17

ioned one of unquestioning deference. But things weren't as they once were, especially not since the war. Of course, Ross had known me since I was a little girl playing with my cousins at Parkview Hall. When we tromped through his gardens, Ross hadn't had any qualms about yelling at us to get out of his flowerbeds.

I watched until the motor disappeared around the bend in the steep drive and the trees hid it from view. I turned to Tate House. I would have rather gone directly to Parkview to see Gwen, but I couldn't arrive in Nether Woodsmoor and not visit my father, which meant I also had to see Sonia. I squared my shoulders.

The front door was unlocked, and I went inside. The airy landscape paintings were gone from their usual spots in the entry hall. A new flocked wallpaper in a pea green shade covered the walls along with a heavy gilt mirror. A stack of paintings rested on the floor, turned to the wall. I recognized the size of them—they were the landscapes, except for the last, larger one.

I flicked through them. I tilted the large one away from the wall, anger bubbling in my chest. I sucked in a breath. It was the painting of Mum. She stood in the garden, a pair of clippers in one hand and a bunch of roses in the other. Her bright smile radiated out from the painting. It had been Father's favorite and had hung in his study.

I gently let it fall back against the wall. This was Sonia's doing, I was sure. I went down the hall to the coolness of Father's study and inhaled the familiar aroma of aged leather. Underlying the scent of old books, was a new smell—beeswax.

I stopped short. Father wasn't at his desk . . . and the desk was clean. Instead of papers scattered across the desk and piles of books teetering on the corners, the desktop was empty except for a desk lamp. In fact, the whole room was tidy. No discarded newspapers littered the chairs in front of the fire, and the usual jumble of magazines and books on the side tables had been cleared away. If I needed more evidence of Sonia's forceful nature, it was here. From the time Father had received a legacy from a distant uncle, which allowed him to retire from being a vicar and move to Tate House to work on his Bible commentary, he'd never allowed anyone in to clean his study.

A voice floated through the open French doors at the back of the study. I made my way across the room, circling around the polished desktop where my father had spent so many hours working on his commentary. The terrace was empty, so I walked around the corner of the house to the little grassy enclave tucked up against the south wall, which had been one of my favorite places to spend a summer afternoon. Father sat at the wrought iron table, his papers and books spread in front of him with various rocks, shells, and a bit of amber weighting down the pages.

He looked up at my approach, and a smile broke across his face. "Olive! Did you tell us you were coming?"

"No, I had a telegram from Gwen yesterday and came straightaway." The cost of the train ticket had cut deeply into my meager resources, but I couldn't ignore a plea from Gwen. I'd reasoned I'd save on food while I was away. And I wasn't making any headway in London. A couple of days away wouldn't set me any further back—I was already about as far back as a girl could get.

I kissed his cheek and drew a chair over to sit beside him. "I'm staying at Parkview for a few days." I'd sent a telegram to Gwen and arranged it.

Voices again drifted through the air, and Father looked down to the garden. "The jobbing gardener is here, and Sonia is with him, giving him instructions. I'm sure she'll be along shortly." Tate House was situated at the top of the wooded hill that overlooked Nether Woodsmoor. The drive and the front of the house were thickly treed, but at the back of the house, the land sloped down in a series of terraced gardens. Mum had spent many hours in the gardens designing the cascades of flowers that flowed down the hillside.

"Don't disturb her on my account."

Father's face was thinner and his cheeks looked gaunt. His skinny neck poking out of his loose collar reminded me of a turtle's neck, wrinkled and vulnerable, as it cautiously extended its head. Father removed his wire-rimmed spectacles and rubbed his eyes. Without his glasses, he looked more helpless than I liked to think he was.

The voices moved closer, and I distinguished Sonia's strident tone. ". . . want those rosebushes moved to the south side of the house . . . espalier . . ."

I looked at Father. "You're letting her move Mum's rosebushes?"

"Tate House is her home now."

Anger sizzled through me. "So you're going to allow her to wipe away everything, change everything? Remove every trace of Mum? There'll be nothing of Mum left by the time she's done. I saw she's taken down Mum's portrait."

He placed a papery hand over mine. It was light and birdlike, and I felt a pang as I remembered how sick he had been. "We have our memories of your mother. That's the most important thing. I thought you'd like to have the portrait. Sonia is sending it out to have it cleaned."

"Oh." My flurry of emotion cooled a bit at the thought of owning the painting.

"Sonia can't take away the memories we have," he said. "Those will always be with us. Rosebushes are just . . ." He shrugged his bony shoulders. "Rosebushes."

I knew he was right, but I didn't like the situation. I placed my hand over his. "You make it difficult to argue with you. You're much too commonsensical."

Sonia came up the steps from the garden. As she stripped off her gloves, she caught sight of me, and her steps checked. Her mouth was naturally set in a downturned curve, but now her expression deepened into a frown as she came across to the table and put down her gloves. "Olive, we didn't know you were coming." She made it sound like an accusation.

"No, it was rather unexpected."

Father said, "Olive is spending a few days at Parkview."

The frown eased slightly. "How nice."

A breeze stirred the leaves overhead and ruffled the pages of an open book in front of Father. He reached out to hold the book open at the point where he was reading, but Sonia beat him to it, deftly placing a marker at the page. "It's time for tea. It should be along shortly." She closed the book and stacked it with the books on the table. "You mustn't overdo it."

I tensed, waiting for his protest. Father never willingly left his studies. I'd often had trouble coaxing him to come to dinner, even when we were expecting guests. But he only smiled and replaced his glasses. "Of course, my dear."

I gave a mental shake of my head, marveling at the changes Sonia had brought about in the short time since she had become mistress of Tate House. Tea arrived, brought by a maid I didn't recognize. After she left, I asked, "Is she new? I don't recognize her."

"Yes," Sonia said. "I'm training her up. Susan left for London last week." Sonia handed me a teacup. "Someone put ideas into her head. No one wants to stay in the country anymore, even in a nice position such as this. They all want to go and become factory girls."

This was clearly a barb aimed at me, and I opened my mouth to defend myself. Father cleared his throat. "And how do you find London, Olive?"

"Yes, have you found anything?" Sonia asked in a tone that indicated it would be beyond the bounds of believability for me to say anything other than *no*.

"Nothing firm, but I have several possibilities."

Sonia's eyebrows flew up. "Oh, you're so much in demand that you can't decide which job to choose?"

I lifted my chin. "I'm sure I'll have some exciting news in a few weeks."

Sonia focused on passing a slice of seed cake to Father, and I shot a look at him as guilt pricked me. He was the most easygoing and usually absentminded of men, but there were certain things that he simply could not and would not abide, like lying, hypocrisy, and cheating. But he was taking the piece of cake and didn't notice what I'm sure was a guilty look on my face.

Sonia selected a sandwich. "I only hope you find a respectable position. Something in an office or a bank. Since you *insist* on working, you must consider your position and how it reflects on your father."

Father said, "Olive always makes me proud. I'm sure whatever she finds to do will be perfectly suitable."

Sonia adjusted the elaborate lace cuffs at her wrists. She wore a long-sleeved white shirtwaist with a high neck. It was tucked into a skirt that fitted tightly about her waist, an ensemble that was stylish a decade ago. With her puffy hair piled upon her head and gathered into a bun, she looked positively Edwardian. Perhaps that's exactly what she wanted. She was only ten years older than me. Possibly her clothes and hairstyle were a deliberate choice, an effort to convey her maturity.

Sonia inspected the sandwich and plucked off a bit of crust that hadn't been cut away. "Perhaps you can stay for dinner tonight? The curate is coming. I'm sure he would be delighted to see you again."

"No," I said. "I'm afraid Gwen has something arranged for this evening." I didn't know if she had or not, but I wasn't about to allow myself to be maneuvered into sitting beside the sweaty curate with his bobbing Adam's apple. "In fact, I should be going. Ross picked me up at the station in Upper Benning and has taken my bags on to Parkview. I'm sure Gwen will be wondering where I am."

"That will work out well. It's time for your father's afternoon rest." Sonia couldn't disguise the relief that shaded her words.

Father said, "No need to fuss, Sonia. I can rest here just as easily."

She placed a hand on his arm. "You mustn't overtax yourself.

You get wrapped up in your books and lose track of time. Before you know it, you will have done too much."

I expected Father to shake off her hand, but he sent her a look of fondness, which she returned.

I set down my cup with a snap. "I really must be going."

I gave Father a kiss on the cheek, said goodbye to Sonia, then went back through the house. I set off down the path through the trees that would take me over the bridge and into Parkview's grounds, the sun hot on my hat and warming my shoulders. That look that they'd exchanged had cut through me. It was as if they'd drawn a circle around themselves, leaving me on the outside.

For over a decade it had been Father and me. Sonia had wormed her way into that pairing and pushed me right out. I increased my pace, trying to slough off the hurt of being excluded. I turned my thoughts to Gwen. She was capability itself. Aunt Caroline was a sweet woman, but she had little interest in household management. Gwen oversaw the day-to-day running of Parkview and enjoyed the task enormously. What Gwen could want my help with, I couldn't imagine.

CHAPTER FOUR

$\mathcal{I}$ leaned over the edge of the bridge, my elbows pressed to the warm golden stone, and watched the river current as it parted and flowed around the limestone piers in a swirl of liquid movement. The swish of the water, birdsong, and the rustle of the leaves as the wind rushed through the trees were the only sounds. I pushed away from the bridge's parapet. On the other side of the bridge, the road twisted away through the trees, but I set off diagonally through the woods, a shortcut that would bring me to Parkview more quickly.

The gate in the wall that enclosed Parkview's grounds on this side was well hidden and covered in ivy, but I went to it unerringly. I pushed back a few strands of trailing ivy, then poked two fingers into a cleft in the masonry of the wall. My fingertips brushed against solid metal, and I extracted the heavy key. I unlocked the gate, replaced the key, and slipped through the gate into the dense wood. A little while later I emerged from the thicket of oaks and stepped onto the drive.

I paused to take in the elegant lines of the Georgian mansion with its portico, pediment, and divided staircase. The graceful lines of the building hadn't changed, but the grounds looked rough around the edges. The lawn around the house had been cut, but where I stood farther away, weeds poked through the gravel, and the shrubbery sprouted pointy new growth that needed to be trimmed.

In the distance, a disappearing figure in tweed and a flat cap climbed up one of the rolling hills and entered a grove of trees, two dogs trotting along beside him. I squinted but couldn't make out who it was. It could be Uncle Leo, who liked to walk the grounds to keep an eye on things. Or it could be Peter, who walked the grounds in an effort to exhaust himself so he could sleep. It seemed he was trying to outpace his memories from the war.

As I neared the house, the front door opened and a blonde figure glided down one side of the pair of curving staircases and met me, arms outstretched. My cousin Gwen hadn't embraced bobbed hair. She still parted her fair hair in the middle of her forehead and smoothed it back into a knot at the nape of her neck, but her fluttery cream-colored linen dress with a dropped sash was the latest style.

She gripped my hands and squeezed. "Thank you for coming."

"Of course. I'd never ignore a telegram from you."

Tall and lean, with brown eyes and a gentle manner, she was one of the most restful people I knew, but today her eyes were troubled. "I'm so glad you're here. It's too late, but at least you're here."

"Too late? What's wrong?"

"It's Violet."

"Isn't it always?" I said jokingly. Five years younger than Gwen and me, Violet had always been the one scampering along behind us, wanting to be involved, pestering us to do exactly what we were doing.

Gwen said, "She's always been a handful, but this is worse than usual."

"Yoo-hoo! Olive, over here." I turned. A figure in pink waved frantically from the edge of the terrace at the side of the house. "Olive, you *must* come up now. I have wonderful news."

Gwen shouted back, "Give her a moment, Violet. Olive hasn't even been to her room."

"But this can't wait," Violet said.

I waved a hand at Gwen. "It's all right. I'll go along now. We both know we won't get a minute's peace until I do."

"That's true, and I'm sure Violet will demonstrate exactly what's wrong."

We rounded the corner of the house and climbed the steps. As we emerged onto the terrace, Violet pounced on us, tucking a blue croquet mallet under her right arm and extending her left hand, fingers splayed. "I'm engaged." The square-cut diamond caught the bright sunlight and refracted it.

"Violet," Gwen said, "you haven't even said hello."

Violet tossed her head, and her short curls quivered against her flushed cheeks. Violet had the same shade of bright blonde hair as Gwen, but that's where the similarities ended. Violet was shorter and rounder than her sister, all bounce and energy.

"I can't help it. It's just too, *too* exciting. Come on, you can meet him. He's here now." She grabbed my wrist and propelled me across the flagstones to the other side of the terrace where another flight of steps led down into the expansive gardens at the back of the house. Beyond the banks of flowers, a game of croquet had been set up on a stretch of the flat green lawn. A dark-haired young man in tennis whites was toeing a red croquet ball, inching it closer to a wicket.

"Alfred!" Violet said. "Come meet Olive."

As we crossed the grass, Violet tucked her arm around my elbow and leaned close. "Isn't he handsome? He's simply the *sweetest* man *ever*. I never have to ask him to fetch me a drink when we're at a party. He always *has* one for me, just when I want it. He's a divine dancer too. *And* he has a lovely motor."

"Well, those are all the top attributes one would want in a husband," I said.

Gwen snorted, and Violet scowled at her. Alfred crossed the grass and met us, a wide smile on his face, which displayed perfectly even teeth that showed up brightly against his suntanned face. Violet released my arm and shifted to Alfred's side as she introduced me.

"Congratulations to you both," I said, aware that Gwen's frown was a counterpoint to Alfred's cheery expression.

He wrapped an arm around Violet and squeezed her in a side hug. "I'm the luckiest man in the world."

Violet looked at me. "Isn't he a dear?" She planted a kiss on his cheek. "We're going to be married in August," she said, her gaze locked with Alfred's.

Gwen crossed her arms over her chest. "Nothing's been decided yet."

Violet pouted. "Daddy's being such a fuddy-duddy. But I'll bring him around." She pressed into Alfred's side.

Gwen said, "I thought you two were playing a game of croquet."

Violet planted a hand on Alfred's chest and pushed him away. "We are. And I'm going to trounce you." She twirled her mallet and ran toward the wickets.

"Care to join us, ladies?" Alfred waved his red mallet toward the discarded mallets on the terrace. "Plenty of room for more players."

"No," Gwen said instantly. "I'm sure Olive would like to have some tea first."

I didn't think it was possible for Alfred's smile to get any bigger, but he exposed a few more teeth. "Perhaps we can play a game of doubles later."

"I'm afraid I feel a headache coming on. I'd better spend some time in the shade." Gwen marched back to the terrace and up the stairs.

I hurried to keep up with her. "Are you feeling unwell?"

She looked a little shamefaced. "My headache isn't a literal one. It's figurative." She shot a glance at Alfred as we sat at a table in the shade where tea had been laid out.

"Well, he's certainly handsome," I said.

Gwen rang for a maid, who took my hat, gloves, and handbag away to my room, then Gwen poured me a cup of tea. "I'm afraid that's his only qualification. I know it's the only one that matters to Violet."

"You forget, he also has a very nice motor and is a divine dancer."

Gwen laughed and handed me a cup of tea. I took it even though I'd already had tea that afternoon. After weeks of my stomach rumbling and growling with hunger, I wasn't about to refuse a drop of tea or a bite of food. I settled into the wrought iron chair and sipped my tea, feeling cosseted. I truly appreciated the rarefied atmosphere of Parkview, probably for the first time in my life.

On the lawn, Alfred was holding Violet's hand as she balanced on one foot to adjust the strap of her shoe. I said, "He seems to be solicitous of Violet."

Gwen watched them, then asked, "What do you think of Alfred? What's your first impression?"

"He smiles too much."

"I knew I could count on you. You're good at grasping the meat of the thing."

I grimaced. "That doesn't sound pleasant."

"It *is* a compliment," Gwen said. "I asked you here hoping you could convince Violet to slow down, to rethink this engagement. You know how she admires you. But it's too late now. She's sent off the announcements to the newspapers."

"I don't think anyone could influence Violet to do anything she doesn't want to. She seems to be set on Alfred."

"Yes, that's the problem. If Mum and I try to talk her out of it, you know she'll dig in her heels."

Aunt Caroline came up through the garden and climbed the steps to the terrace. She held her box of paints in one hand and a canvas shiny with wet oils in the other. "Oh, hello, Olive. We're so glad you could come. Careful, dear. The paint is still wet." She held the canvas away as I gave her a quick kiss on the cheek.

"It's lovely of you to have me."

She propped the painting up against the stone balustrade at the edge of the terrace, then set her box of paints on the table and dropped into a chair. The painting was a combination of blobs and splashes in bright colors. It might be the shrubbery maze . . . or possibly a turtle. I wasn't quite sure, and I knew better than to ask Aunt Caroline.

Aunt Caroline and Father were brother and sister, but if they stood side by side, there was no physical resemblance. Father was dark and on the weedy side, while Aunt Caroline was tall and fair with beautiful skin that she'd passed on to her daughters. Violet had inherited her voluptuous figure. The only thing Aunt Caroline and Father had in common was their ability to delve so deeply into their pursuits that they became absentminded and tended to view the goings-on around them with a hazy, confused air. Many a time, I had taken Father his tea in the afternoon, and he had looked up with the same expression that was on Aunt Caroline's face right now. "Tea?" she said. "I can't believe it's so late."

Gwen handed her a cup. "It is."

The croquet game continued on the lawn. The thwack of a mallet hitting a croquet ball carried through the air, and Violet's blue ball sailed across the lawn to the far side. She smacked Alfred's arm with her palm. "Beast!"

Alfred's reply floated up to the terrace. "Darling, you know I always play to win."

Aunt Caroline put her teacup down with a crack, her gaze sharp and focused. "I don't trust that young man."

One difference between Father and Aunt Caroline was that she occasionally emerged from her self-absorbed fog and came out with a statement of striking clarity. "Who is Alfred Eton? That's what I want to know," Aunt Caroline said. "He's made a few blunders—it makes me wonder."

Gwen asked, "What do you mean, Mum?"

"Did you see him when Violet introduced him? He didn't wait for me to put my hand out. He put his hand out *first*."

"Oh, Mum," Gwen said. "Don't be so old-fashioned. He was probably nervous."

"And he didn't let Violet precede him last night when everyone came down for dinner."

"Things are much more informal now," Gwen said. "You're making too much of it."

Aunt Caroline said, "Well, his behavior is ill-mannered. And that's to say nothing of his friends. That photographer—that Sebastian Blakely—he's not what I consider good company."

"Sebastian is Alfred's godfather," Gwen explained to me.

"And, more importantly, who are his people?" Aunt Caroline picked up a macaron, looked at it, and put it on her plate. "In my day, we courted at home, not out. We knew the families people came from. Alfred is so *vague*. All this about India. Just because he grew up on another continent doesn't mean he can't be specific."

"His father was in the civil service," Gwen said. "I did manage to get that out of him."

Aunt Caroline leaned over her teacup. "But does he have any prospects? As far as I can tell, he doesn't, except assisting that society photographer. And that's certainly not something you can establish a household on."

Aunt Caroline swiveled toward me. "What I want to do is hire a detective, but your Uncle Leo won't hear of it. He says you young people have to live your own lives and we should stay out of it. But I'm not going to let my daughter marry someone I don't know."

I tilted my head. "Even if Uncle Leo won't hear of it, I find it hard to believe that you wouldn't have done something on your own."

Aunt Caroline exchanged a glance with Gwen, then gave me a smile. "You always were perceptive, Olive. Yes, I have made inquiries, but really, I have no idea how to go about it. My friend Antonia told me it will cost at least several hundred pounds to hire a detective."

I glanced across the china and silver spread on the table and the elegant lines of the house soaring above us. "But that shouldn't be a problem?" Parkview might look a little scruffy in certain areas, but surely there weren't deep financial problems here?

"Oh no, dear. I can pay it out of my household accounts."

At this statement, I smiled at Gwen. We both knew it would be Gwen who paid the money out of the household accounts, not my aunt.

"I wouldn't know the first thing about how to find someone like that," Aunt Caroline continued. "I don't want to associate with that type of person—you know, someone not of our class. However, this situation with that rather oily young man must be dealt with."

I had consumed a slice of cake and several of the small sand-wiches. I felt full and content, but as Aunt Caroline's determination penetrated my tranquil state, my heartbeat sped up. I sat up. "I'll do it."

CHAPTER FIVE

"*I*'ll look into Alfred's background," I said. "If you'll consider paying me for it."

The doubtful look that had settled on Aunt Caroline's face intensified. "I don't know, dear. It doesn't seem like a good thing to do. Who knows where this will end? If he's the sort of person I suspect, you could be dealing with some unsavory characters."

"Nonsense," Gwen said. "I think it's a splendid idea. Olive has a knack for figuring things out. Remember how she found Lady Sofia's sapphires last year?"

Aunt Caroline dipped her head in a nod. "Yes, and that would have been terribly embarrassing if it had come out." She studied me for a moment. "I'd forgotten that incident."

Gwen said, "Olive is perceptive and clever. All she needs to do is talk to a few people and find out if what Alfred says is true."

Gwen's words boosted my confidence. She was the sweetest of cousins and tended to be generous to a fault, but she didn't throw out false praise. I turned in my seat so that I was facing Aunt Caroline. "I don't mind doing it. In fact, I would appreciate the chance to do it—as a job. Truthfully, it's looking positively bleak in London."

"No prospects?"

"None." It was much easier to be honest with Aunt Caroline than it was to be with Sonia and Father.

"Well, I don't suppose it would hurt if you asked a few questions." Aunt Caroline gave a small nod and shifted her chair backward. "Yes, give it a try. If nothing else, I can hire a private investigator later." A look of distaste passed over her face, then she brightened. "Hopefully that won't be necessary. Do you think fifty pounds would be enough to start?"

I choked on my tea but recovered. "More than adequate. In fact—"

"If this is to be a proper job, you must have a retainer." Aunt Caroline picked up her macaron. "Gwen, you will be a dear and take care of it, won't you?"

I felt the weight on my shoulders ease. I'd be able to pay my rent and even have a nice dinner.

"Of course, Mum." Gwen lifted the teapot to refreshen our cups. "I knew asking Olive down was a good idea. I'm sure she'll have it sorted out in a few days. How will you begin?"

"I think the place to start is with Alfred himself."

SPEAKING to Alfred proved to be a challenge. Violet and Alfred wanted to be together. That is, they wanted to be together *alone*. I had a devil of a time even finding them after they finished their game of tennis, which they'd switched to after croquet. I was seated off the far end of the table from them during dinner, so I couldn't talk with either one of them then, but I finally ran them to ground in the drawing room after dinner.

They had escaped to the far side of the room. Arms touching, they occupied a settee as they looked through gramophone records. Violet was determined we would have dancing after dinner despite being short on eligible men for partners. Peter had sent his excuses and dined in his room, and Uncle Leo had flatly refused to participate. "Not light on my feet at all, as your mother will tell you," he'd said. Aunt Caroline had confirmed the truth of the statement in the matter-of-fact tone of a long-married woman.

I took a chair beside Violet and offered to hold the records they rejected. After chatting about their tennis game for a few moments, I asked, "Violet, have you met Alfred's family?"

She didn't look up from the albums. "Alfred doesn't have any family."

"Oh, I'm sorry—"

Alfred bumped his shoulder against Violet's. "You mustn't say it so abruptly, old bean. It shocks people."

Violet raised her head, her eyes wide. "But it's true."

"Yes, it is, but you can't toss it out there so casually." He turned to me. "It's perfectly fine. Don't look so horrified. My parents died in a ferry accident in India."

Violet handed me some records. "Nothing but opera and classical music. It's a terribly tragic story—about Alfred's parents, I mean. He's all alone in the world now."

"Except for you, Vi." Alfred sent her a smoldering look, and Violet looked up at him from under her eyelashes.

I cleared my throat. "So you have no other family at all? No one to invite to the wedding?" I hoped talking about the wedding would gloss over my nosiness.

Alfred handed a record to Violet. "This one isn't too bad," he said to her. To me, he said, "My father was an only child, as was my grandfather, who has also passed, along with my grandmother. My mother was an orphan. Their history has a sad beginning but a happy ending because they found each other. They met before my father sailed for India and married within a few weeks."

"And they never returned to England?"

"Didn't want to. I didn't either until last year, when I had a letter from my godfather. He'd heard about the ferry accident and invited me to come back to England."

"Sebastian is a dear," Violet said. "Even if he doesn't want anyone else to think so. He's always saying really cutting things—

very harsh and critical—but he's been incredibly sweet to Alfred. He helped Alfred find his flat in South Regent Mansions, and he's taken him on as a photography assistant."

"So this is the society photographer, Sebastian Blakely?"

"Yes. He takes the most *beautiful* photographs. He can make anyone look good."

"That is a valuable skill, I'm sure."

Violet squeezed Alfred's arm. "You must get Sebastian to teach you all his tricks. Then you can set up your own business, and *you'll* have all the stuffy society matrons insisting you take their photographs."

"He might think that was a bad turn, you know," Alfred said to Violet.

"All's fair," she said with a wave of her hand.

I said, "In love and war, I believe."

"I'm sure it applies to business too," Violet said, focused on the records again.

Alfred shook his head and looked amused. To keep the conversation going, I asked, "So you hadn't met Mr. Blakely before you got his letter?"

"No, but I thought if I was ever going to visit England, it might as well be then. There was nothing to keep me in India. I wasn't sure what to expect, to be honest. But I must say, Sebastian's been grand. Helped me get set up and introduced me around." He sent another look toward Violet.

Before they could get lost in their lingering glances, I said, "India must be a fascinating place. What did your parents do?"

Alfred reluctantly pulled his gaze away from Violet. "Father was in accounting. He had a post in the civil service."

"So where did you live?"

Violet tapped my leg with one of the gramophone records. "He's already told you, silly. In India." She emphasized each syllable as if I were hard of hearing.

"I meant in which city in India?"

"In Delhi."

"What was it like in Delhi?"

"Insufferably hot."

Violet dropped the last of the records onto her lap with a moue of discontentment. "These are all so stodgy." She sighed. "At least we have Sebastian's Silver and Gold party to look forward to. Are you going?" Violet asked me.

"No, I don't know him."

"Oh, that doesn't matter. Sebastian won't care."

"But I don't have an invitation."

Violet waved her hand, brushing away my objection. "It's not one of those starchy old-fashioned parties. You can come with us. It's a Saturday-to-Monday. We're staying with Sebastian at Archly Manor. I'm sure he won't mind if you come. The party is Friday night, and you need to wear something silver or gold. Gwen is coming too—although I'm sure it's only to keep an eye on me. She doesn't usually go to his parties. If you're there, that will give Gwen something to do besides glower at me. Sebastian's parties are the *absolute* best. Last time we played charades, and it was screaming."

"That wasn't technically charades," Alfred said.

"Oh, I know, but it was the most fun I've ever had playing charades." Violet bounced a bit as she shifted toward me. "We were utterly stumped and had guessed every *possible* thing, so Sebastian went upstairs to his studio and came back down wearing a dress, gloves, a wig, and a monstrous hat dripping with flowers. Then he had poor James—that's Sebastian's secretary—lie down on the sofa. Then Sebastian went into this whole act of mincing over and shaking James's hand. Sebastian was Queen Mary!"

"Sounds as if Sebastian is quite the character," I said.

"Oh, he is. I'll fix it up with him for you to come with us." She swung toward Alfred, her face bright. "I know—you could play something for us on the piano."

Alfred said, "Then we wouldn't be able to dance together, silly goose."

"Oh. Yes, that's true. Never mind about dancing, then. You can play, and we'll sing a duet. Something fun." She grabbed his hand and pulled him up. They left me with stacks of gramophone records in my lap.

Alfred was a talented piano player and sang well. He and Violet serenaded us for the rest of the evening. As soon as the party broke up, I went upstairs and sat down at the writing desk in my room. I took a fresh sheet of paper and wrote down everything I'd learned about Alfred. It was a pitifully short list, but it was a start.

OVER THE COURSE of the next two days, I did my best to casually bring up Alfred's background, his time in India, or his parentage. But each time, I couldn't pin him down to anything more specific than what he'd already said. The only details I could get from him about India were that it alternated between horribly hot weather and horribly rainy weather. He'd had a happy childhood in Delhi. His father had enjoyed his job as an accountant, and his mother had thrown herself into colonial society.

I couldn't draw any further information from him, not the name of a friend or acquaintance, anything more specific about his father's job, or even the location of where his parents had met. Over the breakfast table on Friday morning, I renewed my attack. Alfred was eating an egg, and Violet, who was seated at his side, was buttering toast.

I said, "I'd really love to hear more about your time in India, Alfred."

Violet paused with her knife in the air. "I never knew you were so interested in India, Olive. What's brought this on? Are you thinking of going out there yourself? I've heard it's much easier to find a husband there."

Aunt Caroline, who had been going through the morning post, dropped her envelopes and flashed a warning glance at Violet.

"The weather is lovely, and I think it will hold. Should we picnic today?"

Violet said, "That would be spiffing."

"Violet, please," Aunt Caroline said. "Don't use those horrible slang terms. It's not ladylike. Will you go with us on the picnic, Olive?"

"It sounds like a wonderful afternoon, but I have to pass. I have other plans."

I went upstairs, rang for a maid to pack my bag, then went to see Aunt Caroline when I thought she'd be finished with breakfast. I found her in the morning room checking her painting supplies, which she planned to bring on the picnic.

"I'm off to London," I said. "I don't think it's a good idea to press Alfred for more details. It's getting rather awkward."

Aunt Caroline paused, her hands bristling with paintbrushes, and sighed. "Yes, as Violet demonstrated this morning. But what will you do?"

"I'll visit South Regent Mansions. See what I can find out there. I'll try to confirm when he moved in and find out who visits him, that sort of thing."

"Yes, I suppose that's the next logical step."

"Gwen will pick me up tomorrow, and we'll meet Violet and Alfred at Archly Manor for the party."

"I'm not pleased about that party—such extravagance doesn't seem appropriate. So many people are facing such difficult times." She tucked the brushes into her box. "But I know better than to throw obstacles in Violet's way. She'd picture herself a persecuted Juliet at the first opportunity."

"A wise decision, I think. She'd play the role with gusto. I'll let Gwen know anything I discover."

"Excellent," Aunt Caroline said without looking up from her paints.

❧

"SOUTH REGENT MANSIONS," I said later that afternoon as I settled back against the seat of the London taxi. The fifty pounds that Gwen had counted out of the household account resided in my handbag, which I held securely in my lap with both hands clasped over it. *Fifty pounds!* It seemed an enormous amount. A few years ago I would have thought it a trifling sum, but after scrimping and counting every shilling, I had a new appreciation for the value of a pound—and I now had *fifty* of them.

The taxi zipped by a dress shop with scrumptious little hats and beautiful frocks. I turned my gaze to the other side of the street and squashed a sigh of longing. The money was for the investigation into Alfred. I couldn't spend it frivolously. A taxi ride was the most my conscience would allow. Well, and maybe a good dinner. Transportation and food were legitimate expenses.

The taxi pulled up outside the undulating facade of South Regent Mansions in Mayfair. If Alfred could afford to live here, he was certainly doing all right. I paid the driver and gave a generous tip. How wonderful it was to not have to be stingy.

CHAPTER SIX

*N*ot ever having bribed someone, I wasn't quite sure how to go about it. I suspected stating the fact that I was offering a bribe would be gauche, so when the hall porter at South Regent Mansions repeated that he really couldn't say anything about Alfred, I opened my handbag and edged out one of the five-pound notes. Perhaps I should offer *two* five-pound notes? No, better to start low. I glanced around the elegant proportions of the entry hall, which was deserted, but I was sure it wouldn't stay quiet for long. I squeezed the crisp bill in my palm. It made a satisfactory crunching sound as it crinkled. The porter's gaze darted down and lingered on the note.

"Are you *sure* you can't tell me anything else about Alfred Eton?" The hall porter had confirmed Alfred was, indeed, a resident, but that's all he would say.

"No, miss." With his narrow forehead, wide cheeks, and a mustache that covered his upper lip and traced down each side of his mouth, he reminded me of a walrus. His narrow shoulders and broad hips only added to the effect. "I really couldn't say, miss." He slowly drew his gaze away from the money. "I've only worked here a month. Mr. Eton moved in before I came, so I don't know when he arrived."

"What about friends and associates? Mr. Eton must have an occasional visitor."

He smoothed his extravagant mustache while he thought. "No, nothing that would be appropriate to share." The lift rattled and began its descent. The porter looked to the front doors, clearly ready for me to leave.

I narrowed my eyes. "Is it a woman who visits him? Is that why you don't want to talk about it?"

"Wouldn't be right," he said with a note of finality.

I extended my hand. "Thank you for speaking to me."

His eyebrows went up slightly in surprise, but he reflexively reached out to shake my hand. I pressed the note into his palm. "Perhaps you could keep an eye out and let me know if anything changes. I'll drop by again soon." It was hard to tell with the mustache, but I think he smiled.

Not the outcome I wanted, but at least I might have an ally in South Regent Mansions. As I strolled through Mayfair, I considered how to enter that exchange in my expenses. Aunt Caroline wouldn't be happy to see *bribe* listed. Perhaps *incentive pay*. Yes, that sounded much better.

I walked until I came to a telephone box, where I made two calls. First, I rang up Essie Matthews. She wasn't in, but her maid informed me Essie was looking for a new hat and told me which shops were her favorites.

Next, I telephoned Jasper. His man answered. When I asked to speak with Jasper, Grigsby said, "I will inquire as to whether he is available."

A few moments later, Jasper's voice came over the line. I asked, "Does your man dislike all females who telephone you, or is it just me?"

"Olive, old girl! You have to excuse Grigsby. He takes his duty to protect my virtue quite seriously. How are you?"

"I have a job," I said. "It's temporary, but it pays well."

"Sounds intriguing, possibly scandalous."

"It's perfectly respectable. I'm working for Aunt Caroline."

"Well, I suppose you'll do fine as long as she remembers to pay you."

"I got a retainer upfront."

"You *are* going to be a savvy businesswoman."

"I would love to tell you all about it, and I have a small favor to ask. Can you meet me later today?"

"I'd like nothing better. I'll give up the stodgy atmosphere of my club to meet with you anytime, my dear."

I triangulated the shops Essie's maid had named and estimated how long it might take to find Essie. "Shall we say an hour from now, in Hyde Park, near Speakers' Corner?"

"Intent on a stroll, are you?"

"It's far too nice of a day to stay inside."

"You always were an active girl. I suppose I could stand a leisurely amble."

I found Essie in the second shop I tried. She had on a bicorn hat with the brim folded back, which completely covered her dark brown pageboy. She had a moon-shaped face, cinnamon-colored eyes, and pink cheeks. She tilted her head to the side, critically surveying the shop girl who was modeling a wide-brimmed straw hat with a pink sash and a spray of carnations. Essie spun her finger in the air. "Turn."

The shop girl rotated slowly, and I was glad it wasn't me under the hat. Essie nodded. "I'll take it." The shop girl moved away, and I drifted toward Essie. She spotted me and met me halfway, hands outstretched. "Olive, where have you been keeping yourself? I haven't seen you since the Duchess of Seton's ball."

"I've been up to Parkview for a few days." It was best not to tell Essie everything.

"Such a lovely setting. And I hear that the happy couple is there as well?"

"You do keep up, don't you?"

"One tries."

She might not have been interested in writing essays in boarding school, but she had a nose for news—of the society type.

I knew if there were rumors or information—no matter how minuscule—about Alfred, she'd have heard them. The trick would be getting the information out of her without her realizing I was probing for details.

She asked, "Have Violet and Alfred set a date?"

I fingered the appliqué on a beret displayed on a hatstand. "Not yet. Alfred seems a delightful young man."

"Oh, yes. So dashing. And always so *cheerful*. I think he and Violet will do well together."

"And he has such an interesting history."

Essie put a hand on her chest, tilted her head to the side, and said on a sigh, "Romantic India." She leaned toward me. "Of course, I wouldn't want to live there myself, but it does make an excellent story. His father did *quite* well in the east, you know."

I only had to raise my eyebrows to get her to continue.

"You don't know the story?"

"I didn't get the details. You know Violet. She's very much about what's going on now and isn't interested in anything to do with the past. Too boring."

"Yes, but when your deceased father-in-law to-be was a nabob, I think that *is* worthy of discussion."

"Really? I hadn't realized."

Essie nodded. "How do you think Alfred affords his flat in South Regent Mansions? And he's always so well dressed. And his motor! Have you seen it?"

"No, but you're the second person who's mentioned it."

"A stunner. I really *must* get a photograph of Alfred and Violet in it. Now *that* would sell some newspapers."

"I'm sure it would. Colonial son returns to his roots in Derbyshire and makes good," I said, picking a random region and tossing it into my imaginary headline to see Essie's reaction.

"No, it wasn't Derbyshire. Somewhere in the Midlands, a little village . . ." Essie stared at the ceiling for a moment. "Setherwick, that was it. I remember because I misunderstood him. I thought he said Leatherwick. But he said, 'No, *Sether*wick.' I've never been there myself. Alfred said it's a tiny little village, barely a speck on the map."

"And who are his particular friends?"

Essie twisted a hatstand so she could look at the back of a fringed turban. "Sebastian, of course. Can't think of anyone else. Of course, growing up in India, he wouldn't have developed relationships here that go back years and years."

"Yes, that's true."

The shop assistant returned, and Essie asked to see the turban modeled. As I left, Essie said, "Delightful to see you, Olive. Tell Violet I simply *must* have that photo of her. I'll be in touch to arrange it."

I made my way toward Hyde Park. Violet would love to have her photo in the paper, but Aunt Caroline and Gwen wouldn't like it.

Jasper was in the park before me, lounging against a bench, surveying the scene through a monocle. I joined him and said, "You're much too young to use a monocle."

He screwed it into his eye and swiveled in my direction. "I thought it made me look jolly distinguished."

"It makes you look rather foppish."

"Dear me, I best not let Grigsby see it, then." He pocketed the monocle and offered his arm. "Shall we begin this arduous trek?"

"I promise it won't be too taxing."

"Now, tell me all about this commission you have."

I said, "You must keep this completely between us."

"You know I can do that."

"That's why I'm confiding in you." Jasper was one of the few people that I knew who actually *could* keep a secret. I'd learned that many summers ago when I'd been scribbling in a notebook, writing an epic story of love and adventure. It had involved a mummy, a sheik, and—of course—a beautiful woman. I was carrying the notebook with me as I walked to Parkview and had paused on the bank of the river to write down some important detail.

I didn't realize Jasper and Peter were close, or I'd never have the notebook out in plain sight. Their cricket ball sailed into a tree overhead, and a distant buzz sounded, but I didn't realize what it was. Jasper ran up to retrieve his ball just as a swarm of bees descended. I panicked and ran straight over the edge of the riverbank. The instant I made the leap, I realized I was still holding my notebook with my precious story in it. I tossed it to Jasper, who had the presence of mind to notice the bees weren't actually coming in our direction. He caught the notebook and watched me plunge into the river. When I came up sputtering from the shock of the cold water, he raised his gaze from the open pages to me. "You're writing a novel."

I scrambled up the steep bank, water sluicing off my dress. I squished through the long grass and pushed my wet hair off my face. "If you tell a soul . . ." So many emotions surged through me —mortification, anger, embarrassment. I couldn't even finish my sentence.

Jasper closed the notebook with a snap. "Wouldn't dream of it," he said, and his tone had a certainty that I trusted. He wouldn't lie to my face and then later snicker with Peter about it. He handed the notebook back, then took off his jacket and dropped it over my shoulders. "Your secret's safe with me." He picked up his ball and trotted back through the trees to where Peter was shouting for him.

A squeaking sound brought me back to the present as a nurse came toward us, pushing a perambulator with a wheel that needed oil. Jasper and I paused for a moment to let her cross the path in front of us, then I told him about Aunt Caroline's concerns about Alfred Eton. I finished with, "And so you see, because of what you did during the war—"

He looked at me sharply.

"Your work for the Admiralty," I said quickly. I knew it was a touchy subject. Many people had looked down on men like Jasper who didn't fight on the front lines, but Jasper *had* contributed to the war effort, even if it hadn't been on the battlefield. "I thought you might have connections—someone who could find out what Alfred's father did in India."

"Oh—yes. Right. I can make a few inquiries. Old Somerville might remember him. Delhi, you said?"

"That's right."

"I'll see what I can do."

"Might your father have known him?" I asked.

"No. Father was in Bombay."

"Ah."

Jasper didn't often speak of his family, and his tone indicated the subject was closed. His steps, which were already at an ambling pace, slowed even more. "You need to be . . . careful." He whacked a tuft of grass with his walking stick. "Alfred doesn't keep the best company. He spends a lot of time with Sebastian, and that set is rather . . ."

"Fast. Yes, you told me. But I'm not marrying him. It's Violet you should warn off. If there's anything truly unsavory there, I'll uncover it—"

"That's what I'm afraid of," he said.

I ignored his comment. ". . . and that will allow Violet to untangle herself from Alfred before things get too much further along."

Jasper stopped walking and turned to me, leaning with both hands on his stick. "You're determined to do this, then?"

"Yes."

"I see." He straightened, then offered me his arm again as we resumed walking. "I'll see what I can find out."

"Excellent. Thank you."

Our ramble had brought us back to Speakers' Corner, and we parted there. I shook off my irritation at Jasper's reaction. Who was he to tell me who to associate with and what to do?

Instead, I focused on the upcoming house party at Archly Manor. I had several evening gowns Gwen had given me. We were close to the same size, except she was a few inches taller than I was. The only adjustments the dresses needed were shortened hems, and I did that myself, but none of the dresses were silver or gold. I did have a sleeveless white sheath dress. I could make a few adjustments to the dress to make it fit the party theme.

I used my dwindling personal money to buy a tulle fabric shot through with gold thread, then returned to my room. I spent the evening sewing. The long lines of the current styles made it easy to sew the gauzy fabric into a loose overdress that would float around the white dress. With a gold sash tied around my hips, and Mum's pearls, I looked passably fashionable.

The next morning, I kept an eye out the window. When Gwen's mint green Morris Cowley arrived, I grabbed my bags and hurried down the stairs. My lodgings were clean and respectable, but I saw them with new eyes after returning from my short visit to Parkview. The shabbiness of the building stood out to me now. I hurried out the door before Gwen could come inside.

She was about to step out of the Morris. "You're ready?"

"Why do you look so surprised?"

"Because you're usually late."

"Not this time." I stowed my bag and climbed into the seat beside her. "On to the party."

CHAPTER SEVEN

*G*wen and I set out from London for Somerset, and the first portion of the drive was uneventful. It was only after we turned off the main road that we realized Alfred's vague directions left something to be desired. As we approached a crossroads with a faded signpost, I said to Gwen, "Slow down so I can read it. I think *this* may be our turn."

Gwen's foot touched the brake—something she'd rarely done since we'd set off from my lodgings. Gwen, so sedate and measured in her personality, lost all inhibition when she got behind the steering wheel. Her philosophy was to power along at as fast a pace as possible, saying, "If we're wrong, we'll turn around," which we'd already done twice.

I looked back down to the page of scrawled directions. "Yes, take a right here."

Gwen made the turn, then stood on the brake, flinging the directions and the map to the floor. "What is that?"

Arms braced on the dash, I said, "I have no idea."

Now that we'd made the turn, a life-size figure of a clown pointing down the road came into view. Gwen let the motor roll closer.

"It's papier-mâché," I said. It was clothed in a bright harlequin-patterned suit and had a matching floppy hat.

"Sebastian is a bit . . . unconventional," Gwen said. "Perhaps these are signposts to point the way to Archly Manor."

"It would have been more helpful to have one at the actual crossroad," I said.

Gwen returned her attention to the road, and the Morris surged forward. "Sebastian's an artist. He's more into theater than practicality."

We saw three more papier-mâché figures—a mermaid, a knight, and, finally, a unicorn, which guarded the gates of Archly Manor. "They certainly are eye-catching," I said as we passed through the gates. "It makes me wonder what's in store for this party."

"Nothing traditional, that's for certain."

The grounds of Archly Manor were extensive, and it was several minutes before the house came into view. Gwen tapped the brake so I could get a good look.

"Gracious," I said. "Perhaps I should become a society photographer." The white stuccoed mansion dazzled against the green background of the surrounding parkland. A two-story recessed portico lined with Ionic pillars formed the central block of the house. Above it, a balcony enclosed the second floor. Two wings, each with an octagonal design, bookended the entrance block.

"Family money. Violet says Sebastian bought Archly Manor so he could get away. Somewhere to go when he wants to get out of the hustle and bustle of London."

"Pity that it's family money and not his photos that paid for it. I could see myself becoming the dashing lady photographer."

The drive leading to the house buzzed with activity. Gwen threaded between two lorries, then stomped on the brakes to avoid a servant pushing a barrow full of plants. She swept the motor around the man, then jerked us to a stop at the portico by the double front doors. A servant opened the door of the Morris and informed Gwen he'd put the Morris in the old stables then have our bags sent up to our rooms. He drove away around the side of the house.

Gwen and I stood on the sweep for a moment, taking in the activity. On the wide stretch of emerald lawn that gradually dropped down to a lake, gardeners were trimming the grass while others bent over the flowerbeds that surrounded the house. Several men in flat caps and work clothes carried boxes labeled *explosives* down to a boathouse while servants hurried back and forth from one of the side entrances to the house. Other workers tottered along with potted plants, or perched on ladders as they hung Japanese lanterns on tree branches.

A man emerged from Archly Manor's front door. He held two green champagne bottles by their gold-wrapped necks and wore a three-piece suit with a gold watch chain across his vest. He transferred one of the bottles to the crook of his arm and came toward Gwen, his hand extended. He moved with a confident and leisurely stride. "Gwen, so glad you could come." His fair hair was parted in the middle of his forehead and slicked back from his face, which was lean and bordered on gauntness. The sunlight highlighted his prominent cheekbones and the sockets around his eyes, giving him an almost skull-like appearance. The skin stretched tight over the bones of his face was a curious contrast to his obvious youthfulness. He couldn't be more than a few years older than Gwen and me. He was in his early thirties at the most. I wondered if he'd been sick recently.

"Hello, Sebastian," Gwen said. "I don't think you've met my cousin, Olive."

I shook his hand. His grip was strong and his handshake firm. I said, "I hope crashing your party at the last moment hasn't caused any problems."

"Not at all. We're informal here, as you can see." He lifted one of the champagne bottles. "In fact, we're having a little pre-party-party, if you'd like to join us. We're picnicking far away from this chaos." He waved the champagne bottle at a servant carrying a stack of chairs. "Or you may retire to your rooms if your journey was too fatiguing." He smiled as he said the words, but there was a critical edge to his tone, which also held the barest trace of ridicule. "Perhaps you'd like a bit of a rest?"

"I'm not as missish as that," Gwen said. "And I know Olive won't want a rest."

"No, I love a picnic."

"Excellent. This way." He turned his back to the lawn that sloped down to the lake and led us around to the other side of the house. "We're under that large chestnut tree. If you'll excuse me for a moment, I must speak to someone. I'll be with you shortly." He moved away to talk to one of the workers.

I raised my eyebrows at Gwen as we walked to the group gathered under the tree. "I can see why you don't like him."

Gwen's steps paused. "I never said that."

"You didn't have to. I could tell from the way you spoke about him. Meeting him only confirmed my thoughts."

"Really? That's disturbing. Do you think he knows I don't like him?"

"No. He's far too pleased with himself to even wonder about what other people think of him."

"Yes. Smug down to his very bones. That's why I worry about Violet. Alfred is so closely connected to Sebastian, and it's clear that Sebastian doesn't think of anyone but himself. I'm afraid Alfred is cut from the same cloth."

"And neither one of them has Violet's best interests at heart."

"Yes," Gwen said, then glanced back at Sebastian, who was still by the house. "He thinks I'm a dried-up busybody out to spoil everyone's enjoyment. That comment about needing a nap! As if I was Violet's decrepit spinster aunt. Just because I don't indulge in the frivolous life like he and his friends doesn't mean I'm old fashioned."

"You don't have to convince me."

She smiled. "Sorry. He does annoy me."

As we approached the group in the shade of the tree, Violet, who was seated on a blanket and reclining against Alfred's chest, shifted into a sitting position. Alfred rose and greeted us warmly, his grin wide. Violet didn't look nearly as welcoming. "I thought you weren't coming," she said.

"You must have misunderstood," Gwen said. "I said I was arriving later. I went to London to bring Olive." Gwen turned to introduce me to two women in wicker chairs with fashion magazines spread across their laps. The woman closest to me was Lady Pamela. Like the day I'd met her with Jasper at the Savoy, she wore an exquisite gown, this one a flowing cream silk with a lace overdress. "Lady Pamela and I have met," I said.

She tilted her head up slightly so the wide brim of her straw hat revealed one eye. "I'm afraid I don't recall."

"It was at the Savoy."

"How nice."

"With Jasper Rimington."

Her eye narrowed. "Oh, yes. Now I remember. You were in that rather—er—intriguing frock. Of course, I'm sure you had no idea you were dining at the Savoy. Jasper is rather a dear—absolutely spontaneous. And he associates with such . . . eccentric . . . people." Lady Pamela's gaze traveled up and down my ensemble, which was a perfectly acceptable tricot dress in pale green. But beside her frothy garden party dress, I knew I looked dowdy— and she was making sure everyone knew it.

I tilted my head. "And I thought Jasper just enjoyed my arresting eyes and first-class brain."

Gwen coughed as Lady Pamela's eye became a slit.

Before Lady Pamela could launch into a speech, Gwen cleared her throat and indicated the woman seated in the next chair. "Olive, this is Mrs. Reid, Sebastian's sister. She's staying here at Archly Manor with him while her husband is in Brazil."

She dropped her magazine and extended her hand. "Call me Thea. Everyone does." Her clothing was in the same league as Lady Pamela's, and her brunette hair was bobbed, but Thea Reid was probably about ten or fifteen years older than Lady Pamela, who I knew was in her mid-twenties. Thea's plump cheeks were just beginning to show a tendency toward jowls, and her heavily powdered skin looked worn compared with Violet's dewy-fresh complexion.

I shook hands with Thea. "Will your husband return from Brazil soon?"

"Not for months and months. I'd join him, of course, but it's quite primitive there. Certainly not acceptable for the children. And someone has to oversee the workmen." She motioned for me to sit in an empty chair beside her and settled back. "We're updating the London flat. It's completely uninhabitable. Workers in and out all day. It's *too* fatiguing, and they never seem to do *anything* right the first time." Thea held up two magazines folded back at different pages. "What do you think for the cocktail cabinet? The black lacquer with Bakelite or the walnut with chrome?"

"You can't go wrong with either one," I said.

Thea looked critically from one page to the other. "I've engaged Monsieur Babin—he's terribly difficult to get, you know—and he assures me either one will look stunning, but I can't decide."

Lady Pamela shifted in her chair and her handkerchief fell to the ground. Gwen reached out to pick it up, but Lady Pamela snatched it up in a jerky motion. "Just pick the most expensive one. You always do."

Thea said, "I always say it never pays to be cheap."

At that moment, a boy of about seven dropped from the branches of the tree and landed lightly beside me. My startled reaction delighted him, and he giggled.

Thea slapped the magazines down and craned her neck to look around the trunk of the tree. "Muriel!"

I hadn't seen the two people on the far side of the wide tree trunk. A young woman in her early twenties quickly stepped forward. The high waist of her plain gray dress with a full skirt was several years out of date, but her brunette hair was bobbed and lay against her creamy skin, which was now tinged with pink. She sent a sharp look at the boy beside me. He smothered his laughter. She asked, "Yes, Mrs. Reid?"

A man who had been standing behind the tree strolled over. He had a receding hairline, and his expensive suit almost disguised his thickening middle.

Thea said, "Take Paul and Rose back to the nursery. They've had enough time outdoors."

"Yes, Mrs. Reid."

Gwen indicated the young woman as she said, "Olive, this is Muriel Webb. Muriel, this is my cousin, Olive Belgrave."

Muriel murmured, "How do you do?" But her attention was on Paul. She took his hand, and a girl a few years younger than the boy scrambled down the trunk of the tree without help. She dropped the last few feet and landed with a smack beside the man with the receding hairline. He stepped back a pace and examined his trousers for mud. Rose craned her neck and asked him, "Will you be back tonight?"

He shook his head. "No, I have to go into town."

Thea waved the magazine. "Don't bother Mr. Digby-Stratham, Rose. Go along with Muriel. Mum will come up and see you before the party tonight."

As Muriel walked away with the children, Thea twisted around and called, "Muriel, did you take care of that letter?"

"I put it in the mail this morning."

"All right." She half-turned back to our group, then twisted around again. "And what about the striped wallpaper? Did you telephone Monsieur Babin?"

"Yes. It's available but only in blue, not gold."

"Oh! So frustrating," Thea said as she settled back in her chair. "I so wanted the gold."

Gwen caught my eye and gestured to the man with the receding hair line who'd been standing on the other side of the tree with Muriel. "And this is the last of our party. Olive, this is Hugh Digby-Stratham."

We shook hands, and then I asked, "You're not staying for the party tonight?"

He looked as if a foul odor had drifted his way. "No, I'm afraid I can't."

Lady Pamela, who had twisted her handkerchief around her fingers, unwound it. "What Hugh means is he doesn't participate in shallow things. He's far too serious for anything fun."

Hugh did seem to have a starchy personality with his erect posture and his precise movements, but he clearly didn't like Lady Pamela's insinuation he was stodgy. "On the contrary," he said. "I would rather stay, but duty calls." He turned back to me. "I'm afraid I must run. It was a pleasure to meet you." He took his leave of the rest of the group, then marched off across the lawn toward the house with a military stride.

Alfred, who had flopped back down onto the blanket after standing to greet me, plucked a grape from the food spread on the blanket. "Hard to believe stuffy old Hugh has actually gone and fallen in love."

Gwen said, "I don't see why you think it's so surprising." Gwen offered me a sandwich from the picnic basket. I took one, along with Thea, but Lady Pamela waved the plate away and shifted in her chair.

Gwen set the plate down. "I think she and Hugh will get on well together."

With mock horror in his voice, Alfred said, "But she's a *governess*. I bet Hugh had to talk his family around to that."

"Muriel comes from excellent stock," Thea said to Alfred. "The Webbs were an established and well-respected Dartmoor family."

Violet twisted to look around to Thea. "Were?"

"Her parents were killed when she was young."

"Both of them?" Violet asked. "What happened?"

Gwen widened her eyes. "Violet!"

Thea waved a hand. "It's all right, Gwen. Muriel wouldn't mind. Water under the bridge and all that. Her parents were killed in a motor smash."

"That's terrible."

"Yes, I'm sure it was," Thea said as she turned the page of the magazine.

"What happened to her?" Violet asked.

Thea pulled her gaze away from a dress advertisement. "Who?"

"Muriel? After her parents died?"

"Oh, Muriel. She was sent to live with an aunt. Apparently, they didn't get on well, but it all worked out in the end." Thea closed the magazine and picked up another. "Because of that experience, Muriel understands the importance of stability where the children are concerned. She's wonderful at keeping up with my correspondence and my schedule too. So helpful and willing to do whatever is needed. She was kind enough to step in when my previous secretary left."

I thought Muriel might have another perspective on her relationship with Thea. The preemptory way Thea had spoken to Muriel, and Muriel's quick, almost guilty response, told me Muriel was much more interested in keeping her position as Thea's governess-secretary than simply helping Thea. As someone who was desperate for a job, I recognized the signs.

Sebastian arrived and topped off the champagne flutes for those who already had them and handed new glasses to Gwen and me. He caught the end of the conversation and said, "Muriel will be a perfect political hostess. Just what Hugh needs, actually. She'll fade into the background as a proper politician's wife should. She doesn't have enough beauty to distract press attention —or anyone else's, for that matter—from Hugh at all those dreadful ribbon-cutting ceremonies and summer fetes in their future."

I thought his words were harsh. Muriel wasn't unattractive. She wasn't as much of a natural beauty as someone like Lady Pamela, and Muriel obviously didn't have the means of someone like Thea, who used beautiful clothes and cosmetics to delay slipping fully into a matronly stage. But Sebastian was a photographer. Perhaps he analyzed everyone with an artistic eye, assessing whether or not a person was beautiful.

Thea turned a page of her new magazine with a sigh. "Nothing's official yet between Muriel and Hugh. But I can see which way things are going. I'm sure it will be announced soon. The Digby-Strathams recognize what a level-headed girl Muriel is. She's circumspect and attentive to detail. But I *am* disappointed. I'll have to go through that horrid business of finding a new secretary *and* a new governess. So tiresome."

If I'd heard those words a day or two earlier, I'd have made it my objective to show Mrs. Reid what a good candidate I would be for Muriel's replacement, but I was more interested in Alfred's background at the moment. With that thought in mind, I moved to pick up some grapes from the picnic basket, then settled on the blanket near Alfred and Violet.

They didn't look thrilled when I joined them, but Violet was too well bred to not at least make an effort to include me in the conversation. Unfortunately, the conversation centered on the upcoming party, evening gowns in particular. When we exhausted that topic, Violet squeezed Alfred's arm. "But I'm looking forward to the fireworks most of all," she said, then turned to me. "Alfred and I are going to watch them from the balcony at the back of the house." She fixed her gaze back on Alfred. "It'll be too, too romantic."

Alfred tossed away several pieces of grass he'd been stripping apart and said in a disinterested tone, "It has the best view."

I said, "We're boring Alfred with all this talk about the party. Which of your friends are coming tonight, Alfred?"

"Several of the gang will be here." Alfred stood up and extended his hand to Violet. "Come on, Vi. Let's stroll. If they've finished using the boats to get the fireworks over to the island, we can punt about a bit."

I watched Alfred and Violet walk away. I couldn't chase after them and demand to be included in their boating party—that would be far too obvious—so I switched my attention to Sebastian, who was saying, ". . . well, it wasn't quite cricket, but we used to challenge some pompous-looking city gents to a race and taunt them until they agreed. I'm sure Monty will deny this when he arrives, but it was his idea. I'd make a fuss, marking off a starting point on the pavement, very official-like. Then I'd shout, 'Go!' and they'd dash off. Monty would drop back and let the other chap have the lead, then as soon as they ran by a bobby, Monty would yell, 'Stop, thief!' The bobby would sprint off after Mr. Upstanding Citizen while Monty and I raced in the other direction."

"How wonderfully terrible," Lady Pamela said. "You were awful."

"Yes, I was." Sebastian turned to Gwen. "But I'm sure you don't approve."

"It sounds as if it was all in good fun," Gwen said.

"Oh, it was."

"You must tell them about the rag you pulled at university," Thea said. "That one tops all the others."

"I don't think I have time. I must check—"

"You must." Lady Pamela bounced in her chair. "I insist."

"Well, then. I *know* Gwen will disapprove of this joke. I have no excuse, except that I was younger and much more arrogant."

Gwen choked a bit on her tea but managed to keep a straight face. Sebastian gave her a long look, then cleared his throat. "A visiting scholar came to our college, and he was given the royal treatment—given a tour, wined and dined, the whole bit. We decided a few weeks later that another Nobel prize-winning chemist from Germany would drop in unexpectedly for a visit, Dr. Klaus Klausenstine." He threw his hand out in a theatrical manner and pronounced the name with a heavy German accent.

"Who is that?" Lady Pamela asked.

"No one!" Sebastian said. "We made it all up." Sebastian put his hand on his chest and bowed. "You're looking at the good doctor now."

"Didn't someone recognize you?" Gwen asked.

"No. I wore glasses, and I had a large fedora pulled down low. I also glued on a spectacularly curly mustache."

"You speak German?" I asked.

"Not a word," Sebastian said, his grin seeming to cause the skin to strain over the bones of his face. "I nodded and smiled. Even the dean was taken in. It was all going swimmingly until Dr. Heidelberg wanted to chat."

"What happened?" I asked, suspecting I knew the answer. Sebastian was far too shrewd to get caught.

"I had my 'assistant,' a chap who wasn't at university, 'translate' I was unwell and had to leave immediately . . . which I must do now," he said as everyone laughed.

Sebastian stood, saying he needed to check on the party preparations. As he walked away, Lady Pamela jumped up from her chair as well. "I must decide what to wear for dinner." She turned to Thea. "You must come look at my dresses. The silver embroidered frock I picked up in Paris last month? Too much?"

Thea stood and shook out the folds of her dress. "Nothing is ever too much for one of Sebastian's parties."

LATER THAT EVENING I stood in front of the looking glass in my bedroom, which was decorated in a pale green and furnished with a massive canopied bed. The maid who had unpacked my meager belongings earlier that day handed me my only jewelry, Mum's opera-length string of pearls. They felt cool against the back of my neck. I doubled the necklace so that one section formed a choker while the rest of it draped in a longer loop. I powdered my nose and added a touch of red lipstick.

The maid, Jane, a young woman with her white-blonde curls under her maid's cap, stood behind me. Her black gown blended into the shadows, except for the bright white slash of my gloves, which she held in her hands. I turned away from the mirror, and the pearls swung as I took the gloves from Jane.

"Will there be anything else, miss?"

"No, that will be all. Thank you."

Jane left, closing the door behind her.

I smoothed the gloves up over my elbows. Unlike Lady Pamela, I had no trouble choosing my ensemble for the evening. Having only one choice tends to simplify things. In the shadows of my scruffy London room, the dress had looked fine, but against the sumptuous background of Archly Manor, it seemed homespun. I adjusted my sash and departed for the drawing room. I wasn't here to show off my clothes. I was here to find out about Alfred, and the party should be a perfect opportunity to do it.

CHAPTER EIGHT

I entered the drawing room, which I was surprised to see was decorated in a traditional blue toile. I'd expected something much more eccentric, but it appeared Sebastian limited his unconventional taste to papier-mâché. I glanced around the room and realized my sewing skills fell far short of the gorgeous gowns Lady Pamela and Thea wore. I felt dowdy, but at least I got the long strand of pearls correct. Everyone was wearing ropes of them. Violet, Lady Pamela, Thea, and Gwen were draped in them.

Sebastian handed me a cocktail. "You're enchanting this evening."

I sipped the drink, trying to decide if he was serious or mocking. "Thank you."

"Simple lines suit you."

With Sebastian's reputation for making cutting remarks, I initially thought the comment was a snub, but his expression looked as if he was dispassionately assessing my outfit. I decided I'd assume he was viewing me with an artist's eye instead of voicing an insult couched in pretty words.

Thea moved closer to me and fingered the tulle of the overdress. "Lovely. Where did you find this?"

"At a little shop in London."

"You must give me its name." She gestured with her glass at Sebastian. "He's always telling me to cut the flounces and flourishes, but I do love them so."

Thea's ensemble, while cut in a simple tube-like style, was decorated with a dizzying combination of metallic gold embroidery, pink bugle beads, and pearl trim at the neck and hem. A feathered hair clip held back one side of her bob, and a rope of pearls fell below the dropped waist of her gown.

Good manners dictated I should return her compliment, but the only word that came to mind to describe her gown was *overwhelming*, and I couldn't say that. "Your pearls are beautiful."

Sebastian lifted his glass in a faint salute, his eyes dancing with laughter.

Thea patted her necklace. "Mr. Reid brought these back after a business trip to Shanghai. One hundred fifty perfectly matched pearls. Always buy the best, that's what I always say. Mr. Reid agrees with me. He says buying second rate is a false economy."

Sebastian said, "It's bad enough he spouts his maxims constantly. Must you continue to do it while he's absent?"

"Really, Sebastian, you're incorrigible. I don't know why I put up with you."

"Because I'm housing and feeding you, not to mention your brats." Sebastian offered his arm to me. "Come, Olive. Have you met the rest of the houseguests?" He leaned closer as we moved away from Thea, who was sputtering. "Well done, my dear. Her pearls are exquisite and the only thing worth admiring—certainly not that horror of a dress."

Sebastian steered me around the room, introducing me to the remaining guests. The last two members of the dinner party arrived shortly before the meal was announced. Monty Park was tall and fair and had a hearty laugh. I'd danced with him at a hunt ball where he'd stepped on my toes rather heavily. I didn't know the other young man, who was called Tug. He was short and redheaded and seemed to spend most of his time staring at Lady

Pamela. He had to make a conscious effort to pull his gaze away from her when Sebastian introduced me to him.

I didn't have a chance to talk with either Monty or Tug because the butler, Babcock, announced dinner was served.

Ten of us sat down to dinner in the dining room, with its mahogany wainscoting, red-papered walls, and spectacularly ornate plasterwork ceiling. Work-conscious Hugh was absent, but Sebastian's secretary, James Henley, a serious bespectacled young man, joined us. He was seated beside me at dinner and explained in great detail the trickiness of electrifying Archly Manor while preserving parquet floors, ceiling frescoes, and priceless wood paneling.

"It sounds challenging," I said.

"It was." James looked across the table to Muriel. "You caught the end of it when you returned from Paris. Muriel can tell you what a mess everything was."

"Yes, it was hard to do lessons with all the knocking and banging," she said.

The silence stretched, and I cast around for a topic to keep the conversation rolling. "Do you travel often, Muriel? Have you been to the States?"

"Oh, no. I only travel with Mrs. Reid. She went to Paris, and I accompanied her."

"I see. Did you enjoy it?"

"Very much so."

I was glad Monty asked me a question and I could turn my attention to him because conversation with Muriel was hard going. Monty did remember the hunt ball. "I fear I didn't make a good impression," he said. "Or rather, that I made too deep of an impression—on your shoes. I have to apologize. Dancing is not my forte."

"What do you enjoy?"

"I'm a bit of a sportsman. I enjoy golf and horses."

"Buying horses or riding them?" I asked.

Before Monty could answer, Alfred, who was seated across the table from me, asked, "Or betting on them?"

Monty gave him a tight smile, and I had the impression that Monty didn't appreciate Alfred's comment. "A bit of all three." He stared at Alfred for a moment, then said, "There's no law against any of those, is there?"

"No, indeed," Alfred said, his already large grin stretching wide.

"Don't let's talk about horses," Violet said and turned to Sebastian. "Do you have musicians coming tonight? Or will it have to be the gramophone?"

"My dear, would I throw a party without proper music? Of course, I invited a nice little orchestra down from London. They're setting up now."

"Wonderful," Violet said.

Alfred said, "Then perhaps Muriel will serenade us this evening?"

Muriel flushed. "Tonight is for dancing."

Violet, who was seated next to Alfred, tapped his arm. "Beast. Why would you say that? You know Muriel can't—er—I mean . . ."

Muriel smiled at Violet. "You don't have to be delicate about it, Violet. I can't carry a tune to save my life. Alfred likes to tease me about it."

"Well, he shouldn't," Violet said, then turned to Alfred with a bounce. "I know! Why don't *you* sing for us tonight, Alfred?"

He shook his head. "No, Muriel is right. Tonight is for dancing."

Lady Pamela, who was seated beside Sebastian, put her hand on his arm. "I want to know about this music in America that's all the rage. You were just there. Tell us about it."

"That was several months ago," Sebastian said.

Lady Pamela twitched a shoulder and adjusted her necklace. "But you heard the music, didn't you? You went to shows?" She reached up to smooth her hair. She'd been constantly moving her hands throughout dinner—twisting the rings on her fingers or fiddling with her silverware.

"Of course."

"Well, then, tell us." Lady Pamela waved off a footman offering the next course. I was seated diagonally across the table from her and could see she ate like one of Jasper's society girls. She mostly pushed the food around her plate and ate only a few bites.

Sebastian grinned at her. "Scandalous stuff, let me tell you. Wild and loose-limbed and sure to drive the papers to declare it will cause the downfall of society."

"Superb! You must demonstrate," Lady Pamela said.

"Oh, no. I'm not that talented. You'll have to go to the clubs in London to see the real thing. The foxtrot is as wild as I get."

"Spoilsport," Lady Pamela said with a pout.

IT WAS ONLY after dinner that things began to get a little wild. Motor after motor arrived and disgorged glittering partygoers who fell on the buffet tables in the reception hall like swarms of locusts. They danced in the ballroom and poured out onto the terrace. As the rooms became more and more crowded, the guests eventually spilled onto the lawn that went down to the lake.

As the number of partygoers climbed, I inched my way around the ballroom. My hopes of buttonholing Monty or Tug, who I'd learned were friends of Alfred's, were totally impractical. After dinner Violet had recruited me to fix a comb that had fallen out of her hair. I'd asked if Monty and Tug were Alfred's friends. She'd said, "Yes, I suppose so. He does mention them often." Violet was determined to dance every dance, so she and Alfred constantly circled the floor as best they could among the sea of glittering dresses and black ties, but neither Monty nor Tug were around them, and I didn't see either of the men anywhere in the ballroom.

Thinking they might be in another part of the ground floor, I went into the hallway that connected the ballroom with the entry to the house, the rococo reception hall with its gilded Georgian portraits and landscapes. People were rushing back and forth through the corridor. Screams, shrieks, and applause sounded from the direction of the reception hall. In the midst of all the movement, a still figure in the shadows against the wall caught my attention. It was Thea seated in a chair, listing to one side, her fingertips pressed to her forehead.

I went across to her. "Are you all right?

Thea moved her hand an inch and squinted at me. "I'm afraid I'm not feeling well. One of my migraines coming on."

Her face was washed out and had a pinched look. A giggling, squealing group of young women hurried by. Thea grimaced and covered her eyes.

"Is there anything I can do for you?" I asked.

"Lady Pamela was supposed to bring me one of her headache powders. She said they work wonders, but she disappeared." Thea motioned down the hall without opening her eyes. "I believe she went into the dining room."

"I'll see if I can find her for you."

The dining room was deserted except for a woman sitting in a man's lap in the chair at the head of the table. They were very . . . *involved* and didn't notice me. I closed the door and moved to the next room, a sitting room. I opened the door, and Lady Pamela jumped up from the seat beside a cherrywood piecrust table. Two young women beside her started and turned.

"Lady Pamela," I said. "Thea is waiting for you—"

Lady Pamela rushed toward me, grabbed both my hands, and swung me around in a circle. "Oh, Olivia, didn't I tell you Sebastian gives the most *divine* parties? Just too, too divine!"

I was too startled to remind her my name was Olive, not Olivia, as I noticed the pupils of her eyes were enormous, leaving only a thin line of her green irises around the dark center. She twirled me around once more, then released me, and I bumped into the piecrust table and sent the flower arrangement on it rocking. Lady Pamela dashed out the door with the other two young women. As I steadied the vase, Lady Pamela reappeared in the doorway. "My handbag. I must have left—"

"Here it is." The bag had to be hers because the sparkly black and silver sequins matched her dress exactly. It lay on the table, half open, the contents spilling out. I replaced a compact and a cigarette case, and reached for the handkerchief. When I picked up the gauzy fabric, two bright jewels fell onto the table, square-cut emeralds edged in rows of diamonds. The facets of the stones reflected against the polished grain of the tabletop. I was surprised Lady Pamela wasn't wearing such beautiful jewels, but perhaps she'd decided green didn't go with her black dress. I replaced the jewelry in the bag. Lady Pamela snatched the bag from me and rushed out the door again.

My fingers felt gritty, and I rubbed my thumb across my fingertips. A layer of fine powder coated my fingers. I went back to the piecrust table and switched on the light beside the flower arrangement. Specks of white powder dusted the shiny surface.

I returned to Thea and found her in exactly the same position I'd left her. She asked, "Did you find the headache powders?"

"No, and I don't think you should take any type of powder from Lady Pamela. I'm sure the housekeeper will have something you can take."

"Yes, I suppose Mrs. Foster will have something. I should go to my room, I think." She said the words as if she were contemplating a trek to the Arctic. She could barely keep her eyes open against the glare of the lights coming from the reception hall, and she cringed at every loud noise.

I couldn't leave her in this rowdy crowd. "Let me help you." I reached for her elbow and steadied her as she came to her feet. We moved slowly down the hallway and emerged into the reception hall. "Oh my," Thea said.

A young man in evening attire was perched on a silver platter at the top of the stairs at the center of the red carpet runner.

Anyone would have looked absurd poised at the top of the stairs, seated on a massive serving tray, but against the ornate flourishes of the plasterwork on the walls and the formal Georgian artwork, he looked even more ridiculous.

Someone shouted, "Go!" and he rocketed down the staircase on the platter as if it were a sled. I'd never actually seen a cowboy ride a wild horse, but I supposed it would look something like the young man bucking and bouncing along the treads. He landed on the marble floor with a clatter, and a chorus of applause broke out.

Thea leaned against my arm. "I don't know if I can—I mean, will they let us through, do you think?"

"I'll see that they do." I turned so that I wasn't facing Thea and said in a loud voice, "Coming through. Excuse us. She needs some air."

I counted on the fact that these partygoers were familiar with people who couldn't handle their drink, and everyone scurried out of our way. With my arm under Thea's elbow, we climbed the now deserted stairs. Once we reached the first landing, the voices surged again as they resumed their sledding game.

A footman waited at the landing. He came forward, his hand up as if to bar our way, but then he recognized Thea. He stepped back and let us pass. As I helped her up the last flight of stairs, I asked, "Why is the footman blocking the stairs?"

"Oh, Sebastian always does that when he has a party." Her voice was faint. I could tell going up the stairs was a great effort for her, so I wasn't going to ask anything else, but she went on, "No guests above the ground floor—it's his single rule. His studio and photography equipment are upstairs. He's extremely particular about them. He doesn't care a fig for the rest of the house, but if someone damaged anything related to his photographs . . . well, I don't know what he would do."

"But aren't there other staircases leading upstairs? Surely the servants have another staircase?"

"Oh, yes. But a footman blocks that one as well. Sebastian is thorough. He would never take chances with his precious pictures."

Thea indicated which room was hers, and we went inside. I rang for a maid as Thea slowly lowered herself into a chair. "Your maid will be here soon," I said as I turned off all the lights in the room except for a single table lamp in a far corner.

Thea spoke with her eyes closed as she massaged her temple with one hand. "My maid didn't accompany me. She's sick and stayed in London with her sister."

"Would you like for me to ask for Muriel, then?"

"No, she's with the children. I'd rather she stayed with them. On a night like this, I know Paul will be tempted to sneak out to watch the fireworks, and it's better she stay there to keep an eye on him."

Jane entered, throwing back the door. She caught it before it hit the wall and closed it gently. Jane stood for a second with her back to the room, and I saw her shoulders rise and fall as she took a deep breath. When she had helped me dress for dinner that evening, she'd been deferential and helpful, but as she turned, she had a different air about her. Her cheeks were flushed, and her eyes sparkled, but as soon as I explained Thea needed headache powders and possibly a sleeping draught, some of the pent-up energy that seemed to be buzzing around Jane faded. "Yes, ma'am. I'll see to it."

I closed the door with a click, navigated around the party on the stairs, and returned to the ballroom. After the quiet dimness of Thea's room, the exuberance of the ballroom was a shock. Voices shouted over the din of blaring music, and the crush was so tight I could barely see beyond the four or five bodies packed around me. I pushed between two people and bumped into Tug. I said, "I've been looking for you."

He leaned far too close and fanned me with sour, alcohol-laced breath. "Brilliant. I say, care to dance?"

I thought of the fifty-pound retainer Aunt Caroline had

already paid me. "Let's," I said. At least it was an upbeat number, which meant I wouldn't have to fight to keep him at arm's length.

The song was already half over, but we shoved through the throng to the dance floor. When I had a chance, I asked, "Have you known Alfred long?"

He shook his head. "I don't know where Alfred is."

"No, I said—"

Tug continued, "He and Violet had a dust up. Trouble in paradise, I think."

"Oh, dear," I said, diverted from my original train of thought. "What about?" An argument between Alfred and Violet might not be such a bad thing. If Alfred and Violet broke things off, Aunt Caroline and Gwen wouldn't have to worry anymore. Of course, it would also mean I was out of a job. I pushed that thought away.

"No idea. A woman, probably."

"Why do you say that?"

"Well, Alfred is quite the ladies' man—" He blinked. The fact that I was Violet's relative must have risen through his alcohol-soaked brain. "I mean—er—that—"

"Quite." I would have left him squirming except he could be a good source of information about Alfred, so I rescued him. "How *long* have you known Alfred?" I asked, shouting to be heard over the music.

"A while, I suppose. Hard to keep track of time, don't you know."

"Where did you meet him?"

"At a party."

The song ended, and a ripple of excitement flowed through the dancers along with the word *fireworks*. I was carried along with the tide as everyone rushed outside to watch the fireworks, and Tug and I were separated. I wasn't actually that sorry to see him go. I broke away from the crowd and let them surge down to the lawn. I drifted across the terrace and down the stairs to the lawn, keeping an eye out for Gwen. The last time I'd seen her, she'd been in the ballroom, trying to keep an eye on Violet.

"Hello, Olive."

I turned and saw Monty. He raised his lighter to a cigarette, and the flame highlighted his face for a moment. He offered his cigarette case. "Would you like one?"

"No, thank you."

He closed the case and tucked it away. "I believe if we stand over here away from these trees, we'll have the best view of the fireworks."

A whine cut through the air, and the sky above us exploded into a starburst of light.

"How are you enjoying the party?" I asked. Unlike Tug, Monty seemed to be as sober as he had been earlier in the evening.

The tip of the cigarette glowed red, then Monty blew a stream of smoke away from me. "Sebastian always puts on a good show." Several fireworks went off, one after another, sparkling against the black sky as the lake mirrored the explosions. A trace of acrid smoke drifted across the lake, but it wasn't enough to set off an asthma attack.

"Where *is* Sebastian? I haven't seen him."

"Probably watching from one of the balconies. It's the best view—" Monty glanced over his shoulder at Archly Manor. "What the—?"

I swung around at the intensity of his tone. Two figures struggled on the balcony. Silhouetted against the faint light coming from the open door behind them, it was impossible to distinguish anything more than a dark blur. The high-pitched drone of another firework lifting off sounded, then a bright explosion lit up the façade of the house. For just a moment, it revealed a man with dark hair in evening dress and a woman with short blonde hair in a sparkly dress. As the twinkling light of the firework faded, one figure went over the balustrade.

CHAPTER NINE

*A*fter a stunned second, I set off at a run toward Archly Manor, my thoughts jumbling together. Violet and Alfred —they'd planned to watch the fireworks upstairs. Had that been Violet on the balcony?

Beside me, Monty sprinted toward the bulk of the house where patches of light shone from open windows. I was nearing the base of the terrace steps when I felt the familiar constriction in my chest as if a band were squeezing my lungs, cinching down tighter and tighter. I dragged in a ragged breath and told myself to calm down.

Monty didn't notice I'd slowed my pace. With his long stride, he widened the distance between us and raced up the shallow steps. My breathing evened out once I slowed down to a less frantic pace. By the time I reached the top of the stairs, Monty was already on the far side of the terrace under the balcony.

He stood completely still for a moment, staring down at the flagstones, then he spun away, a hand over his mouth. I had my breathing under control and headed for him. He stepped into my path and caught my upper arms in his hands. "Don't go over there."

I didn't have to go closer to see it was a man stretched out on the ground. His torso and upper body were in the shadows, but his black-clad legs were visible in a bar of light coming through one of the open doors. The unnatural angles of his lower limbs and the utter stillness could only mean one thing.

It wasn't Violet. I drew in a breath, which came easier than it had a few moments ago. "Who is it?"

"Alfred."

I looked up to the balcony, but it was deserted. The fireworks continued to explode overhead, creating a flashing effect that intermittently lit up the house and Alfred's body. I turned away and swallowed hard. My surge of fear that it was Violet who had fallen faded, and I felt shaky with relief. I was grateful it wasn't my cousin lying crushed and broken on the flagstones. But the whole situation was terrible—awful. And at the same time, I almost couldn't believe what I'd seen. It was so . . . fantastic. People weren't pushed off balconies, and yet, Alfred's body lay unmoving just a short distance away.

". . . the police."

The final words of Monty's sentence penetrated my thoughts. "What? Oh, right. The police—yes, of course." They would have to be called.

Monty said, "Find Babcock—the butler, you know—and have him ring up the local police station. Can you do that?"

At his mollycoddling tone, I straightened my spine. "Of course. If I can't find Babcock, I'll do it myself."

Monty raised his eyebrows, but I swept away before he had a chance to say anything else. As I left, I heard him calling for one of the footmen to create a barrier around Alfred, and for someone to alert the footman on the stairs to hold everyone upstairs. My steps stuttered for a moment, but I pressed on. Of course Monty was right. Someone—a woman, in fact—had pushed Alfred over the balcony, and she might still be upstairs.

As I dashed across the terrace, my foot skidded. I caught my balance and saw the luminescent glow of several pearls by my foot. I picked up the strand of about ten pearls that had come to rest in the mortared groove between the flagstones. They looked valuable, and I didn't want to leave them there, but I didn't have my handbag with me or pockets in my dress. I hesitated for a second, then slipped them into my glove, where they lodged against my forearm, cool against my skin.

The musicians were taking a break, and the ballroom was empty. I sped on to the reception hall, where the furniture had been pushed askew. Plates of half-eaten food and empty glasses littered the tables and the edges of the stair treads. Babcock was picking up the large silver tray that the revelers had abandoned at the foot of the stairs. I rushed to his side. "You must ring the police. Tell them to come at once. A man—Alfred Eton—has been killed, pushed off the balcony."

Babcock straightened slowly, the tray in his hand. Butlers always seemed to maintain an impassive expression, but I'd startled him enough that his eyebrows actually rose. "How unfortunate. I will see to it immediately."

"Thank you." I took a few steps up the stairs. "And I suppose you'd better find Sebastian and let him know what's happened."

"Of course, madam." He tucked the tray under his arm and glided over to the telephone positioned on a table under the stairs.

The footman on the landing recognized me and stepped aside, allowing me to trot up the next set of stairs. Another set of footfalls sounded as someone sprinted up from the reception hall. Monty spoke to the footman, instructing him not to let anyone come downstairs. I was too worried about Violet to stop and speak to Monty.

As I made my way down the corridor, I peered into the rooms on the back of the house that looked out toward the lake and the fireworks display. Alfred's door was open, but the room was empty. The other rooms on this side of the hall were occupied by Lady Pamela and Thea. I didn't think Violet would be in either of those rooms. Perhaps I was wrong. Perhaps Violet hadn't come upstairs with Alfred to watch the fireworks? But I should check Violet's room—just to make sure. Violet, Gwen, and I had rooms on the other side of the hall that looked out over the front of the house.

Lady Pamela's door opened. She stepped out and closed the door with a snap. I didn't want to engage in another rendition of *Ring Around the Rosie,* so I moved to the far side of the hall out of her reach. But Lady Pamela wasn't interested in games. As she neared me, I saw her pupils still were large and dark, but now her attitude seemed more angry than euphoric. She wore a new gown, a shimmery pink shift decorated with seed pearls.

She saw I'd noticed her dress. "That idiot Tug spilled his drink all over me," she said, then sailed down the corridor to the stairs.

I tapped on Violet's door. Lady Pamela's autocratic voice floated back to me, her words clipped. "Stand aside this instant." Obviously, the footman was following instructions. Monty's voice rumbled soothingly.

A voice on the other side of the door called, "Come in."

I stepped inside. Violet's room was similar to mine, except instead of pale green and gold striped wallpaper with cream furnishings, this room had a lavender color scheme. Violet was seated at the small writing desk positioned between two long windows on the far side of the room. Her back was to me. She remained bent over the desk, her pen scratching across the paper. "Have you come to apologize?" Her tone was frosty.

"No."

She whipped around. "Oh. I thought you were Alfred."

So she and Alfred were on friendly enough terms that she would expect him to come to her room. It appeared that their relationship was on a much more intimate level than Aunt Caroline or Gwen imagined. "What are you doing?" I asked. It wasn't like Violet to be shut away in her room while a party was going on.

"I'm writing a letter to Alfred to explain to him *exactly* how angry I am."

"Oh." I cleared my throat. "I'm afraid I have some bad news." I stopped, not sure how to go on. I couldn't say it as baldly as I had to Babcock. My news would shatter her. I paused, feeling sick at the thought of what she would have to face.

A tap sounded on the door connecting Violet's room to Gwen's next door. "Violet, are you in there?" The door opened an inch, and Gwen poked her head into the room. "I thought I heard voices. Hello, Olive. I haven't seen you for hours."

"I know; I wondered where you were."

"There was a bit of an upheaval in the kitchens. I went down to smooth things out."

"Only you would get roped into running someone else's party," I said, glad for the momentary distraction.

"I couldn't leave the poor cook on her own. She had no idea how many people would arrive for the party."

Violet closed the lid on the writing desk and turned sideways in her chair. "She must be new. Sebastian's parties are always like this. The word spreads and more people arrive. In fact, this one seems a little bit mild. People probably won't even remember it in a few weeks despite the fireworks."

That awful feeling in the pit of my stomach intensified. This party was certainly not going to be forgotten. "Violet, I'm afraid I have some bad news—"

Violet jumped up from her chair and crossed the room to Gwen. "What have you done to your hand?"

Gwen stepped fully into the room. She had been holding her hand pressed to her waist, but now she extended it. She had a towel wrapped around it. "Someone dropped a champagne flute, and I cut myself picking it up."

"Oh, Gwen," Violet said. "Why didn't you call for someone to clean it up?"

I went to Gwen and gently pulled back the towel to examine her hand. "Because Gwen likes to handle things herself and not cause a fuss. It doesn't look bad. It's not deep, and the bleeding has stopped." A red scratch ran along her palm from the base of her thumb down to her wrist.

"It's nothing," she said. "I came up to put a plaster on it."

Gwen dabbed at the cut with the towel. "I'll be back in a moment. Then why don't we all go down and watch the end of the fireworks?"

"That's not a good idea," I said. "In fact, I'm surprised they're still going on." Even though this side of the house overlooked the drive and we couldn't see the fireworks going off over the lake, I could still hear the pops and booms as the fireworks continued. "But I suppose they haven't sent anyone over there to tell them to stop."

"Why would they stop the fireworks?" Violet asked.

"There's been an—" I was going to say 'accident,' but that wasn't right. Alfred's fall hadn't been accidental.

Gwen tilted her head. "What's wrong, Olive? You're awfully pale. Aren't you feeling well?"

"I'm fine. It's—here, come over to the chairs." I drew them both over to the wingbacks positioned in front of the empty fire and had them sit down. I grabbed the chair from the writing desk and dragged it over. I blew out a breath, then I took one of Violet's hands in both of mine. "I'm so sorry to have to tell you this, but Alfred was pushed off the balcony—"

Violet blinked. "What?"

"Alfred was pushed off the balcony—"

Violet jumped up. "Where is he? I've got to get to him. Why didn't you tell me when you first came in?"

She turned for the door, but I caught her hand. "He's—that is —he didn't survive the fall."

Gwen drew a sharp breath. Violet stared at me for a long moment. Her face became hard. "I know people play pranks all the time, but this is beyond cruel. How could you even say something like that?"

"It's not a prank." I had expected hysterics and was ready to pull Violet into an embrace and smooth her hair as she sobbed on my shoulder, but she continued to stare at me as if my words didn't make sense.

"But he can't be. He *can't*. He's here—just across the hall—in his room. We were going to watch the fireworks, but he was being completely insufferable."

"So you were with him on the balcony?" I asked. "Who else was with you?"

"No one. I mean, I didn't even go onto the balcony. We argued downstairs before the fireworks began. He was being so stubborn —I couldn't stand it, so I—I left him in the hallway and came in here. He's still out there, on the balcony outside his room. He *has* to be. If something had happened to him, I'd know it." She put her hand on her chest. "I'd know it inside."

"I'm sorry, Violet."

"No. Take it back." Her tone was harsh. "It's not true."

I said gently, "I'm not lying to you."

Violet's fierce expression shifted and her brows wrinkled. "No. You're wrong," she said, but her tone wasn't as fierce as it had been.

Gwen stood, put her arm around Violet, and moved her back to the chair, where she gently pushed her into the seat. Using her uninjured hand, she pulled a blanket from the bed and tucked it around Violet's legs.

Violet stared at me for a long moment, then said, "What happened?"

I mentioned what I'd seen from the lawn but didn't describe Alfred's body on the terrace.

"He was pushed?" Violet asked. "That means he was killed— someone murdered him."

"Yes." I looked at Gwen, but she was ringing for the maid, probably to request a cup of tea or a sleeping draught for Violet.

I turned back to Violet in time to hear her murmur what sounded like, "Then it *was* true."

"What's true, Violet?" I asked.

"Nothing," she said in a low voice. "It doesn't matter now."

∾

THE POLICE ARRIVED, collected the names of the partygoers, and then sent them off. It was nearly three in the morning when a knock sounded on the door of Violet's room. The police had asked that Gwen and I remain in Violet's room with her until we were called for an interview.

Violet still huddled in the chair. She had cried a little, but mostly she stared, lost in her own thoughts. Gwen had hovered and tried to convince Violet to take a sleeping powder, but Violet only shook her head. She didn't move or react when a maid with dark curly hair and a long nose stepped into the room. "The police inspector would like to see you, Miss Olive."

I stood up. "Where is he?"

"In Mr. Blakely's study. I'm to take you."

I followed the maid out the door. A police constable stood outside Alfred's room. I glanced into it as we walked by. The room was packed with people. The bright flare of a flashbulb temporarily lit up the balcony.

The footman guarding the landing on the staircase was gone. We stepped around the debris from the party that still covered the stairs. As the maid and I neared the ground floor, a maid passed through the reception hall with a teapot on a tray. The soothing aroma of freshly brewed tea drifted in her wake. Thinking of Violet's near-catatonic state, I said to the maid who was walking with me, "After you take me to the inspector, could you see that Jane brings up a fresh pot of tea to Violet's room?"

The maid gripped the sides of her apron as her gaze skidded to the left and right. "I can't."

"You can't?"

"I mean, I'll see to it, but Jane can't. She's gone."

"Gone?"

She lowered her voice. "Jane packed her clothes and left. Marched out the front door, she did. I saw her myself. She used the telephone under the stairs, bold as you please, to call Mr. Brown, then left."

"Mr. Brown?"

"The taxi service in the village. Jane told Mr. Brown to meet her at the front gates."

"When did this happen?"

"It must have been a little before midnight. The fireworks started not long after she left." The maid who had passed us with the tea tray a few moments earlier came out of the little room at the end of the hall that was Sebastian's study. She left the door ajar. The maid with me indicated the study door. "The police inspector is in there. I'll see to the tea for Miss Violet," she said. She was obviously flustered because instead of escorting me into the room and announcing me, the maid ducked her head and scurried away, leaving me outside the door.

A male voice rumbled on the other side of the door. ". . . don't hold with all these rambunctious young people. Pack of trouble, that's what they are. Haven't had a moment's peace since Mr. Blakely moved into the neighborhood. Motorcars tearing through the village at all hours. Constable Phiney had to run them out of the fountain on the green last month. Splashing about in it after midnight. You mark my words, this is nothing more than a lover's quarrel gone bad. The young woman was probably drunk, or she's a drug fiend. She gave her intended a shove—that's what happened."

Indignation blazed through me. Calling Violet a drunk or drug fiend! This police officer hadn't even spoken to her. He couldn't know a thing about her yet.

A different voice, also male but more muted, replied, "Remains to be seen, Inspector. We'll do our part tonight, then I'll ring Scotland Yard. This is a matter for them. With all of these posh names, we definitely need the Yard in on this."

It wouldn't do Violet any good if I lost my temper. I took a deep breath through my nose, squashed down the outrage I felt on Violet's behalf, and rapped on the panel of the door. A rotund man with a bald head was seated behind a desk at one end of the room. He didn't look up from his examination of an open pocket watch on the desk.

The other man in the room had a thatch of coarse brown hair, a luxurious mustache, and was dressed in tweed. He was more courteous. He rose from a chair that had been swiveled away from a credenza with a typewriter. He extended his hand. "I'm Chief Constable Warren."

I shook his hand. "Olive Belgrave. Pleased to meet you."

"This is Police Inspector Jennings."

The man behind the desk finally lifted his bulky frame from his chair a few inches and gestured to the chair in front of the desk. "Have a seat."

"I'm glad you wanted to see me," I said. "I can tell you one thing straightaway. Violet didn't do it."

The inspector lifted a plump hand. "Let's not get ahead of ourselves." He checked the watch, which was centered on the desk. "First, name and residence." He jerked his head toward a man in the corner, a young constable with a shiny pink face and a pencil poised over a notebook.

I gave my name and my London address, at which the inspector raised his eyebrows. "Not one for swanky digs, then?"

"It's temporary."

"And this Miss Violet Stone is a relative?"

"My cousin. As is her sister, Gwen."

"Naturally, you would defend this . . . Violet Stone."

"Naturally. But it *is* the truth. I know Violet. She wouldn't do something like this. She told me she left Alfred in the hallway and went into her room."

"So she admits she was upstairs?"

"In her room, not on the balcony."

He made a noise that indicated disbelief, then looked at the watch again. "Right. Moving on. About the balcony. I understand you saw the whole thing from the lawn?"

"What little there was to see in the darkness." I described the struggle and the brief glimpse of the figures when the firework lit up the house.

Inspector Jennings drummed his chubby fingers on the desk. "And your cousin Violet, she has blonde hair?"

"Well, yes, but that doesn't mean she was on the balcony. Plenty of people at this party have blonde hair."

"But she was the only one who had had an argument with the victim." Inspector Jennings gave me a perfunctory smile and checked the pocket watch. "I believe we've taken enough time with you, Miss—er—Belgrave. That will be all." He looked at the constable. "Have her escorted upstairs. Let's have the fiancée in next."

CHAPTER TEN

J woke with a start. Why had I been sleeping in a chair?

The room was dim, but sunlight radiated around the closed green drapes. Oh, yes. It all rushed back—Archly Manor, Alfred's death, and that police inspector who seemed to have decided Violet was guilty.

I straightened and massaged the kink in my neck.

Last night Gwen had insisted on accompanying Violet to her interview with Inspector Jennings. I had returned to my room and sat down in the chair beside the empty fireplace, but I'd left the connecting door between my room and Gwen's open, thinking I'd hear them when they returned. I must have slept through any noise they made.

I stood and rotated my shoulders, then stretched my arms. I still wore the white dress with the gold overdress, but it was creased with wrinkles. I walked to the windows, drew back the curtains, and blinked against the bright sunlight.

It was a gorgeous summer day with a bright blue sky above the dense trees. I opened the window, and a breeze ruffled the drapes. Some of the paper lanterns had fallen out of the trees and were scattered across the lawn. The morning dew had coated them, and now they had a sad, deflated look.

A servant moved across the grass, picking up the lanterns, bits of trash, cigarette butts, and discarded plates and glasses. The grinding noise of an engine filled the air, then a lorry with the name of a caterer emblazoned on the side came around the house from the back entrance and lumbered along the drive toward the main gate. The police must have finished on the terrace and ground floor. Last night, they'd banished everyone from the north side of the house where Alfred had fallen.

I went to the connecting door between my room and Gwen's, which was still slightly open as I'd left it. I pushed it back another few inches. Gwen sat in front of her dressing table, her loose hair spread across her shoulders. She was wrapped in a dressing gown and held a brush in her hand, turning it over and over as she stared at the glass. My movement, reflected in the mirror, caught her attention. "Oh, good. You're up. I didn't have the heart to wake you when we came back from speaking with the police."

"How did that go?"

Gwen put the brush down and rubbed her forehead. "Terrible. That awful man from the police thinks Violet pushed Alfred. And I think the only reason he didn't arrest her last night is because an inspector from Scotland Yard will be here later today."

"I had the same feeling about him—that he suspected Violet, but that premise is absurd. Heaps of people came to the party. And who knows how many of them came upstairs?"

Gwen looked up. "What do you mean? Sebastian had footmen stationed at the main stairs as well as the servants' staircase to prevent anyone from wandering into the rooms above the ground floor."

"Well, yes, but who's to say someone didn't slip past a footman or perhaps bribe their way upstairs? And even if we're only considering people who could legitimately get beyond the footmen, Violet wasn't the only one upstairs."

"Someone else was up here at that time?"

"Yes. Reams of people, actually."

"Who?"

"Lady Pamela, for one. She came out of her room when I came upstairs to find Violet. Thea had retired to her room with a headache, and I know Jane was tending to her. Who knows who else was on this floor at that time? Anyone could have been lurking behind all the closed doors."

"I was up here too." Gwen smiled briefly. "But I don't think the fact that I—or anyone else—was on this floor will have any impact on what the police think. They seem to have made up their minds." She aligned the brush with a comb. "I had to telephone Mum this morning. It was awful. She's so worried. On top of everything else, Father has come down with something." Gwen said, her voice wavering.

"Gwen, what's happened?"

"The doctor suspects it might be the . . ." Gwen took a breath. "The flu."

"Oh, Gwen. I'm sorry. That's awful. I'm sure he'll be fine, though." After the horrible flu epidemic a few years ago, just the word *flu* sent a chill through me.

Gwen blinked and sniffed. "Yes, I'm sure he will be too. It's all that tramping around the estate. Mum said it was especially damp a few days ago, and he was out the entire day. I'm not going to tell Violet. She has enough to worry about right now." Gwen picked up her handkerchief and blew her nose. "The doctor's quarantined everyone at Parkview. Otherwise I'm sure Mum and Father would already be on their way here. Father's contacted his solicitor, but the solicitor is in Ireland." Gwen tossed the handkerchief onto the dressing table. "Everything is so terrible right now. When word gets out in Nether Woodsmoor, Mum'll be devastated. The whispers. You know how monstrous people can be."

"Yes, I know—they can be vicious, especially in a village." I pressed my lips together, remembering the gossipy murmurs I'd heard in Nether Woodsmoor as a child about Mum . . . and about me too. After Mum rode a bike through the village wearing trousers, I could still hear two of the old biddies as I waited behind them at the chemist. Unaware of my presence, Mrs. Nettlebury said to Mrs. Taylor, ". . . what can you expect? She is *American*, after all. Common—not up to our standards at all. I have no idea what the dear vicar sees in her." Since something as innocuous as my mother's clothing set them off, I hated to think what the reaction of some of the villagers would be to the news that Violet was caught up in the investigation of Alfred's death.

I moved across the room and sat on the end of the bed. "Don't worry about Uncle Leo. You know he's as strong as an ox. He'll be fine in a few days. Just think of what a horrible patient he is and be glad you're not the one trying to convince him to stay in bed and rest."

Gwen's nervous fingers were fiddling with the brush again, but she made an effort and a tiny smile appeared. "Yes, that is true."

"And as far as the police's opinion about Violet, we'll just have to find someone else for them to consider."

Gwen stopped fingering the brush. "Do you think it's possible? To find someone else? And is that quite . . . fair? To divert their attention onto someone else?"

"Gwen, dear, you have to stop being so tender hearted. Is it fair to suspect Violet simply because she was on this floor? Really, that's all they have to go on," I said.

Gwen's forehead wrinkled. "No, it's not right of them to decide it was Violet with so little to go on." Her face cleared and she swiveled fully toward me. "You can do it."

"Of course I'll do anything to help Violet." We'd grown up together. I would do everything I could to help Violet. Gwen, Violet, and Peter were like siblings to me. And Gwen was right about the scandal. It would devastate Aunt Caroline. Uncle Leo didn't mind things like that so much, but Aunt Caroline wasn't so lost in her painting that she wouldn't notice the sting of gossip.

Gwen's face became animated. "No, I mean you can investigate this, like you were investigating Alfred."

"But that was different. I was only looking into his background."

Gwen said, "It's not that different. You've already found out some information, like who was on this floor. Now you just need to find out who had a motive to push Alfred over the balcony."

"When you put it like that, it doesn't sound at all like meddling in a police investigation."

"You wouldn't be meddling. A few questions here and there." She came over and sat on the bed beside me. "I don't know if you heard that Violet and Alfred argued, and several people over-heard them."

"Tug mentioned it to me."

A look of distaste crossed Gwen's face. "Not a very pleasant young man."

"So you danced with him too?" I asked.

"You mean, did I try to keep him at arm's length to stay out of range of the fumes?" She grinned, then turned serious again. "In any case, the fact that Violet and Alfred argued . . . well, I'll be the first to admit she has a temper, but Violet would never do anything to actually hurt Alfred."

"Yes, I agree."

"But the argument is awfully significant—at least in the eyes of that police inspector. Last night, he kept going on and on, asking Violet about it. She said it was about whether they should sit out a dance or not, which I don't believe for a minute. So that's three things against Violet—her relationship with Alfred, she was on this floor, and she and Alfred argued."

"This inspector from the Yard may be completely different from the local police inspector. The Scotland Yard inspector may have an open mind."

"But what if he doesn't? No, you've got to do it." She straight-ened, her face alight. "I know. I'll pay you."

I opened my mouth to protest, but Gwen squeezed my hand. "I know you need the money."

"I don't think—"

"I won't hear anything else about it. Consider this an extension of our earlier decision to have you search out the truth about Alfred," Gwen said in her best lady of the manor voice, then her shoulders sloped and worry filled her expression. "You will do it, won't you? You're so *good* at this kind of thing. I'd be hopeless at it. You're marvelous at finding things out."

"I wasn't actually doing that well where Alfred was concerned. It had all been a dead end, in fact."

"Please. We'll work together. You're miles better at something like this than I am, but I'll do what I can."

"Yes, you do tend to see the best in everyone. If I left it to you, you'd never have the heart to name another suspect."

She laughed. "I wouldn't go that far—it *is* my sister we're talking about—but you're right. I do tend to assume the best."

I couldn't turn her down. I patted her hand. "While I, hard-hearted working girl that I am, don't have any such qualms."

I BATHED and changed into a pale yellow dress with white piping on the sleeves and collar. It was too frivolous for a job interview, but it was perfect for a country house visit. I couldn't do anything about the dark circles under my eyes, but I dusted my face with powder and added a touch of color to my lips. I selected a long necklace of bugle beads, which reminded me of the pearls I'd found on the terrace. I probably should've given them to the police inspector, but after his immediate assumption of Violet's guilt, I'd decided to hold onto them and give them to the inspector from Scotland Yard. When I'd taken off my gloves, I'd left the pearls inside them. With all the confusion around Alfred's death, a maid hadn't been up to tidy my room or put my clothes away.

I went to my dresser and shook out the glove. The string of pearls rolled across the dresser, milky white and perfectly matched. I dropped them in my handbag. The pearls were the least of my worries. If the inspector from Scotland Yard wasn't reasonable, I would still do everything I could to make sure he widened his investigation beyond Violet. I'd made a promise to Gwen, and I'd fulfill it. It seemed the best place to start was with the other people who had been on the second floor last night.

It was only a little after eight. I was sure that Lady Pamela wouldn't emerge from her room for hours, and Thea was probably still asleep as well, so I couldn't make any progress there, but I could find out more about Jane. She'd definitely been buzzing with strong emotion when she had come to Thea's room, and she'd left Archly Manor shortly afterward. I rang for a cup of tea. When the maid brought it, it was the same dark-haired young woman with the long nose who had escorted me downstairs. I wondered if she'd gotten any sleep at all. She put the tray down and was about to leave when I asked her, "Has Jane returned?"

"No, miss. I don't expect she will. I think she's gone to London to stay with her sister."

"Did Jane go to London often?"

"As often as she could. Her sister works in a bank. Jane said that someday she'd be able to work there too. I thought it was all talk, but I suppose it has to be true, now that she's gone and left. After Mr. Eton spoke to her so harshly, I'm not at all surprised she left."

I hadn't heard about this. "Something happened between Jane and Mr. Eton?"

"Oh, nothing, I'm sure . . . a small misunderstanding." She moved toward the door. "If that will be all . . ."

"No, wait. It's important. Jane and Alfred argued?"

She gave a small nod.

"And what did they argue about?"

"I don't know, miss. I only saw them from down the hall. Mr. Eton was rather looming over Jane, pointing at her. He was mad —I could see that by his face. He was frowning and jabbing his finger at her. She pushed his hand away and said something . . .

impertinent, I thought, by the look of it. Then Jane walked away. That's all I saw, I promise. I didn't hear a word they said."

I couldn't draw any more details out of her, so I dismissed her, drank my tea, and ate the buttered toast on the tray. I left my room by the door that opened onto the hallway. I walked past Gwen's door and knocked on the door to Violet's room. I'd convinced Gwen to lie down and rest for a while. She hadn't slept at all, and I didn't want to disturb her. The doors on the other side of the hall were closed. Light showed under Alfred's door, but Lady Pamela's and Thea's doors were still closed and no light showed from under them.

I tapped on Violet's door. No response came from the other side, so I peeked inside. Violet, wearing a lilac dressing gown, was curled into the corner of one of the chairs positioned in front of a roaring fire, her head resting against the wing. Without lifting her head, she glanced at me, then returned her gaze to the fire.

"Goodness, Violet. It's stifling in here."

"I can't seem to get warm."

"Then you should get dressed and come outside. It's a beautiful day, and the sun is bright. It will be hot soon."

"I don't want to see anyone. I don't want to talk to anyone either." She shifted her shoulder, turning away from me slightly. I sat down in the chair across from her. "Violet, I know you're upset about Alfred."

"It's awful," she said in a small voice that was unlike her usual robust tone. "I don't want to think about it, but it's all I *can* think about. And then there's that ghastly policeman. He thinks *I* pushed Alfred. It's like an endless carousel in my head. First Alfred and then the police. I was afraid that they were going to take me away. And then what would I do? What would Mum and Daddy do? They'd be crushed—absolutely crushed."

"Then I suggest you help me prove you didn't do it." I spoke with the starchy tones that Nanny at Parkview used on Gwen, Violet, and Peter when they were young. Violet was already distraught, and I didn't want to give her any reason to become more emotional than she already was. I wanted to ask her about the argument between Alfred and Jane but decided to hold off. She was in a fragile state, and it wasn't the right time to fire questions at her.

She looked at me out of the corner of her eye. "But how can we do that? I was in this room, alone. There's no way to prove that."

"No, but we can prove that someone *else* could have been on the balcony besides you."

Violet turned. Her hair was pressed flat against her head where she'd been leaning on the chair. "Like who?"

"Well, there are lots of people who might be possibilities."

"Who?"

"Lady Pamela, for one. She was upstairs at the same time you were. I saw her when I came up to find you. I'm sure she's sleeping now. It would be incredibly bad manners to burst into her room and ask her about last night, so we can't talk to her right now, but I intend to talk to the footman who guarded the landing. I'll find out who else came upstairs. Then there's also the maid, Jane, who left sometime last night and hasn't returned. I want to discover where she's gone."

At the name of the maid, a spark of interest appeared in Violet's eyes, but then she dropped her gaze to the arm of the chair and ran her finger over a seam. "Anyone else?"

"Thea had a migraine." With the extreme pain Thea had been in, I couldn't picture her wrestling with anyone to shove them over a balcony. "She was either asleep or incapacitated from her headache, but I'd still like to talk to her later today when she finally comes out of her room."

Violet traced the seam, giving it all her attention. "I suppose I could get dressed."

"Excellent idea."

I went downstairs and asked Babcock where to find the footman who had guarded the landing during the party. If he was curious as to why I was asking about a footman, Babcock didn't show it. With his face impassive, he told me George had gone to retrieve the breakfast tray from the nursery and would be down shortly.

I trotted up the stairs to the first floor, then went down the hallway to the narrow set of stairs at the end of the corridor, the servants' staircase that ran from the top floor to the kitchen on the ground floor. I climbed the bare wooden stair treads to the next floor and met the footman as he backed out of the nursery door, a tray with empty plates balanced in one hand.

I didn't want to startle him, so I waited until he'd closed the door and turned in my direction. "Hello, George. I'm Miss Belgrave."

"Yes, miss. I remember you from last night."

I eyed the full tray, which had to be heavy. "Excellent. I won't keep you. I have a question about last evening. Who went upstairs shortly before the fireworks began or right after?"

He wasn't quite so schooled as Babcock in keeping his expression blank, and a flare of surprise showed on his face for a second before he cleared it and said, "Besides yourself, I saw Miss Violet and Mr. Eton as well as Lady Pamela and . . ." He stared over my shoulder as he thought. "And Miss Stone."

"What about Mrs. Reid?" I asked. "Did she leave her room after I brought her up?"

"No, miss." He adjusted his grip on the tray.

"I'll walk with you to the stairs," I said and turned. He followed me as I asked, "And Jane, the maid. What about her?"

"She came up, but that was earlier, when you were with Mrs. Reid."

"And did she come down?"

"Yes, miss. She was carrying her suitcase."

"And she didn't go back up later?"

"No, miss."

We reached the staircase, and I nodded to it. "What about these stairs? Could someone have come up or down them?"

"No one did."

"How do you know that?"

"Tommy was on duty at the base of these stairs. I spoke to him last night, and he said no one came by him."

"He's sure?"

"Yes. You can speak to him if you like, or Cook. Anyone going up these stairs would have to go right by her too."

"Thank you, I'd like to do that."

George nodded, and I preceded him down the backstairs, which I think shocked him a bit, but I didn't see the point in retracing my steps to the main staircase then walking around to the kitchen through the main rooms of the house when I could go directly down from where I was.

I emerged into the kitchen, startling the servants into a brief silence. I smiled and crossed to the cook. "Sorry to disturb you, but I have a question about last night."

"Don't we all, dearie. Don't we all. I'm Mrs. Finley," she said. "How can I help you?"

I smiled at her, glad she was the informal type. I looked over my shoulder to the stairs. "Did anyone go upstairs last night?"

"Heavens, no," she said. "That's the one thing Mr. Blakely won't hold with—people stumbling about upstairs unsupervised." She picked up a skillet and waved it back and forth as she shook her head. "No, Tommy stood on guard the whole evening. As I told the police, he's a good lad and wouldn't let someone slip by." She pointed the skillet at me. "And they'd have to get by me as well."

The staircase was in plain sight of most of the kitchen, so I didn't see how someone could have gotten by unnoticed. Cook leaned in and said, "George and Tommy wouldn't let anyone go upstairs. It'd be their job if they did, and neither one of them would want that."

I asked after the maid who had brought my tea that morning. I learned her name was Milly, and I found her in the ballroom, scrubbing the floor where a drink had been spilled. She scrambled to her feet as I crossed the parquet.

"Hello, Milly. I have another question about Jane. Do you know where her sister lives in London?"

"Yes, miss. She has a room not far from where she works."

"But do you know what part of town it's in?"

"No, but the address is on a stack of letters. Jane left them in the dresser in our room. She was in such a hurry when she packed that she forgot them. I found them this morning and put them aside for her. I know she'll want them."

"It's important I get in touch with Jane. Could you get one of the letters for me?"

"Yes, miss." Milly left and returned with a stack of envelopes. I copied down the return address from one, then went to look for Violet in the breakfast room, but she hadn't appeared.

She must have changed her mind and decided to stay in her room. I asked for Gwen's motor to be brought around. I knew Gwen wouldn't mind if I borrowed it. While I waited, I wrote Gwen a note, letting her know I was using her motor and I'd be back later. I penned a second note to Violet and sent it upstairs to her. The mint green Morris Cowley rolled to a stop on the sweep as I pulled on my gloves. The chauffeur held the door for me, and I climbed in. I released the lever, and the motor was rolling forward when Violet dashed out the front door. I applied the brake.

She gripped the top of the door. "Where are you going?"

"To London."

Her eyebrows shot up. "You can't do that."

"Why not?"

"The police won't like it."

"Did the police specifically tell us we couldn't leave?"

"Well . . . no."

"Then it will be fine, I'm sure. And I *am* coming back. I'm only going to dash up to town and find out what happened with Jane. I got her sister's address from one of the maids. It should only take a few hours at the most."

"I want to come with you."

"Then climb in."

Violet's grip on the door tightened. "You don't think we'll get in trouble?"

"I have no idea. If we do, we'll beg for forgiveness."

One corner of Violet's mouth turned up. "That's usually how I operate."

"I know. I'll wait while you get your hat."

CHAPTER ELEVEN

*a*s Violet and I zipped through the sun-speckled shade of Archly Manor's grounds, I swung the steering wheel of the Morris back and forth, following the curves of the road, readjusting to driving on the left side of the road. I'd last driven in America and was glad to have a few acres to recalibrate my brain to English driving. By the time we came to the gates, I felt confident and swung the motor toward the little village closest to the estate. The papier-mâché unicorn guarding the gate was gone, and I wondered if some of the partygoers had taken it with them when they left. It would be just the sort of thing that set would find hilarious—driving back to London with a huge unicorn sticking out of their motor.

The summer sunshine was warm, but the breeze kept it from becoming too hot. Violet had been silent, and I left her to soak up the sun and feel the wind pulling at her hair and clothes. When I slowed down in the village and rolled to a stop in front of a cottage with a blue door and white shutters, she said, "I thought we were going to London?"

"We are. But first, one quick stop. Wait here. I shouldn't be a moment."

The blue door opened, and I introduced myself to a woman

who wore a housedress and apron and had her dull brown hair pulled back into a bun. I explained I was looking for Mr. Brown.

"He's out. Off to Finchbury Crossing."

"To the train station?"

She looked over my shoulder to the pale green car. "That's right. I don't suppose you're wanting to hire him."

"No. I only want to ask him a question about last night. Did he get a telephone call from Archly Manor late last night?"

"That he did. Nearly midnight. Picked up a young woman at the gates, he said. Drove her to Finchbury Crossing and waited until the last train arrived. He saw her safely on the train to London. Said he didn't feel right about leaving her there at that time of night."

"Thank you, that's helpful. When will he return? Later this afternoon?"

She confirmed this was the case and seemed slightly offended that I obviously wanted to hear the story from her husband.

I returned to the motor.

"What was that about?" Violet asked.

I was glad to see the interest in her eyes instead of dazed blankness. I explained, and she asked, "So you thought Jane might not have left?"

"I didn't know. Best to find out exactly what she did rather than speculate, don't you think?"

"Yes, I suppose so."

"What do you know about the argument between Jane and Alfred?" I asked, skimming along the road to London.

Violet's chin came up. "Nothing. Alfred was absolutely unreasonable. He refused to tell me what it was about."

"And then you and Alfred argued?"

"Yes."

"Did it happen often? Alfred arguing with the servants . . . or anyone else?"

"No, of course not."

Her response was so quick that I looked away from the road, but her head was turned away, and I couldn't see her expression.

Violet said, "I think I'll try and sleep a bit." She put her head down on the seat, closed her eyes, and didn't move until we arrived in London.

∼

JANE'S SISTER lived at a much better address than I did in London, a neat little terraced house almost in Kensington. I parked the motor and gently shook Violet's shoulder. "We're here."

Violet blinked and sat up, a confused look on her face.

"We're in London at Jane's sister's lodging house."

Violet straightened her hat and smoothed her dress. "So what do we do? Ring the bell and ask to speak with her?"

"We won't have to do that if we can catch her before she gets too far." I tilted my head in the direction of a woman with short white-blonde curls in a flower-print dress who had come out of the front door of the house. She walked quickly down the stairs and past us, moving at a good clip down the sidewalk. She never looked our way. Violet twisted her head around to watch her, then looked back at me. "That's Jane? Are you sure?"

"I think so. It's amazing what a bob and new clothes can do." I climbed out of the car and hurried after the woman. I caught up with her at the next corner as she waited for a break in the traffic. "Jane?"

She turned, and her eyebrows rose. "Miss Olive?"

"It is you," I said. "You look a bit different with your hair shorter, but I thought it was you." The fair-haired bun that had rested at the nape of Jane's neck was gone. Her hair curled in short tendrils framing her face.

She touched the ends of the curls. "It's quite different. I'm not sure if I like it."

"It's very becoming," I said as Violet arrived at my side. Jane eyed her with what seemed to be a wary expression. I glanced at

Violet. She had a scowl on her face as she studied Jane's new look. Tension vibrated in the air between them. Perhaps bringing Violet along hadn't been the best idea. I'd thought the change of scene would do Violet good, but the animosity she was projecting toward Jane might make it hard to convince Jane to talk to us.

I said to Jane, "You look as though you're in a hurry, but I'd like to ask you a few questions if you can spare a few moments. Something rather . . . tragic . . . happened last night at Archly Manor after you left."

Everyone loves a mystery, and the intrigue must have piqued Jane's interest because she checked her wristwatch. "I do have a few minutes. There's a Lyons this way."

Once we were settled at a table and served tea, Jane said, "I suppose this is about why I left so suddenly, isn't it?"

"Yes," Violet said. "Why did you leave your post and scurry away in the middle of the night?"

I sent Violet a warning glance as Jane said, "It was a silly thing, to leave like that. Of course, if I'd not had my sister to go to, I wouldn't have done it." Jane had been stirring her tea. She put the spoon down with a click. "I'd had enough. I wasn't going to put up with it anymore. I considered staying through the end of the month, but . . ." She pressed her lips together for a moment. "I know he's your fiancé, but he can be . . . bothersome."

Violet looked a little surprised at this burst of honesty from the former maid. A day ago, I doubt that Jane would've ever made that statement, but this was a new woman. The bobbed hair and bright frock weren't the only change. Her attitude was no longer self-effacing.

Violet's hand tightened on the handle of her teacup. I asked hurriedly, "It was last night that he bothered you?"

Jane had been about to take a sip of her tea, but she set her cup down and looked directly at Violet. "I know you're jealous and think he was flirting, but he wanted money."

Violet dropped her gaze from Jane to the tabletop. I turned back to Jane. "I'm not sure I understand."

Jane opened her mouth, took a small breath, then made a huffing sound. "There's really no way to say it politely." She placed her hand on the table in front of Violet. "I don't want to hurt your feelings, but I swear it's true. It was blackmail."

"Blackmail?" I repeated, and several people in the restaurant turned to look at me. I was stunned. I'd expected her to say Alfred had made unwelcome advances. I lowered my voice and leaned over the table. "What exactly happened?"

She pushed her teacup away and settled her hands in her lap. "I'll tell you the whole thing, then perhaps you'll understand. Mr. Eton often stays at Archly Manor. One morning when he was staying at the manor, he found me in Mr. Blakely's study. I was using the typewriter." She pushed her shoulders back. "I've been learning to type. My sister said that the bank would have an opening soon, and if I could type, I had a good chance of being hired because she could give me a recommendation. She had her instruction books and sent them to me. I couldn't afford to go to a secretarial school, but Mr. Blakely had a typewriter, so I got up early and snuck downstairs before most of the household was awake to practice."

I waved off a waitress approaching our table, and Jane went on, "Mr. Eton wasn't an early riser. I don't know why he was up at that hour, but he saw me, and he knew I had no business using the typewriter. I suppose I looked guilty when he startled me. He only made some comment about how he'd never seen a maid who could type. He told me to get on about my business and leave everything as it was. I did take the practice book with me, but I was so flustered that I left the paper in the typewriter." She sighed. "I thought that was the end of it, but a few days later, he told me that if I didn't pay him two shillings that week, he would tell Mr. Babcock. Mr. Eton had kept the paper I'd accidentally left in the typewriter, you see. He said it was evidence, and he'd show it to Babcock if I didn't pay."

"And you were afraid you'd lose your position even though you were doing it before your day officially began?" I asked.

"Mr. Babcock is not the most lenient of people." Jane closed her eyes for a moment, then said, "I gave Mr. Eton the money. I realize now it was a stupid, *stupid* thing to do because the next week he wanted more money. He went away for a few weeks, and I thought it was over, that he'd forgotten it. A bit of fun with the maid, you know? But last night he cornered me and said, 'Don't forget, you owe me three weeks' worth now.'"

She looked out the window. "I don't know what came over me last night. I decided I didn't want to do it anymore, and I told him so." She turned to Violet. "You saw part of that, I think."

Violet gave a little nod of her head.

Jane's voice was stronger as she said, "I told him I wouldn't put up with it anymore and told him to leave me alone. He laughed and said, 'We'll see about that.' It made me so angry. That was when you called for help with Mrs. Reid," Jane said, looking to me. "Once I had her comfortable, I went upstairs, changed out of my uniform, packed my bag, and marched down the stairs. I knew there was a late train out of Finchbury Crossing. If I hurried, I could catch it and be in London and with my sister in a few hours. I had enough money saved up for the train fare and to pay Mr. Brown to get me to the station."

"So you caught the train at what time?"

"At midnight."

Violet, who had been so silent, said, "Alfred's dead."

Jane looked as if someone had slapped her. "Dead? But how? Was there an accident?"

"He was pushed off the balcony during the fireworks," Violet said.

"Oh, how horrible." Jane looked away, her thoughts obviously turned inward, but then her gaze flew back to Violet. "I'm so sorry. I didn't know—"

Violet nodded, and Jane's sympathy must have moved her because Violet's eyes glistened with tears and she sniffed. "Thank you."

To give Violet a moment to compose herself, I turned the

conversation back to Jane. "Because of Alfred's death, I'm sure the police will contact you."

"Oh, that's true. How terrible. I'm sure my sister's landlady will be appalled, but I suppose I'll have to talk to them. Everything happened exactly as I said."

I believed her. Jane hadn't seemed to be keeping anything back or trying to avoid answering our questions. The fact that Alfred had tried to blackmail her was shocking, but I didn't think she was making it up. After all, it would be so much easier to lie and say he'd pressed his attentions on her. I said, "I'm sure they'll want to confirm certain things with you, like what you've told us as well as the fact that you gave Thea—Mrs. Reid—a sleeping powder."

She nodded. "Yes, poor thing."

"So you made it for her?" I asked.

"Yes, she was in terrible pain and was keeping as still as possible. She asked me to mix the packet into the water and then wait while she drank it so I could take the glass away."

"And you saw her take it all?"

"Oh, yes. She needed it."

I looked at Violet with raised eyebrows, indicating that if she had any questions she should ask them now. Violet shook her head, and after a few more minutes, Jane said she had to leave. Milly had given me Jane's letters that she'd left behind at Archly Manor, and I gave those to Jane before she left.

As we stepped onto the pavement and moved in the opposite direction from Jane, I said to Violet, "You knew, didn't you?"

CHAPTER TWELVE

*V*iolet picked up her pace. "Why would you think I knew anything about Alfred blackmailing a maid?"

I hurried to keep up with her. "Because you weren't surprised."

Violet's steps halted, and her gaze dropped from my face. "Yes, I knew," she mumbled, her chin tucked into the collar of her dress.

"How did you find out Alfred was blackmailing her?" I asked. "*Did* you overhear the argument between Alfred and Jane?"

She looked around the crowded street. "Not here. I'll tell you on the way back to Archly Manor."

She remained silent until we were settled in the motor and I was navigating through the traffic of London. I glanced at her out of the corner of my eye. She stared through the windshield, gripping her handbag. She didn't look at all like the carefree young woman of a few days before whose only concern had been dancing at a party.

Once the traffic thinned and we were on the outskirts of London, I said, "So how did you find out about the blackmail?"

Violet's hold on her handbag tightened. "I *knew* Alfred wasn't telling me everything. I could tell there was something between him and Jane. That dratted comb fell out of my hair again, and I'd gone to fix it. When I came back down the hall to the ballroom, Alfred and Jane were over to the side in a dark corner. I couldn't hear what they said, but they were arguing rather fiercely. He leaned in and said something with great emphasis."

"And you couldn't hear them?"

"No, but I could see Jane's face. She had the last word. Alfred wasn't happy. When I asked him about it, he would only tell me that it didn't matter—that it was nothing." She turned away. It was harder to hear her voice as she said, "I jumped to the same conclusion that you did, that Alfred was . . . flirting with her. Alfred wouldn't say anything else. I went off to dance with another chap."

Trying to make him jealous, I thought.

Violet went on, "I danced three or four dances with other boys. Then, because it was getting close to midnight, I went off to find him."

"And I bet you asked him about it again?" Violet was one of the most persistent people I knew.

"He couldn't expect me to just forget it. I found him at the side of the ballroom, laughing with some chaps as if nothing had happened. When he saw me, he said it was time for the fireworks, and we should go to the balcony upstairs for the best view. I went, but I asked him if he was ready to talk about what had happened, and he refused. And that was the last time I spoke to him." Violet's voice trembled. She took a handkerchief out of her handbag and pressed it to her eyes. "I didn't speak a word to him on the stairs. I wanted him to realize just how angry I was."

I tried to work out the timeline in my head. Alfred and Violet went upstairs shortly before the fireworks started, and I'd seen Alfred pushed over the balcony at the beginning of the fireworks display. Something was off. I slowed the motor as we caught up to a lorry on a narrow stretch of the road. "But you said you never went outside on the balcony—that you went to your room instead. How could you know he was blackmailing Jane if he didn't tell you before the fireworks started?"

Violet jerked the handkerchief away from her face. "Because I was so infuriated I couldn't stay in my room. I waited a few minutes, then slipped into Alfred's room. He was on the balcony, and I knew he didn't see me because his back was turned to me. He never turned around. Alfred had this little book, a notebook —" She made an impatient gesture, waving the handkerchief. "It makes more sense if I tell you about the notebook first. Alfred and I argued about it."

"That's not particularly surprising. All couples disagree."

"I suppose. Alfred had a small black leather notebook. I asked to borrow it one day to make a note, but he wouldn't let me have it."

"And that piqued your curiosity, but I don't see what it has to do with Alfred's death."

"I'm getting there. You need the background to understand it properly. Where was I? Oh, the notebook. He wouldn't let me see it, so of course I was curious. Don't look at me like that. You'd be exactly the same way."

"Yes, I suppose I would be. I am a terribly curious creature."

Violet said, "Alfred and I were to be married. If he wouldn't share his notebook with me, what else was he hiding?"

"A good question." I didn't add that Alfred had obviously been hiding quite a bit more than a notebook.

"So I decided I'd find it and take a quick peek. Oh, I know that's not the done thing, but as I said, he was going to be my husband, and I couldn't have him hiding things from me. Yesterday I stopped by his room to ask him a question. As I walked in, he put the notebook away in the middle drawer of the writing desk. So last night, when I was so upset, I decided I'd take his idiotic notebook and see what was so private that he wouldn't share it with me."

She focused on smoothing her gloves as she said, "I slipped into his room while he was on the balcony watching the fireworks. I pulled out the drawer, and there was the notebook." She lifted her chin. "I took it back to my room."

"Was there anyone else on the balcony with him?"

"No, not that I could see, but the balcony stretches along the back of the house. Anyone from the other rooms on that side of the house could have come out onto the balcony from their room and joined him there."

"That's true." Lady Pamela and Thea had rooms farther along the corridor on that same side of the house. The French windows from their rooms would open onto the balcony.

I inched the motor forward, hoping to pass the lorry when the road opened up. "So, what was in the notebook?"

"The first part of it was random jottings, bits and bobs. Nothing important. A note to telephone his tailor, a reminder to order more milk. Can you believe it?"

"It does seem odd. Did you look through the whole book?"

"I did, and I was feeling indignant by the time I got a few pages into it. They were such trivial things. Why would he keep me from looking at it?" Her gaze dropped, and she plucked at the trim on her handbag. "But in the last few pages, I found a list of names . . . of a sort. Across from some of them were dates and amounts of money. A folded-up piece of paper was tucked in the back. It was typewritten and obviously the kind of thing you'd type up if you were using an exercise book. The quick brown fox jumped over the lazy dog—that kind of thing."

"Jane's typewriting practice."

"Yes. I didn't realize what it was then, of course."

"So Alfred was blackmailing more people than Jane." Aunt Caroline and Gwen's instincts had been right about Alfred. He wasn't a gentleman. I'd thought he was a slippery one—that too-ready smile—but even I hadn't expected him to be a blackmailer.

"It does look that way."

"You said there were names listed?"

"Sometimes. One was a single initial J, which must have been Jane. And then there were some that had to be nicknames."

"Such as?"

"Well, there was a *Lady Snooty* listed. I figured that had to be Lady Pamela."

"Most likely."

"That was the most obvious one. The others . . . I wasn't sure who they could be," Violet said.

"Well, this is interesting."

"What do you mean?"

The road finally widened, and I shifted gears. We zipped around the lorry. "Blackmail is an excellent motivation for murder. Do you have the notebook with you?"

"No."

"You left it in a safe place, then?"

Violet didn't answer, and I turned toward her. "You *did* hide it? I suppose it's safe enough in your room . . ."

She raised her chin. "No, I burned it."

"You burned it?"

"The wall! Watch out for that wall."

I was so shocked I'd let the Morris drift to the spongy earth at the edge of the road. I jerked the wheel, brought the motor back onto the road, and slowed so I could turn to Violet. "Don't you realize you destroyed a piece of evidence that could be used to show other people had a motive to want to hurt Alfred?"

"I realize that *now*, but when I found out Alfred had died, I was so shocked. I wasn't thinking straight. I knew I shouldn't have the notebook. I couldn't get it back into his room, not with the police in there. And I didn't know how long it would be before the police might want to search my room. When they found that notebook, how would I explain having it? I'd have to tell them I'd been in Alfred's room. The footman had seen me come upstairs with Alfred. If the police figured out that I was in Alfred's room before he died, then what would I do?"

I tapped the steering wheel. "The fire in your room this morning. You weren't cold. That's when you burned it."

"It seemed the best thing to do at the time."

"You didn't save anything from it?"

"No. I stirred the fire until even the cover was gone."

"I have a pencil and some paper in my handbag." I pushed it across the seat to her. "I suggest you reconstruct the list as best you remember."

CHAPTER THIRTEEN

*B*y the time we arrived back at Archly Manor, Violet had recreated as much of the information from the list as she could remember.

We turned through the gates, and I pulled over in the shade. Violet handed me her list. "This is all I can remember."

Violet had not excelled in penmanship, and writing while the motor was moving made her notes even harder to read, but I was able to decipher the first name. "Lady Snooty," I read. "I agree, that's probably Lady Pamela, which is interesting." I thought I probably knew what Alfred was blackmailing Lady Pamela about, but I didn't share that information with Violet. I went on to the next word. "Muncher? Any idea who that could be?"

Violet shook her head. "Not the faintest."

"And no amount was listed beside this name? Or couldn't you remember?"

"No, that one was blank."

"Perhaps Alfred tried to blackmail this Muncher person but wasn't successful. Perhaps Alfred's list contained blackmail targets as well as people he'd been successful in getting money from."

Violet threw herself back against the seat. "It's hopeless. The only one that we have any idea about is the initial *J*. But we know that Jane was on the train when Alfred died. The only thing we've accomplished today is to *eliminate* Jane as a suspect."

On the way back to Archly Manor, we'd stopped again at the house with the blue door and the white shutters, and I'd spoken to Mr. Brown. He'd confirmed he'd picked up a young woman with blonde hair at the front gates of Archly Manor a little before midnight the previous evening. He had driven her to Finchbury Crossing, the nearest train station, and waited until he saw her board the last train to London. I knew it was the last train to London, and it didn't stop at any nearby villages. I'd checked the train schedule when I was in London in case Gwen couldn't bring me to Archly Manor.

Violet said, "We're not making any progress."

"I disagree." I tapped the list. "We know Alfred was holding something over these people. Any one of them could have decided they didn't want to continue to pay and pushed him over the balcony."

"But most of the amounts are so small—trifling, really. Would someone really kill to avoid paying a few pounds?"

I ran my gaze down the column where Violet had noted the amounts of money. The smallest amount of money was listed next to the initial *J*, while the rest were mostly a few pounds, except for the amount beside the name Lady Snooty.

"I can't say for sure those amounts are exactly right, but they were all small." Violet pointed to Lady Snooty. "Except for Lady Snooty. I'm sure it was ten guineas."

"Yes, most of these amounts are fairly minor, but think about it. Would you want to go on paying a few pounds every week for who knows how long—possibly the rest of your life? And what if Alfred asked for more? Or decided that he'd rather sell his infor-mation to the newspapers?"

Violet shifted in the seat, frowning. "I still find it hard to believe Alfred was doing this. I didn't know him at all. Mum and Gwen were right."

It seemed the fact that her sister and mother had accurately assessed Alfred's character bothered her almost as much as his duplicity.

"And what do you mean, sell the information to the newspapers?" Violet asked. "They wouldn't care if Jane was typing away hours before dawn in Sebastian's study. That's not anything the gossip sheets would be interested in."

"But we don't know what information Alfred had on these other people," I said, thinking of Lady Pamela. I'd heard her father was a stickler for propriety. Lady Pamela wouldn't want hints linking her with drugs in the papers, but I didn't share that information with Violet. I loved her, but Violet had a tendency to speak before she thought.

I turned my attention back to the list and deciphered the next scrawl, which was the abbreviation *Dr*. "Who do you suppose was the doctor? The one here in the village or someone in London?"

"Who knows? It's so vague. It could be anyone."

"No, it couldn't be anyone. Let's see what we can work out. Did Alfred ever mention going to the doctor? Was he sick recently?"

Violet shook her head. "No."

"What about your friends? Do you know any physicians?"

"No."

"Or it could be a professor. What about that? Anyone like that in your circle of friends?"

Violet gave a little laugh. "No. None of our friends are brainy."

"Well, we'll start with the doctor here. What do you think about the last one, Songbird?"

"Again, no idea. No one in our circle is known for being an excellent singer—except Alfred, of course. No one could sing as well as he could. I can't think who it could be."

"Well, we'll just have to find out, won't we?"

I released the brake, and we rolled on through the extensive grounds around Archly Manor, the dappled shade streaming over us as we followed the curving road. I said, "I wouldn't be surprised if the inspector from Scotland Yard arrives this afternoon. He might already be here."

Violet gripped the seat and turned fully toward me. "Scotland Yard?"

"I overheard the police inspector and the chief constable. They were set on handing the case off to someone else. All of the attention and notoriety it will get has made them want to wash their hands of it as quickly as possible. You should tell the Scotland Yard man about Alfred's notebook."

"Oh, I'd much rather *you* do it. I'll get flustered and say something wrong and end up arrested."

"I doubt that. And if I tell them about it, I believe it's called 'hearsay.' You're the only one who actually saw the notebook."

"And burned it." Her shoulders drooped.

I stopped the motor on the sweep in front of Archly Manor. As soon as we stepped inside the reception hall, a new police constable met us. "Miss Belgrave and Miss Stone? Please come with me. Inspector Longly wants to see you."

Violet shot me a distressed look. I smiled encouragingly and followed the constable down the hall. Violet caught my arm and spoke low. "I don't think I can do it again—answer all those questions. I know they'll try to trip me up and confuse me, and I'll say something wrong."

"Nonsense, you can't say anything wrong if you stick to the truth."

The constable escorted us to the study. A man, probably in his early thirties, with light brown hair and a thin mustache was seated behind the desk where Police Inspector Jennings had been the night before. The man had what I supposed would normally be a friendly, open countenance, but at that moment, he was frowning and looked severely put out. He stood and focused on Violet.

"Miss Stone?"

"Yes." Her reply was barely a whisper, and I was slightly amazed to see my normally fiery and energetic cousin answer in such a subdued manner.

"I'm Inspector Longly. The investigation into your fiancé's death has been handed over to my department, and I have a few questions for you."

Violet swallowed. "Of course."

"But first, I must ask, why did you leave Archly Manor?"

Violet twisted the handle of her handbag. "It was—well, you see . . ." Violet glanced at me.

I stepped forward. "I'm afraid it's all my fault, Inspector." I extended my hand. "I'm Olive Belgrave, Violet's cousin. I ran up to London today, and Violet decided to come with me."

He glanced down at my hand. What I thought was a resigned expression chased across his face. He extended his hand. Not his right hand, but his left. The light coming in from the French windows behind him silhouetted his figure, but as my eyes adjusted, I realized his right sleeve was empty and pinned to his jacket. After a moment of shuffling my handbag and gloves, I extended my left hand, and we shook hands.

He motioned to a pair of chairs for us, then moved around behind the desk. "Why did you think it would be fine for you to take a little jaunt up to town?"

Violet and I took a seat, and I said, "We weren't told to stay here at Archly Manor, and we were returning within a few hours. I didn't see how it could be a problem."

"It is very much a problem when an investigation is ongoing and the people I need to interview are not present."

"But we're here now. It's not even teatime. Surely your investigation hasn't been thrown off that severely by not being able to speak to us right away. In fact, I bet you only arrived here an hour or so before us."

"My arrival time does not matter," he said, but I saw a slight upturn at one corner of his mouth for a brief second. "Now, what was so urgent that it required both of you to go to London?"

"One of the maids packed up her belongings and left during the party last night," I said. "She had had an argument with Alfred, and I thought that she was just as viable a suspect as my cousin."

"So you're doing my job for me?"

"I couldn't be sure you would be more open minded than your associate who interviewed me last night. It was clear that he'd decided Violet was the guilty party and would look no further. I felt it important to present you with other options."

At the mention of Inspector Jennings, Longly sighed. "You intended to force my hand?" His tone was less heated than it had been.

"If necessary." I allowed my spine to touch the back of the chair. His anger had burned off, and I didn't think he'd snap at Violet.

"I assure you I won't seize on one suspect to the exclusion of all others. Everything will be considered." The door opened and a constable with a notebook entered. "Good, we can begin now." Inspector Longly turned to Violet. "I'm afraid I have to ask you to go over everything again. It's important we have all the facts clear and down on paper."

Violet gave a small nod.

Inspector Longly said to me, "If you'll wait in the reception hall, I'll send for you in a moment."

I gave Violet's shoulder a pat on the way out, then went to the reception hall and paced up and down, unable to sit. About a quarter of an hour later, Violet came out of the study and gave a slight shake of her head as she passed me and went up the stairs. The constable was right behind her, and he escorted me back to the study, where I took the same seat as before.

Inspector Longly said, "I understand from your cousin that the trip to London was fruitless."

"I wouldn't say that. We now know exactly where Jane was and that she couldn't have pushed Alfred over the balcony. I suppose you would consider it unproductive in one sense, but it seems to me that finding out the truth of the situation is just as important as finding another viable suspect."

"An admirable sentiment, and one I agree with. Your cousin informs me you can give me the former maid's new address in London."

The constable took it down, then Inspector Longly said, "We'll of course verify everything you told us." He left the subject of Jane and took me back through what I'd seen of the struggle on the balcony.

"You can't be more specific than that—blonde hair and a sparkling dress?"

"No, and I've tried to remember more—believe me, I have." I'd spent most of the drive to London trying to tease out some small detail that had escaped me. I shook my head. "As much as I'd like to give you some other bit of information, I can't. That's all I remember. It all happened so quickly. It was more of an impression than a clear memory."

Longly nodded. "Yes, well, if that's the case, I appreciate you having the restraint to *not* make up a helpful distinguishing detail that would clear your cousin."

"I doubt that would work."

"It wouldn't."

I supposed that Violet's warning shake of the head meant she hadn't said anything about Alfred's notebook, which I thought was a mistake. Inspector Longly was not a short-sighted fool like Jennings. I suspected Longly was a man who would pursue all the leads he could find, and it seemed a shame to hamstring him. When he asked my opinion of Alfred, I said, "My aunt and my other cousin, Gwen, were convinced that he wasn't . . . a gentleman, shall we say."

"They thought he was . . . what? A fortune hunter?"

"No, Violet doesn't have a large dowry or the possibility of a massive inheritance. No, it was more that they thought Alfred was rather unsavory," I said, choosing my words carefully.

"And what did they base this opinion on?"

"Nothing substantial. Alfred made several social blunders. He didn't let Violet precede him up a staircase, and he didn't offer his hand at the correct moment during introductions." I sighed. "It sounds like nothing, but there was something about him that was . . . it's difficult to describe. He was overly friendly, as if he was working extra hard to make sure you stayed on his side."

"And what did you find out about Alfred Eton?"

I hesitated, and he said, "Your cousin Gwen told me the family had asked you to look into his background."

"In that case, you should know I was incredibly unsuccessful at uncovering information about Alfred. I couldn't get him to tell me more than the barest facts about his childhood or parents. I came to the party hoping to meet some of his friends and confirm what Alfred had told me, but I didn't achieve that goal either." I told him the small amount of information I had gathered.

Longly said, "I'm sure the Yard will be able to gather a few more particulars."

He took me through what I'd seen on the balcony a second time. "You're sure it was a woman with blonde hair on the balcony with him?"

"Yes, I'm sure, but that's all I'm positive about."

Inspector Longly put down the pencil he'd been holding in his left hand and ran his fingers over his chin as he stared at his hand-written notes for a moment. "Your account tallies with Monty Park's version, so I have a tendency to think what you say is fairly accurate. Unfortunately, he couldn't give us any more details either."

Longly closed his notebook, reached for an envelope, and shook it gently. Four strands of pearls spilled onto the notebook. "Now, why do you have a surprised expression on your face?"

"Because—" I reached for my handbag and took out the

pearls. I handed them to Inspector Longly. "I found these on the terrace after Alfred fell. My foot skidded across the top of them. I picked them up and put them in my glove."

He took the string of pearls and laid them down beside the other four strands. "These four strands were found in Alfred's pocket." He touched the row of pearls I'd given him. "Where exactly did you find these?"

"They were in front of the doors to the ballroom, the first set of doors."

"Did you find any other jewelry?"

"No, that was all I saw."

He swept all the pearls into the envelope. "Thank you for your time. That will be all."

I was at the door when he said, "Oh, Miss Belgrave, I'm specifically instructing you to remain on the grounds of Archly Manor. No more jaunts to London."

"That's fine. I don't think I'll need to make any more trips."

I LEFT Inspector Longly and went along to the drawing room, which had a subdued atmosphere. Sebastian sat on the far side of the room conversing in low tones with Lady Pamela, who was draped across one end of a scroll-arm settee. Thea looked a bit pale but otherwise seemed to have recovered. She had button-holed James, Sebastian's secretary, who looked at me as a cast-away would gaze at a distantly passing ship. Thea was describing the pickled paneling in her London flat, her voice carrying across the room. ". . . quite expensive. But as I always say, it never pays to be cheap, you know." I gave them a wide berth and went to join Gwen, who stood at one of the open French doors that looked out over the terrace and the west gardens, a teacup and saucer in her hands.

"Oh, there you are," she said as I came to stand beside her. The window was open and the scent of roses and honeysuckle drifted inside. "I heard you return, but by the time I got downstairs, you'd been swept off to the inspector. Was he terribly angry with you? Was it grim?"

"No, it wasn't horrible at all." In a low voice, I told her everything Violet and I had learned, and her tea grew cold as she listened without moving.

She kept her voice down as well, but anger vibrated through it. "So Alfred was a cad—blackmailing people and threatening maids."

"Yes, you were right about him."

"But I never suspected he was as bad as that." Her teacup clattered against the saucer as she set it down on a table.

"Unfortunately, I don't think Violet told the police about the notebook. Did you speak to her after we returned from London?"

"No, she went directly to her room. She said she had a headache and took a sleeping powder." Gwen rubbed the bandage on her hand. "I think she doesn't want to deal with it anymore, poor lamb. I'm sure the revelations of the last few hours are a lot for her to take in."

"We'll have to convince her to tell Inspector Longly about the notebook. He seems a competent sort."

"If you say so." Gwen's cheeks turned pink.

"He seemed to be interested in getting to the truth. Didn't you have the same impression?"

"He had quite a few pointed questions for me."

"You have to admit he seems to be better than the local police inspector."

"Possibly."

It wasn't like Gwen to come down so firmly against someone, but perhaps it was because she felt defensive for Violet.

Gwen glanced out the window, then surveyed the room before lowering her voice. "I can't help but worry for Violet. I spoke to one of the maids whose brother is a police constable in the village, and he says that there's no evidence against anyone other than Violet. What if they arrest her because there's no one else?"

"Of course there are other suspects. Jane and Thea are washed out, but Lady Pamela was upstairs."

The door opened and Muriel entered with Paul and Rose. They went to Thea, and James escaped with the agility of a mouse fleeing a momentarily distracted cat. He murmured something about a telephone call and left the room.

I gripped Gwen's arm. "Muriel! I'd completely forgotten about her. She'd have been upstairs too, in the nursery. Granted, it's the floor above the bedrooms, but she was upstairs."

Gwen shook her head. "But Muriel has dark hair. And you said the woman on the balcony was a blonde."

"There are such things as wigs, you know."

"But Muriel?" Gwen looked across the room. "She's such a mouse. I don't think she could do something like that."

"Do you want another suspect or not?" I asked.

"You're right. Put Muriel down as a long shot."

"And then there's Lady Pamela," I said. "She said Tug spilled his drink on her and she went upstairs. When did *that* happen? How long was she upstairs? Did it even happen? Maybe she spilled her drink to give herself an excuse to go upstairs."

"And I thought the fierce inspector might have frightened you out of asking questions. He read me the Riot Act when I told him you were gone. I should have known better."

"It's my innate curiosity. Even if I wanted to stop asking questions, I don't think I could. Apparently, we're all going to be trapped here at least until the inquest, and I'm not going to sit around doing needlepoint."

"Although you do lovely needlepoint," Gwen said with a mischievous look in her eye.

"Thank you, but you know I can't do anything productive while something is on my mind." When Gwen had asked me to help Violet, I'd been reluctant, but talking with Jane and learning about Alfred's notebook had fanned my curiosity. I wanted to help Violet, but I also wanted to figure out who else Alfred had been blackmailing.

"Yes, you are a bit single-minded at times. But I don't think Inspector Longly will be happy. He was extremely cross today when he found out you and Violet were gone."

"Then he'll just have to be grumpy. There's no law against asking questions."

CHAPTER FOURTEEN

$\mathcal{T}$he high-pitched voices of Thea's children increased the noise in the drawing room and brought a sense of energy. I wasn't paying attention to their chatter until Paul's voice carried across the room, ". . . we'll be *murdered* in our beds," he said with relish.

Rose's chin wobbled, and Thea scowled at Paul. "No more talk of that." She patted Rose's hand. "No need to worry, dear. The police are here, and they'll take away the person who did that horrible thing soon." Thea's gaze strayed to Gwen, who stood with her back to the room, but Gwen had heard the exchange. Her shoulders stiffened and red suffused her cheeks.

"Muriel," Thea said and motioned to the open French windows. "Take the children to the garden. It will take their minds off things."

Muriel was raising a fresh cup of tea to her mouth. She took a little sip, then set it down. "Yes, Mrs. Reid."

"Remember, you don't have to worry," Thea said as she squeezed Rose's hand again. Then Thea pointed a finger at Paul. "And no more statements like that from you, young man. You know they upset your sister." Muriel herded the children outside through the other open French door. Their squeaky voices, a counterpoint to Muriel's muted alto replies, faded as they moved away through the banks of flowers.

Gwen's gaze was fixed on the garden as she said in a near whisper, "This is awful. If the police don't find who really did it, suspicion will hang over Violet for the rest of her life. I'm going upstairs. I don't care to speak to anyone right now." Gwen left the room, pointedly avoiding Thea. But Thea was flicking through the pages of a magazine and didn't notice Gwen's snub.

With a frisson of anger simmering through me, I decided I'd better avoid Thea as well. I joined Lady Pamela and Sebastian. Lady Pamela turned her head slightly as I approached. "Oh, Olivia, isn't it the most awful thing?"

Sebastian stubbed out his cigarette. "Don't be a cat, Lady Pamela. Her name is Olive, as you very well know. I don't know why you persist in these petty games. It doesn't gain you anything."

Lady Pamela smiled slowly at Sebastian. "You're terribly direct. It will get you in trouble someday, I'm sure, but it's rather attractive."

"I always say exactly what I mean," Sebastian said.

Lady Pamela pulled her attention away from Sebastian and said to me, "I'm all out of sorts. I do apologize, Olive."

"I think we're all out of sorts at the moment. It's a terrible thing to have happened."

Lady Pamela reached for a cigarette. "It's certainly ruined the party."

Sebastian took out his lighter. "Now there, I disagree with you. There's nothing like a murder to add a little cachet to a party."

Lady Pamela drew on the cigarette, then whipped it out of her mouth. "Now who's behaving badly?"

Sebastian saw my face and added, "Of course it's tragic and most unfortunate."

"Yes, it is," I said firmly. "Alfred didn't have any family, did he? Will you be handling all of the arrangements?"

"The arrangements?"

"For the funeral. You were his godfather."

Sebastian's blasé manner slipped, and he actually looked uncomfortable. "I—well, I daresay I shall have to."

Lady Pamela swept her hand through the air, leaving a trail of smoke. "Sebastian, you're such a goose. You'd actually forgotten you were his godfather, hadn't you?"

"No, my dear. I've been caught up in other things. Great geniuses like myself do that, you know. Total immersion in our work to the point that the rest of the world fades away."

"Sounds lovely," Lady Pamela murmured. "Perhaps I'll become a genius. How would one go about it?"

Irritation prickled across my skin. They were treating Alfred's death as a party game.

Sebastian looked away from Lady Pamela to me and amended his expression from frivolous amusement to something more somber. "I do apologize. I'm treating things far too lightly. You see, I don't like reality. I prefer the artificial world of my studio. I can control everything there. It's like being a little god—quite addicting. When the real world is too much, I retreat there. I go up to my darkroom and shut myself in. No one can bother me there. I've been developing photographs."

His manner was still somewhat flippant, but I sensed an earnestness behind his words. I asked, "Is the darkroom part of your studio upstairs?"

"Yes. I'll show it to you if you'd like."

"I'd be interested in seeing it."

The door opened, and James reentered the room. He crossed to Sebastian and whispered something in his ear. Sebastian pocketed his lighter and stood. "I'm afraid you'll have to excuse me. I have an urgent call I must take."

He left, and Lady Pamela's gaze skimmed around the room. I knew she was looking for some way to escape from me. I said, "I suppose the police have already talked to you?"

"So tedious, all those questions. Where was I? How long did I stay upstairs? Who else did I see?"

"But all important."

She lifted her shoulder. "I suppose."

"You really don't have any interest in knowing who killed Alfred?"

She raised her eyebrows. "It's obvious. Violet did it."

"Do you really think that?"

"Well, it seems the police do. In fact, I'm surprised Violet is still here. I thought they would've taken her away by now."

"Did you actually see her in Alfred's room?"

"No, the only person I saw upstairs was you."

She seemed to enjoy imparting that detail. I was sure she'd also informed the police of it. I wondered if she'd gotten my name right.

I ignored the barb and asked, "And you didn't hear anything from the balcony when you were changing your gown?"

"No. The doors to the balcony were closed in my room." Her eyes sparked with interest as she really focused on me for the first time. "Why so many questions?"

"Because Violet didn't do it."

She laughed, throwing her head back, exposing the long column of her neck and the edge of a pointy collarbone. "Of course she did. Who else is there?"

"You."

That wiped the smile off her face. "Are you accusing me of pushing that slick little social climber off the balcony?" Her voice was full of aristocratic hauteur.

"You were upstairs."

"You *are* accusing me! I'm astounded. Me? You think I did it?"

"I'm merely stating you had opportunity as well as Violet. Why should the blame immediately fall on her?"

Lady Pamela's lips curved into a little smile. "Because I am Lady Pamela Withers, and my father is Lord Harlan. The police will think long and hard before even insinuating I had anything to do with it. Violet is simply Violet Stone. Her father is only a baronet."

"So because Violet's family connections are not as *impressive* as yours, she *must* be guilty."

"Exactly. Besides, I wasn't the one who argued with Alfred. That's common knowledge."

I glanced around the room to make sure Thea was still absorbed in her magazine and no one else had entered. "But he was blackmailing you."

She froze, one skinny arm raised to her hair. She stroked her hair away from her face. "If you repeat a word of that, I will vehemently deny it. And you have a lot less social standing than Violet. You'd do well to remember that." She stood and stalked out of the room.

Thea closed her magazine and tossed it aside. "What's gotten into Pammy?"

"I suppose we're all a little on edge."

"Yes, it has been a trying day." Thea crossed the room and sat down beside me. "I want you to know that we all think Violet is a sweet girl and hope things work out for her as well as possible."

"You mean we should hope the authorities are lenient?"

"Well, yes. I suppose that's the best you can expect at this point."

"There's not a shred of real evidence against Violet. She had an argument with Alfred, and she was upstairs. But quite a few other people were there too, including you."

"Me?" Her eyebrows disappeared under her heavy fringe. "I was asleep."

I tilted my head to the side. "But can you *prove* that you were asleep in your room?"

Her gaze skittered around the room. "I suppose not."

"Then you know exactly how Violet feels. I suggest you keep your insinuations to yourself. They're particularly hurtful to Gwen."

"But then that means if Violet didn't do it, someone else here did."

"Yes, that's true."

Thea's hand went to the neckline of her dress. "That's . . . such a disturbing thought. We may not be safe here." She jumped up. "I must speak to Muriel about the children and call a maid to have our things packed."

"I'm afraid no one is allowed to leave."

"Not allowed to leave?" Her voice was shrill. "What do you mean?"

"Until the police complete their investigation, we all have to stay here."

"Why that's—that's unacceptable. I'll have Sebastian speak to the inspector." She hurried off. I shook out my skirt and left the drawing room. I'd managed to offend two women in the space of less than an hour, but I didn't feel much remorse. Their attitudes toward Violet were inexcusable.

I found Tug and Monty in the billiard room. They had given up their game and were sitting in club chairs, drinking whiskey. Monty offered to get me a drink, but I declined and sat down in another chair beside them. "Tug, you're just the person I wanted to talk to."

He looked a bit stunned. "Oh?"

"Yes. Did you spill a drink on Lady Pamela during the party?"

"Still complaining about that, is she?" Monty asked.

"It was a complete accident," Tug said. "Someone hit my elbow, and before I knew it, I'd soaked her."

Monty said, "She was furious."

Tug snickered. "That's putting it lightly."

"You were there too?" I asked Monty.

"I wasn't beside Tug, but everyone within about a thirty-yard radius heard Lady P's screech," Monty said. "Why do you ask?"

"I heard her gown had been ruined, and I was curious about what happened."

Tug seemed to take my answer in stride, but Monty gave me a long look. He put down his drink. "I think I'll take a stroll in the garden. Would you like to come with me, Miss Belgrave?"

"That would be lovely."

As we left the room, Tug reached for the whiskey. I said to Monty, "I wouldn't leave him alone with that decanter too long. At least, not if we want him to be coherent at dinner."

"I'll come back and put away the drink in a moment." He stepped back so I could go through the door to the terrace first. We went down the steps and into the garden with its boxwood hedges and masses of flowers. Our feet crunched on the gravel path as Monty said, "The inspector from the Yard interviewed me."

"Yes, I know. It seems we alibi each other."

He smiled fleetingly. "Handy that we were together, wasn't it? I am glad the police aren't hectoring me as they are your cousin." He turned and walked sideways as he asked, "Did they ask you about the cufflink?"

"No—well, Inspector Longly did ask me about jewelry, but he never mentioned a cufflink."

"Hmm. Perhaps I shouldn't have said anything to you, then. Well, too late now, isn't it? I suspect that you're the sort of person who will pester me until I tell you what I know, so let me save us both a great quantity of time and tell you. But first, I suppose you'd better swear not to tell."

"I swear," I said, feeling a bit like I was humoring a small boy.

"Good. I suppose that will do. When the police . . . er . . . checked over Alfred on the terrace, he was missing a cufflink. They searched all the flagstones and even the gardens nearby."

"They must not have found it."

"No, and I think it came off as he went over the balustrade."

"Why do you think that? He could have lost it earlier during the evening."

Monty shook his head. "No, he had both of them before he went off to find Violet before the fireworks began. He and I were talking, and he adjusted his cuffs. I saw both cufflinks. Later, before the police shooed me off of the terrace, I heard someone up above on the balcony pointing out a gouge in the stone. A long, deep scratch, he called it. Apparently they could tell from the position of . . . er . . . the *body* that it was where Alfred had gone over. The scratch was at that exact spot on the railing. They speculated a button or tie tack had caught on the stone as he went over. Shortly after, they went over—um—the body rather thoroughly. That's when they noticed the missing cufflink."

"What did the cufflinks look like?"

"Silver with his initials engraved on them."

"When you saw the cufflinks, what part of the evening was it?"

Monty frowned. "Not long before the fireworks."

"And was Violet with Alfred?"

"No, that was a bit of a sore spot with him, in fact."

"What do you mean?"

"Oh, I said something about him managing to get away from Violet—bit of a joke, you know, because they'd been dancing together all night. But he took it the wrong way. Bit off my head, actually."

"What did he say?"

Monty tugged at his collar. "Don't remember exactly."

"Yes, you do. You don't want to make me uncomfortable because it wasn't flattering toward Violet, right?"

Monty sighed. "Yes, that was it. Said she was a pushy baggage."

"Not flattering at all," I said. Their conversation must have taken place after Alfred and Violet had argued while Violet was dancing with other boys.

We walked a few steps in silence. Why hadn't Longly asked me about the cufflink directly? Monty linked his hands behind his back. "So you're checking up on suspects?"

I looked at him out of the corner of my eye. "Perhaps."

"There's no perhaps about it. You're conducting your own investigation, something the inspector wasn't too happy with earlier today. He took out most of his frustration on Gwen."

I grimaced. "That's not what I intended."

"So what have you found out?"

I considered for a moment whether I should tell him or not, but he was with me when Alfred was pushed off the balcony. We had both watched it happen from the lawn, so Monty couldn't have been involved. "You must promise not to tell anyone else."

"It's juicy stuff, then."

"That's not a promise."

"No, all right. I officially promise not to breathe a word of what you say—nary a syllable shall pass my lips."

"That's better. Violet and I went to London today and talked to Jane, a maid who left last night."

The corners of his mouth turned down as he raised his eyebrows. "My, you have been busy."

"Jane was well away from the house before Alfred was killed. But Jane, Lady Pamela, Thea, and even Gwen were upstairs—oh, and Muriel and the children as well. I wonder if Muriel let the children watch the fireworks or if she put them to bed . . ."

We circled around a flowerbed and headed back to the house. "My governess wouldn't have let me watch the fireworks, but Muriel seems a bit more lenient."

"That's another thing I'll have to check on."

"Anything else?"

"Nothing specific." Unlike Inspector Jennings, I wasn't about to air my suspicions until I had something to back them up. And I wasn't going to mention Alfred's blackmailing scheme either.

"You realize the police are set on your cousin as a suspect, but you disagree?"

"Yes, and I'm going to do everything I can to help Violet."

"I can see that. Be careful." He squinted at the gleaming white exterior of Archly Manor. "Remember, if you're right, and I think you are—I don't see Violet murdering Alfred—then someone in that house is a murderer."

CHAPTER FIFTEEN

S unday passed quietly. It was as if we were waiting for the inquest, which had been scheduled for Monday. I hadn't expected Sebastian's household to attend church, and no mention was made of going to the service, so Gwen and I spent the morning strategizing in the sitting room, another room decorated in the rococo style but with a lighter touch. The over-the-top curves, flourishes, and gilding had been kept to a minimum. Lady Pamela, Thea, and Violet weren't early risers, and the men were playing a game of billiards, so we didn't have to worry about being disturbed.

"I think our best chance is to see if we can find out who these people are." I tapped the list Violet had made.

Gwen pursed her lips as she stared at the paper. "I hate to have a defeatist attitude, but it does seem daunting."

"Well, we have to try. We've already figured out Lady Snooty and the initial *J*, so that only leaves three. We *are* making progress."

"I suppose." Gwen smoothed a strand of hair off her forehead and drew the paper closer. "I've no idea about Muncher or Songbird. No idea at all."

"Then you work on the doctor. You met the cook and house-keeper on the night of the party. Find some excuse to speak to them again and see if Alfred had any contact with the local doctor."

"I suppose I could do that."

"Good. I'll work on the other two."

Gwen pushed up from her chair and moved to the door slowly. I said, "You're not on your way to your execution, you know. You're only asking a few questions."

Gwen smiled. "You're right, of course." She straightened her shoulders. "Just a few questions dropped here and there," she muttered to herself. "Here goes."

Poor Gwen. She hated subterfuge, but she'd do anything to help Violet, even something that went against her natural inclinations. I tucked the paper away in a pocket and followed her out of the room.

The billiard game had broken up, but I heard voices out the open window and walked through the shrubbery until I found the men. Sebastian stood behind a camera on a tripod that was set up in a sunken portion of the garden, waving his hand. "Over to the left."

Tug stood a little way down the path from Sebastian. He took a step away from a statue of Venus, which was set on a stone plinth.

"No, *your* left," Sebastian said. "Yes, another step—wait. Back a half step. There. Don't move."

Monty sat on a stone bench positioned on the upper portion of the garden. He asked, "Care to join me?" I sat beside him, and he said, "It's a bit like an amphitheater, being on this raised bit of ground. Excellent seat for the show."

"How did Sebastian convince Tug to get into his tux at this time of day?"

"Promised him the immortality of being photographed by one of the world's greatest artists. That's Sebastian, in case you didn't know."

"Are his photographs any good?"

"Amazing, actually."

"Really? Why doesn't he have any hung around Archly Manor?"

"Don't know. I suppose it's his fragile artist's ego. Sebastian thinks of himself as a genius, but the slightest tidbit of criticism crushes him. Sends him right off into a foul mood. Strange creatures, these creative types."

Sebastian directed Tug to lean on the plinth and look up at the Venus statue. "And don't squint."

"Can't help it," Tug said. "The sunlight is too bright not to."

"Then pretend it's overcast. Immortality, my good man. Do you want it or not?"

"How did Tug get his nickname?" I asked.

"Haven't the faintest."

"Did Alfred come up with it? He was a fan of nicknames, wasn't he?"

Monty frowned. "Occasionally, yes. He called Sebastian *the artiste*. Sebastian liked it."

"Any more?"

"Hmm . . . I wonder why you're asking. Could it be because of your interest in finding his killer?"

"Perhaps. Can you think of any more of Alfred's nicknames?"

"Let's see . . . *dormouse*, that's what he called Muriel."

"She does seem timid."

"And he called Babcock—well, ah . . . perhaps that's not one for mixed company. Oh, here's another. You know what a prig Lord Harlan—Lady Pamela's father—is?"

"I've never met him, but I've heard he's a stickler for propriety."

"Too tepid a description, actually," Monty said. "Once Alfred was attempting to describe Lord Harlan as *Mr. Pompous*, but he'd —Alfred, I mean—had rather too much to drink, and it kept coming out as *Mr. Pom-Pants*." Monty sighed as he looked across the garden. "That was a jolly good time. I ran into Lord Harlan at my club not long after, and I nearly slipped and called him Mr. Pom-Pants. I'm terrified now I'll actually speak the words aloud sometime."

"So Violet was right about Lord Harlan, that he's strict?"

"Imagine Hugh in thirty years' time. They're not related, but it's a fairly accurate picture."

"Then her father is the opposite of Lady Pamela," I said.

"Yes. He's doing all he can to bring her in line with his expectations—limits her funds, that sort of thing."

"Really? I assumed Lady Pamela was quite well set up."

He shook his head. "She never pays her own way. I bought the train tickets to get us here—first-class, of course. Why do you think she spends so much time with Thea?"

I tilted my head to the side. "They aren't very alike." The women weren't the same age, and they were at different stages of life. Thea was a matronly mum of two children, fighting every sign of aging, and she was several years older than Lady Pamela, who was single and childless.

"Thea likes the distinction of having an aristocratic friend, and Lady Pamela likes Thea's open purse." Monty lifted his chin toward the two men in the garden. "It's why Lady Pamela lets Tug tag along after her. His father is generous with his allowance, and Tug is more than happy to lavish dinners, outings to night-clubs, and the best champagne on Lady Pamela."

"Smile wider," Sebastian said to Tug. "Pretend that's Lady Pamela you're looking at. There—perfect."

LATER THAT AFTERNOON, I was the first one down to tea. The empty day had stretched out endlessly. I wanted to talk to the other members of the house party, but Thea remained in her room most of the day, and Tug rowed Lady Pamela around the lake for hours.

Monty and Sebastian closeted themselves in Sebastian's study and smoked cigars. The slow passage of time grated on me. I liked movement and accomplishing things, but it was impossible to make progress when no one was around.

As I entered the drawing room, a flicker of movement caught my eye. A foot slithered under one of the blue toile settees. I walked over, dropped to my knees, and found myself looking into Paul's face. He held a large slice of cake in one hand, and crumbs dusted the corners of his mouth.

"Needed a bite to eat?" I asked.

He swallowed and licked the crumbs from his mouth. "Er— yes. Muriel doesn't let us eat until they bring our tea to the nursery, and that won't be for *hours* and *hours*."

"Oh, I don't think it's actually that long from now."

"But it *feels* like it."

"I imagine it does." A boy with as much energy as Paul was probably hungry all the time. "Then you'd better slip out now while you have the chance. Go out the doors to the terrace and the west garden. I'll keep your secret." However it was obvious that a large chunk of cake was missing from the table where tea had been laid out.

A grin split his face. "Thanks." He wiggled out from under the settee, holding the cake so that it didn't brush against the furniture or himself—quite a feat of dexterity, actually.

He was almost to the door when he turned back. "I don't do this all the time, you know."

"I'm sure you don't." It suddenly struck me that Paul could answer one of my questions. "Paul, the night of the party, did you watch the fireworks?"

His eyebrows lowered, and his mouth flattened into a line. "No. Muriel wouldn't let us."

"But I think you were probably determined to see them, right?" He hesitated. I said, "It's okay, I'll keep this secret too. Did you slip out and watch them?"

He nodded.

"Muriel didn't see you?"

"No. I'm quiet."

"I noticed. Did Muriel stay in the nursery?"

His gaze shifted over my shoulder. He whispered, "Yes," then melted out the door.

I turned. Muriel stood in the doorway, scanning the room. "Paul's slipped away again. Have you seen him?"

"He's not in here," I said.

She pounced on a bright bit of paper on the floor. "Fruit gums. Paul's been in here. And I told him to throw the wrapper in the trash." She crumpled the paper and stuffed it into her pocket as she made a quick circuit of the room, looking behind the furniture. "I'd better check the kitchen. He has Cook keeping back sweets for him too."

Muriel left, and I sent up a quick prayer of thankfulness I hadn't been hired as a governess. It would have been me chasing after schoolboys and probably keeping up with my mistress's correspondence too, as Muriel had to do for Thea.

Everyone drifted in for tea. No one commented on the missing slab of cake, but Babcock did sigh when he checked the table. Nearly half an hour later, Muriel appeared with Paul and Rose. Paul avoided my gaze as they entered, but when Muriel was turned away, I winked at him. He giggled, then stifled the sound as Muriel turned sharply toward him.

I'd hoped to compare notes with Gwen while everyone was sipping their tea, but we weren't able to separate from everyone for any length of time. It had to wait until later when we went upstairs after dinner. I clinched the tie of my dressing gown and tapped on the connecting door before going through.

Gwen put down her brush and turned from the glass. "Don't get your hopes up. I'm afraid I wasn't successful. The doctor hasn't been summoned here in months, and he hasn't dined here either. Apparently, Sebastian doesn't invite the local neighbors to his events."

"Well, I didn't make much progress either. Alfred was fond of nicknames, but the nicknames Monty remembered weren't Muncher or Songbird. And according to Paul, Muriel stayed in the nursery during the fireworks. Maybe we'll discover something new tomorrow at the inquest."

CHAPTER SIXTEEN

*T*he inquest was held late Monday afternoon, and it was the most boring event I had ever attended. The Chief Constable, Inspector Longly, and the police surgeon made sure it was as low-key as possible. The pearls, the missing cufflink, and any other interesting tidbits of information were not mentioned. The pressmen packed into the back of the room must have been disappointed. Word was out about the tragic Silver and Gold party, which had been written up in all the London papers with degrees of exaggeration varying according to the sensationalism of the paper.

Violet, pale and subdued, answered the questions put to her but didn't volunteer any additional information. The notebook went unmentioned, and I made a mental note. I had to convince Violet to tell the inspector about it. Monty gave evidence, describing what we'd seen from the lawn, but I was told I wasn't needed and sat in the audience on a hard chair.

Lady Pamela treated the inquest as a social event, arriving in a gorgeous frock and executing a pirouette for the waiting reporters, who had arrived and set up camp in the village pub and outside the gates of Archly Manor. Inspector Jennings, while not a thorough investigator, in my opinion, was excellent at crowd control, and saw that the reporters were kept back from the gates of the estate. Because of the police's vigilance in guarding Archly Manor, the inquest was the first close-up glimpse the reporters were able to get of the attendees of Archly Manor's Saturday-to-Monday. I'm sure they thought it was a shame the proceedings were so flat and boring. A verdict of *murder by person or persons unknown* was returned. Inspector Longly stated that we could leave, but I suspected he or one of his people would follow us discreetly.

By the time we returned to Archly Manor, it was time to dress for dinner. Gwen and Violet decided we would leave early the next morning. Dinner was a bit strained, with only Thea droning on about the advantages of solid wood over veneers when it came to cabinetry. When the men joined us in the drawing room, Tug suggested dancing as he gazed at Lady Pamela, but Thea vetoed the idea. "Inappropriate after what happened . . . um . . . with Alfred, I think."

"Perhaps we could have some music, though," I said, thinking of Alfred's list of nicknames. "Something subdued. Perhaps someone could sing—?" I broke off as Sebastian, who was standing behind Thea's chair, made a cutting motion, his hand at his throat.

Thea perked up. "That would be all right as long as the songs are ballads. I could—"

"No," Sebastian said firmly. "None of your caterwauling tonight, Sis." Thea scowled, but Sebastian squeezed her shoulder briefly and said to me, "You'll find us a decidedly unmusical group, Olive. I'm afraid none of us are talented in that area. Let's have bridge instead."

Lady Pamela, Monty, Tug, and I played a few half-hearted rounds of bridge, but none of our minds were on the game. Violet spent the evening turning the pages of a magazine. Gwen moved the pieces of a jigsaw puzzle around until another bridge game formed and she took a place at the table, but she missed two obvious plays. James was her partner, but Gwen's absentmindedness didn't seem to bother him. The secretary only murmured, "It's fine. So difficult to catch some of these things."

When Thea declared she had to go upstairs and check on the progress of the packing of her trunks, we all retired to our rooms. I slept fitfully and awoke early the next morning.

I was on my way down to breakfast when I heard a shriek as I passed Violet's door. I paused on the threshold. Milly stood in the middle of the room, both hands covering her mouth as she stared at something on the floor. She was obviously in the middle of packing Violet's clothes. The doors to the wardrobe were open, and folded clothes sat in a neat tower next to Violet's sponge bag and pink enamel-backed brush and hand mirror.

"Are you all right, Milly?"

She jumped and jerked around to face me, her hand to her chest. "Oh, it's you, Miss Olive." She looked down at the floor again and then back to me.

"Whatever is the matter?" I walked into the room and around the end of the bed. She seemed to be frightened of a pile of clothes on the floor.

"She did it," Milly said. "I didn't want to think Miss Violet murdered Mr. Eton, but she did."

"What are you talking about?"

Milly pointed to the clothes in the floor. "The cufflink—it's caught in her dress."

My stomach plummeted, and a coldness came over me. "The cufflink? How do you know about it?"

"Inspector Longly, miss. He told us about it and said to look for it." She glanced back to the crumpled pile of fabric. "It's just like he described—silver with Mr. Eton's initials. It has to be his, and it's caught on the dress Miss Violet wore the night of the party."

I stepped forward. "Let me see."

Milly shook her head. "I'm not to touch it. Inspector Longly said if we found it, to leave it and call the police immediately."

"So Inspector Longly informed the servants the cufflink was missing?"

"Only two of us, miss. Me and Tabitha. We're taking care of the ladies. He made us promise to keep it a secret and said it was very important." Her eyes widened even more. "I shouldn't have told you. He said not to tell anyone."

"I expect he'll realize you were shocked and spoke without thinking." I picked up the dress.

Milly sucked in a breath. "Oh, don't do that, miss. He said to leave it exactly as it was."

"But I doubt that you found it in a pile on the floor."

"Well, no. The dress was in the wardrobe. I took it off the hanger and was about to lay it on the bed to fold it in tissue when I noticed a bit of metal caught in the bow. When I saw it was a cufflink, I was so surprised, I dropped it."

"Very understandable. Since it was in the wardrobe, it won't hurt to look at it properly." I draped the dress across the bed. It was white silk embellished with silver bugle beads and sequins. The sash at the dropped waist was elaborately beaded and caught to one side with a bow sewn to it.

I didn't notice the extra bit of metal at first glance because it blended in with the silver beads, but I saw it when I looked closer. The silver cufflink was lodged in the beading in a crevice where the fabric was drawn into the bow. "Did you put this dress away after the party?"

"Yes, miss."

"But you didn't notice the cufflink then?"

"No, miss. But that was when the house was in such confusion. I would have normally taken it away so that it could be washed, but Miss Violet told me to hang it up. She would have it seen to later when she returned home."

"So you hung it up but didn't notice the cufflink caught in the decoration then?"

"No, but I was working quickly, and it barely shows." Milly twisted her hands together at her waist. "I should tell Mrs. Foster so she can contact the police."

"Yes, you had better do that." I realized after a second or two that Milly still stood beside me. "Yes?"

"I think I should lock the door before I leave. It's what the inspector would want, don't you think?"

"Yes, you're absolutely right." I left the room with her. She locked the door with a key from her pocket, then she hurried down the hallway to the back staircase that would take her down to the servants' hall.

I went in the opposite direction, speeding down the stairs and along to the dining room, where Violet was pushing eggs around her plate. Monty and James sat at the other end of the table. James was saying, ". . . fortunate that the reporters have shoved off."

"Back to London now that the inquest is over?" Monty asked.

"Yes, apparently they've given up on us."

"You're an optimistic chap. I'm sure they'll be back. It will make it easier to get to the train station, though. We can be thankful for small favors."

I slipped into the seat beside Violet and waved away the servant who offered me coffee. I kept my voice soft as I said, "Milly just found one of the cufflinks Alfred wore the night he died caught in the trim of the dress you wore that night."

Her fork clattered to her plate. "What? That can't be possible."

"I saw it myself. It's definitely a cufflink, silver, with the initials *A* and *E*. I heard from—" I glanced at the other end of the table. James was reading a letter, but Monty was watching us. "Well, it doesn't matter now where I heard about it, but it seems the police think Alfred lost the cufflink as he struggled against whoever pushed him." The word was out about the cufflink. I didn't have any qualms about breaking my word to Monty. Violet needed to know what had happened. The color had drained from her face as I spoke. I asked, "Did the police ask you about Alfred's cufflinks?" She stared at me, her thoughts obviously miles away. "Violet, did the police ask you about these cufflinks?"

She blinked. "Yes, they wanted to know which ones he wore

that night, and I described them. They never said one was missing."

Monty told me he'd seen both the cufflinks in Alfred's cuffs shortly before the fireworks began. Perhaps Alfred had lost one between that time and when he was killed. "Could Alfred have lost the cufflink earlier, perhaps on the way up the stairs? Could it have fallen off and snagged on your dress then?"

"Maybe."

"And you didn't notice it caught in the dress when you changed into your dressing gown later?"

"No. And I would've seen it if it had been caught in the fabric."

"Perhaps not." I described where the cufflink was on the dress. "It's possible it was caught in the crevice by the bow and you didn't notice it—or that's what I'm afraid Inspector Longly may think."

Violet pushed back her chair. "I must tell Gwen." She left the room, and I followed her, but Monty pushed his chair back and caught up with me before I cleared the door of the dining room. "What's happened?"

"Someone is trying to make sure Violet takes the blame for Alfred's death," I said. "I'm afraid I broke my promise and told Violet what you said about the cufflink. I felt she needed to know."

"Quite all right. It's not cricket to go planting incriminating evidence, what?"

"Thank you for not being upset." I gave him my most brilliant smile and hurried upstairs to Gwen's room. I tapped on the door and peeked inside, expecting to see Violet and Gwen talking. But Gwen was alone, propped up in bed with a tray across her lap. "Thank goodness we can leave today," she said. "Are you packed? I've instructed them to bring the Morris around at nine. Will you be ready?"

"Where's Violet?" I asked.

"I don't know."

"She didn't come to talk to you?"

"No. I haven't seen her this morning."

I walked to the connecting door and tried the handle, but it was locked. The door from the hall into Violet's room was still locked.

I checked my room, but Violet wasn't there either. I went back down to the morning room and made a quick circuit through the ground floor. I went back upstairs and paused in the hallway, considering whether or not Violet would go up to the next floor, but only the nursery was up there.

Gwen opened her door and came into the hall. Her dressing gown floated around her legs, and her hair rested in loose waves across her shoulders. "Why are the doors to Violet's room locked? Something's wrong, isn't it?"

A deep male voice boomed up the stairs. ". . . official police business." Inspector Jennings's bald head appeared first, then the rest of his bulky body came into view as he labored up the stairs. Mr. Babcock, looking as put out as his butlerly demeanor would allow, was one step behind him.

A rustling sound behind us signaled the arrival of the housekeeper, Mrs. Foster. The metal keys on her ring clicked as she flicked through them. "I'm afraid it's true, Mr. Babcock," she said as she unlocked Violet's door. "It's a matter for the police." She sent a blistering look at me and Gwen as if it were our fault the police had again invaded Archly Manor. "I'll leave you to oversee things, Mr. Babcock," she said and rustled away down the hall.

"What is it? What's happened?" Gwen asked.

I drew a breath to explain, but then another head appeared, bobbing up the stairs at a much faster pace than Inspector Jennings. It was Inspector Longly, taking the stairs two at a time. He crested the stairs, then his steps stuttered when he saw Gwen and me in the hallway. "I—uh—the front door was open . . ."

Gwen seemed to realize she was in her dressing gown and pulled the lapels together.

Longly gazed at Gwen with a dazed expression. "I—ah—had a

message . . ." He swallowed. Pink bloomed in Gwen's cheeks as Longly muttered, "New—um—developments . . ."

Inspector Jennings popped his head out of Violet's doorway. "Come along, then. You'll want to see this."

"See what?" Gwen asked.

"Evidence," Jennings said with a triumphant air. He turned to Longly. "On her dress."

Jennings escorted Longly into the room with the air of a proud father showing off a new baby. Babcock followed them, and Gwen and I crowded into the doorway. Jennings and Longly bent over the sparkly dress, which was still spread across the bed. They were so focused on it, they didn't notice that Gwen and I had followed them into the room. I explained to Gwen in low tones what had happened.

"But that's impossible," Gwen said. "Violet wasn't even on the balcony."

I kept my voice down as I replied. "It's not impossible."

"What do you mean?" Gwen asked in her normal tone of voice. She released the collar of her dressing gown and fisted her hands as if she were ready to take on the two police officials.

"Someone put the cufflink on Violet's dress to make it *look* as if she were on the balcony."

Longly swiveled away from the dress and said to Babcock, who still looked pained at the early morning intrusion of the police, "I need to speak to Miss Violet right away. In the study, I think, if Mr. Blakely doesn't mind."

"I'll see to it." Babcock glided away, conveying his disapproval in his tone and posture.

"I don't think that will be possible," I murmured more to myself than anyone else. They hadn't noticed yet that Violet's luggage was gone.

CHAPTER SEVENTEEN

 nce Babcock returned with the news that Violet couldn't be found, Jennings called for his constables. While they searched Archly Manor from the attics to the scullery, I did another fruitless tour of my own, then went to the drawing room. Gwen stood at the French windows, her hands clenched together as she watched the constables searching the garden.

The police search had included every cupboard, nook, and cranny in the house. Sebastian retreated to his studio and was angry when a constable insisted on searching that room and his darkroom. Lady Pamela was still in bed and had screamed when a constable entered her room. Thea had huffed and gone on about the inconvenience of it.

After she told Longly she had no idea where Violet had gone, Gwen retreated to her room. I hadn't followed her. I knew she needed to be alone. Gwen was like that—she often went off on her own to sort things out. I was relieved to find her in the drawing room. She'd changed into a day dress and looped her hair into an untidy bun. I wanted to talk about my suspicions. I didn't think either one of the police officials would be interested in my theories, but I knew Gwen would.

As I joined her, she kept her gaze focused on the gardens as she said, "I'm so afraid something else . . . has happened." She swallowed. "I keep picturing Violet hurt or unconscious somewhere."

"I don't think that's what's happened."

"What do you mean?"

"I don't think Violet's been attacked. I think she left."

Gwen turned to me. "You mean she ran away? Why? Why would she do that?"

"She's frightened. Someone is doing everything they can to make sure she looks guilty of Alfred's murder. I don't blame her for doing a bunk."

"But how can you be sure she's left?"

"Some of her clothes along with her sponge bag and valise are gone."

Hope filtered into Gwen's expression. "Really?"

"Yes. When I spoke to Milly this morning, she'd folded a stack of clothes. They were on the bed, but they're gone now, along with the other things."

"But how could she leave without anyone seeing her go?"

"When she left me in the breakfast room, she said she was going upstairs. Were you in your room?"

"No, I was in the bath."

"Then Violet must have gone through your room and used the connecting door to get into her room."

Gwen nodded. "Yes, she could have done that. We didn't lock the connecting door."

"It wouldn't take more than a few minutes to go to her room, grab a few things, then slip back downstairs. Lady Pamela and Thea were in their rooms, and I was downstairs speaking to Monty in the breakfast room," I said.

"But then where did Violet go? She's not in the house or in the gardens." Gwen glanced out the window. The search had widened. Now the constables were moving along the lawn to the parkland beyond the formal gardens.

"I have an idea. Let's check something." I led Gwen through

the frills of the rococo reception hall then down the corridor to Sebastian's study. I nodded as I walked in the door. "I thought I remembered seeing a telephone in here."

"Why is that important?" Gwen asked.

I crossed to the French doors behind the desk and peered at the handle. "Look, it's closed but not locked." I used the edge of my skirt to cover my fingers as I gently gripped the handle and pushed the door open.

Beyond the terrace that ran along the west side of the house, a small area of lawn sloped down to a belt of trees. I walked back and forth a few steps until the sun slanted over the grass at the perfect angle. "Gwen, come stand exactly where I am. You're taller than I am, so duck your head a little bit and look at the grass. What do you see?"

"The lawn and trees."

"Do you notice anything interesting about the grass?"

"Well, it's cut evenly."

"What else?"

"I don't see—oh, footsteps in the dew!"

"Yes, that's it."

A layer of dew coated the grass on this side of the house, which was still in the shade. I peered at the first footprint in the droplets. The footprint was small and curved, a lady's shoe. The grass had been slightly compressed underneath it but not totally flattened.

"I can see a trail of footprints," Gwen said, her voice excited. "They go all the way over to the trees." Then her tone turned puzzled. "You think that Violet is in the woods? I know she's frightened of being blamed for Alfred's death because of the cuff-link, but it's not going to do her any good to hide in the woods."

"No, I doubt she's hiding in the woods. I think after she collected her things, she went to Sebastian's study and made a telephone call to Mr. Brown. She requested his taxi service."

Gwen looked from me to the trees and back again. "I suppose that's possible."

"Violet was following Jane's example. She knew about Mr. Brown. We stopped there on the way to London. Violet probably gave Mr. Brown the same instructions Jane did. I bet he picked her up outside the gates and took her to Finchbury Crossing."

"So you think Violet isn't even on the estate?"

"Exactly. The question is, where did she go from the train station?"

"I may not be smart enough to find footprints in the grass, but I can answer that," Gwen said. "She'd go home to Parkview Hall."

"Do you really think so? Won't that be the first place the police look after they exhaust all possibilities here?"

Babcock came through the doors from the study to the terrace. He held out a tray. "A telegram for you, Miss Olive."

"Thank you." I took it, and Babcock melted away as I ripped the envelope open. It was always better to open it quickly rather than let my thoughts get carried away with all the horrible possibilities a telegram could contain.

"What does it say?" Gwen crowded close to my shoulder. "Oh, it's only Jasper. I thought it might be from Mum, saying Violet had arrived at Parkview."

"It's much too soon for that. It would take Violet hours to get to Derbyshire."

"Well, I'm sure that's where she'll go. And I'm going there now." Gwen headed back to the house.

"Do you think Inspector Longly will let you leave?" I asked.

"Just let him try to stop me. I'm not under suspicion. He has no reason to hold me." She swept through the door, then returned a moment later. "Aren't you coming?"

I looked up from the telegram. "No, I'm going to London to speak to Jasper."

CHAPTER EIGHTEEN

*J*asper met me on the platform when I emerged from the train. "Hello, old thing."

"I didn't expect you to meet me here," I said.

"I had to see for myself that you were all right. Quite a house party, what?"

"Rather."

Jasper leaned toward me with a confidential air. "About that commission you gave me . . . I have news."

"I can't wait to hear it. Your wire was incredibly vague."

"A ploy to get you here quickly."

"You couldn't have telephoned? Not that I'm not glad to see you, but . . ."

"Frightfully public things, telephones. You never know who's listening in."

"That is true. What's your news?"

"All in good time, old bean. First, food. Have you had lunch?"

"No, but I've been well fed for the last few days at Archly Manor. I'm not starving like I was that day you took me to the Savoy."

Jasper offered his arm. "Nevertheless, *I'm* feeling peckish today."

Over a sizzling steak, I told Jasper everything that had happened at Archly Manor. "And now Violet has disappeared. Gwen thinks she's gone back to Parkview Hall, but I'm not so sure."

"Why?"

"Because I think Parkview is where Gwen would go if she were in trouble, but I don't think it's where Violet would go. Besides, it's the first place the police will look. Violet is savvy enough to know that."

Jasper put down his cutlery. "But Violet's not smart enough to realize running away makes her look guilty?"

"I'm not saying her thinking is flawless, I admit that. I think she fled on instinct, but once she was away from Archly Manor, I bet some of her natural deviousness came out. Violet will do her best to confuse the trail."

"Where do you think she went?"

"A friend's, most likely. I telephoned Parkview and spoke to Aunt Caroline before I left Archly Manor. I have a list of friends Violet was especially close to during the season last year. I'll get in touch with as many of them as I can today." Aunt Caroline had also said that Uncle Leo was feeling much better, and she expected the doctor to lift the quarantine soon. I was so glad to hear the news, especially with Gwen going there. I didn't want her to become ill on top of everything else.

Jasper drummed his fingers on the table as he looked at me out of the corner of his eye. "You're loyal. Maybe too loyal."

"How could I be too loyal? What do you mean?"

Jasper stopped drumming his fingers. "If anyone has a reason to be devoted to the Stone family, it's me. They welcomed a rambunctious, clumsy boy into their home every holiday for years on end—something my own family wouldn't do. But loyalty should have limits."

"If you're saying I'm blindly loyal, you're wrong. I genuinely don't think Violet killed Alfred."

"Now I've made you angry. Of course you're backing Violet.

For what it's worth, I don't think Violet's the type to shove her intended off a balcony either. But your determination to prove Violet is innocent combined with your tendency to run at life headlong, well . . . you're like quicksilver." He swished his hand through the air in a serpentine motion. "Someday those lightning decisions of yours will get you into trouble. I'd rather not see that happen."

Irritation flared through me. "Thank you for your concern, but I'm well able to govern my actions. If I were as hotheaded as you seem to think I am, I'd—I'd have removed Sonia from Father's life long ago," I said with a little smile to show I was teasing.

"Well, there's proof positive I'm wrong, then," Jasper said, and the tension that had sprung up between us eased. "You've shown great restraint there."

The waiter removed my plate, and I put both hands on the table, stacking one on the other. "All right. You've kept me in suspense long enough. What have you uncovered about Alfred?"

"It's taken me quite a while to track down the truth, but I can assure you no one with the surname of Eton was employed as an accountant in Delhi in the civil service any time in the last fifty years."

I hunched forward, pressing my hands into the tablecloth. "You weren't able to find evidence of his father as an employee in India?"

"Not a trace. I made a thorough search, calling in a few favors —for which you owe me greatly, by the way. We'll discuss that later."

"Oh, admit it. You were actually interested."

"I have no idea what you're talking about. I merely executed a favor for a friend." Jasper grinned as he spoke.

"And I thank you." I bowed my head. "But no matter what you say, I can tell this caught your attention." I gazed across the restaurant. "If Alfred's father was never in India, was Alfred ever there?"

"Excellent question," Jasper said. "I looked into it. I couldn't find any mention of an Alfred Eton either."

"Interesting."

"You don't seem shocked."

"If you'd told me this a few days ago, I would have been shocked, but after discovering Alfred was blackmailing people, I can't say it's surprising he would lie about his past. I wonder if anything Alfred told us was true."

"Doubtful," Jasper said. "Did Alfred mention anything else, any scrap of information? A place or person? He might have slipped up and given a bit of his real background."

"Oh." I sat up straight. "He mentioned—no, it was Essie—she told me Alfred said he grew up in a tiny village . . . what was its name?" I reached for my handbag and pulled out the list of information I'd written down when I first started investigating Alfred's background. It seemed like I'd made the list weeks ago, but it had only been a few days earlier. I unfolded the paper. "Setherwick. That's where it was."

"Never heard of it."

"Neither have I." I put my napkin on the table. "I need an atlas. Do you have one?"

"I'm afraid my rooms only have gramophone records and books of the most unedifying sort."

"Really?" I asked, momentarily distracted. "What sort of books do you read?"

"The most lurid detective fiction imaginable. I'll loan you one sometime. I think it would appeal to your curious side. My nonfiction section is rather thin."

"We need an atlas."

One taxi ride and a quarter of an hour later, we were at the British Museum, poring over an atlas only slightly smaller than the table it rested on. I checked the index twice and shook my head. "No Setherwick here."

Jasper heaved the unwieldy cover closed. "Let's check another to be sure."

In the second atlas, I trailed my finger down the list of towns and villages that began with the letter *S*, then I shook my head.

"It doesn't exist, does it?" Jasper asked.

"No. And now the question is, who was Alfred Eton, really?"

I WOULD HAVE PREFERRED to continue my search into Alfred's background, but the search for Violet had to take priority. Jasper was kind enough to send me off to Mayfair in a taxi. Several of Violet's friends lived within a few blocks of each other, and I'd be able to visit all of them on foot.

It was an unproductive search. Two hours later, I returned to the train station, picked up my valise from Left Luggage, and walked to my room at Mrs. Gutler's boarding house. Even though I had money to pay a bus fare, I couldn't bring myself to spend it when I had no urgent need to get home quickly.

Walking allowed me to think over the question of where Violet could be and who Alfred could have been. The other question hovering in my mind that night as I unpacked was why would someone take a fake name and pursue an engagement with a young society girl? Wouldn't Alfred have been found out eventually? Or had he hoped his charade would never be discovered? Perhaps he had fake papers—a birth certificate and other documents that would "prove" his identity—and he wasn't worried about being caught.

Being one's own maid gives one quite a bit of time to think. I sorted my clothes to send to the laundry around the corner, mended a hem, and reattached a feather to one of my hats. I had plenty of time to think through those questions, but I didn't come up with any satisfactory answers. I had one more of Violet's friends to speak to the next day, and I laid out my green tricot dress with its matching hat and dropped into my creaky little bed.

Lady Buxton-Wimburry lived an hour outside of London in a Victorian home. She was not helpful at all. She hinted that Violet's behavior was beyond scandalous and that she wouldn't let her daughter associate with her in the future.

I bought a sandwich and a newspaper for the return train journey to London. I almost wished I had one of Jasper's lurid detective novels to take my mind off things. Nothing exasperated me more than unanswered questions, and once my mind started on a track of trying to figure something out, it wouldn't stop.

I rattled the newspaper as I flung it open. I should've expected it, but I was still stunned when I turned a page and saw a picture of Violet and Gwen alongside a story recapping the events surrounding Alfred's death. The article had no new information. The writer merely rehashed the details of Alfred's death, exaggerated the excesses of the Silver and Gold party, and did their best to sensationalize the inquest—a difficult task, considering how dry the proceedings were. I was skimming through the text when a line caught my attention.

Alfred Eton, lately of the swanky South Regent Mansions, was known to be one of the Bright Young People about town, mixing with Sebastian Blakely and Lady Pamela Withers.

I folded the paper, anxious to get back to London. I knew exactly where I needed to go.

I breezed into the elegant and modern entry lobby of South Regent Mansions and gave the hall porter who resembled a walrus a friendly smile. "Hello. I stopped in a short while ago and made some inquiries about Alfred Eton."

He looked at me for a long moment, and then his face cleared. "Oh yes." He shook his head. "Poor sod."

"I suppose so." I didn't consider Alfred a poor sod—besides being a blackmailer, he'd deceived Violet—but I suppose he didn't deserve to die for either of those things. "Have the police been here?"

"Yes, been and gone. Didn't find anything of use, apparently."

"And has anyone else been here?"

"I'm not sure what you mean . . ." He sent a significant look at my handbag.

I removed two five-pound notes from my bag along with the newspaper open to the article about Alfred's death. I held the folded notes against the newspaper and handed the whole thing to him. "Perhaps one of these young women?"

The money disappeared into his large palm as he took the newspaper. Either the larger bribe or the fact that Alfred was dead loosened his tongue. "Yes, she's been here." He held the paper out, his finger pointing to Gwen's face.

Gwen? He had to be mistaken. I pushed the paper back to him. "Are you sure?"

"Oh yes. It was this lady right here."

"Not the lady with short hair?"

"No, the young lady had long hair, and she was quite upset."

"When was this?"

He frowned at the ceiling. "It would've been a few days before you came the first time."

What was Gwen doing at South Regent Mansions?

"Miss?"

I realized he was holding out the newspaper. I took it. "Thank you." My thoughts reeled. Sweet, straightforward Gwen had come to South Regent Mansions? Why hadn't she told me? And why had she come in the first place? Could she and Alfred—? No. Gwen would never do that to Violet. And Gwen truly thought Alfred was a cad. But then why visit Alfred's flat? "How often did you see her?" I asked, hardly believing I was asking the question.

"Just the once."

I gathered my thoughts and remembered I had another question for the hall porter. "Did a doctor make a house call on Mr. Eton?"

"No, miss. In fact, he hardly ever had any visitors."

"I see."

"Will there be anything else, miss?"

"Yes," I said slowly, "one other thing. I'd like to peek inside Alfred's flat. Could you make that happen?" I reached into my handbag again.

The hall porter could make it happen, and I made it worth his while, handing over almost all of my remaining bank notes to him. The expense was worth it if it got me into Alfred's flat with no fuss. But no more taxis or buses for me. I'd definitely be walking from now on.

It didn't take long for the hall porter to procure a passkey from one of the maids who cleaned the flats. I rode the lift up to the sixth floor, where the lift boy unlatched the grate. I felt his gaze on me as I walked to Alfred's flat, unlocked the door, and stepped inside.

CHAPTER NINETEEN

*T*he door of Alfred's flat opened into a short, narrow hallway. To my right, a few steps down the hall, was a small kitchen. As instructed, I left the key on the countertop beside the sink. The next door, also on the right, opened into the bathroom.

Two doors, side by side, faced me at the end of the hallway. The doorway on the left opened into a living area with a curved wall of windows, giving a view of the courtyard below. I intended to go into the living area, but I heard a slight rustling noise from the other doorway, which opened to a bedroom.

"Violet, it's me, Olive." I poked my head into the bedroom.

Violet came out from behind the door, an iron lamp base in the shape of a curvy female figure clutched in her hands.

"You weren't going to bean me over the head with that, were you?" I asked.

"I didn't know it was you, did I? How did you know I was behind the door?"

"A hunch, but even if I hadn't realized you were in here, your clothes would've given you away." I gestured to the bright dresses spilling out of her valise onto the unmade bed.

Violet put the lamp base down on a bedside table. "How did you find me?"

"I'm ashamed to say it's taken me far too long to figure it out. I realized you'd run away from Archly Manor, but I spent yesterday and part of today speaking to your deb friends."

Violet gave a little shudder. "I'd *never* go to one of them. They might welcome me, but their mothers—they'd act like I had some sort of fatal disease."

I didn't want to agree with her, but the atmosphere at the homes I'd visited had been decidedly frosty.

Violet said, "Well, as long as you're here, we may as well be comfortable. Come through to the living room."

Violet dropped onto a brown button-backed sofa with square lines. Greasy waxed paper, teacups, and glasses covered a side table next to the sofa. "Excuse the mess," Violet said. "The maids have been told not to clean this flat, so there's no service."

I sat in a chair with a tubular metal frame. "How did you get into the flat?"

"With Alfred's key."

"Did you take it from his room when you took the notebook?"

"No, silly. Alfred gave it to me weeks ago. When Mum and Daddy were so upset with me about him, Alfred gave me a key and told me if things got too grim at Parkview to come stay here. Oh, you needn't look so scandalized. It wasn't like *that*. He was usually gone. He spent a lot of time at Archly Manor. He meant I could stay here when he wasn't here."

"So did you visit him here?" I asked, wondering if the hall porter *had* been mistaken in the identity of the woman who'd visited Alfred's flat after all.

"No." Violet looked down at the sofa and picked at one of the buttons on the upholstery. "I could never get up the courage to do it." She looked at me from underneath her lashes. "I like to think I'm avant-garde, but I'm actually quite conventional. It's a rather lowering discovery."

"Aunt Caroline would be so relieved to hear that."

"Don't you dare tell her."

"You have to keep her on edge, is that it?" I asked.

"It's why I get so much. Gwen never pushes. I do. Mum and Daddy know I'm going to push, so they give in to me more than they do to her."

I didn't say anything about the hall porter identifying Gwen as a woman who had visited Alfred. Instead, I asked, "How did you get past the hall porter?"

"I made a friend of the lift boy. He was easy to bribe with sweets. He kept a lookout and let me know when the hall porter was gone. He whisked me upstairs, and no one was the wiser."

"And your lift boy, has he been bringing you food?"

"His taste runs to fish and chips, which I am getting a little tired of."

"You've been here since yesterday?"

Violet nodded. "I came directly here from Archly Manor."

"I thought so. Gwen was sure you'd gone to Parkview Hall, but I didn't think you would do that."

Violet looked horrified. "I'd never go back *there*. Not now—not after they found that cufflink. I'm sure that's the first place the police went to look for me."

"I believe you're right." I'd heard from Gwen that the police arrived shortly after she did and made a complete search of Parkview Hall. "Your parents are distraught."

Violet jumped up and walked to the curved windows. "I'm sure they are, but I'm distraught as well. Don't they realize if I go to Parkview I'll be arrested?"

"I don't know if that's exactly true."

She turned quickly from the window. "But it's a possibility."

"An outside possibility, I'd say."

She crossed her arms. "I'm not going back there."

"Well, you can't stay holed up here indefinitely."

"I don't see why not."

"For one thing, this flat will probably be let soon. They might even start showing it."

Violet frowned. "I hadn't thought of that."

"I suppose it's a question of who owns it. Did Alfred rent the flat?"

"I have no idea. He never said."

"You don't know?" I asked.

"Alfred and I had better things to talk about than property," Violet said. "That's something Daddy would be interested in, not Alfred." She plunked down on the sofa again.

"Violet, I discovered something about Alfred you should know." My tone must have conveyed the seriousness of what I was about to say because she looked up, her eyebrows drawn together. She held completely still as I told her what Jasper and I had discovered. When I finished explaining that the village Alfred said he was from didn't exist, she blinked several times and then dropped her head back against the sofa and stared at the ceiling. "I felt as if something else was coming—something terrible about Alfred that I didn't know." She closed her eyes briefly and rocked her head back and forth against the cushion. "I didn't know him at all."

"He never told you anything except his fake name and the made-up bit about India?"

"No. Never. He didn't want to talk about his past, but I thought it was because the death of his parents bothered him. One doesn't push about things like that."

"Of course not."

I looked around the flat, which had an impersonal feel to it. The contemporary furniture was serviceable and plain. No portraits or photographs were displayed, and no books, magazines, or newspapers had been randomly discarded. "I hoped to have a look around the flat, but it doesn't feel as if Alfred lived here long."

Violet tilted her head. "How did *you* get in?"

"I bribed the hall porter."

Her eyebrows went up. "Well done. I didn't think of that."

"What do you say we have a look around? Perhaps we'll find some hint of who Alfred really was."

Violet sat up. "Let's take this place apart."

Violet tackled the job with a ferocity that surprised me. From the living room, I could hear her slamming drawers and muttering to herself as she went through the bedroom. It didn't take me long in the living room. I looked through the few drawers in the side tables, which were empty, then checked the drinks cabinet, but it only contained liquor. I went to join Violet, but stopped short on the threshold of the bedroom. "It looks like a bomb went off in here."

She looked up from her seat on the floor. "What?"

"The room. It will take forever to put everything back."

She waved a hand. "Never mind that. Come look."

Printed playbills surrounded her. "I found them in an envelope under his socks. Vaudeville—Alfred was a *performer*. Here, look at this." She thrust one of the playbills at me and pointed about halfway down the list of performers to a photo of two men in tuxedos. The younger man was definitely Alfred, but the name listed under his photo was different.

"Clyde Roberts?"

"It has to be him. It's the only name in common on all of these." Violet was sorting the playbills into stacks. "That one is the most recent—last year—and shows he had a partner, but these others, the older playbills, all list Clyde Roberts in various acts—singing, dancing, and acting."

I read the name of Clyde Roberts's act from the playbill, "The Dapper British Gents. Tap dancing and repartee most posh—"

The *snick* of a key sliding into the lock of the flat's front door startled both of us.

CHAPTER TWENTY

*V*iolet and I exchanged an alarmed glance, then she hunkered down behind the bed. She would be hidden from the view of anyone walking down the hall, but I was in the bedroom's doorway. The handle of the front door turned. I stepped behind the open bedroom door, but didn't have time to shut it before the front door opened.

Someone with a heavy tread strode in, shoving the door closed. I looked through the crack between the door and the frame, then mouthed the word *Sebastian* to Violet.

Her eyes widened as she popped up from behind the bed to have a look. I waved her back down, but she ignored me.

Sebastian had been in the process of pocketing his keys as he walked down the hall, but he glanced into the living area and came to a sudden stop, his hand half in his pocket. He surveyed the room, then his gaze darted to the bedroom.

Violet stood up, hands on her hips. "Sebastian, you gave me a terrible fright. What are you doing here?"

He let the keys fall into his pocket and frowned at her. The hall was dim and the light coming in from the living room highlighted the hollows around his eyes and gaunt cheeks. "I think the question is, what are *you* doing here?"

"Staying for a few days while I figure out what to do. Alfred wouldn't mind. How did you get a key?"

A small smile crossed Sebastian's lean face. "It seems I should ask the same thing of you. This is my flat."

"Your flat?"

"Yes, I lent it to Alfred."

Violet swallowed and seemed to be speechless for a moment. I decided it was time to announce my presence. I stepped out from behind the door. "Hello, Sebastian. This being your flat makes perfect sense." I handed him the playbill Violet had given me. "I have the feeling you were the one person in London who knew Alfred's true identity."

He stared at the playbill a moment before he took it from my hand. He blew out a long stream of air through his nose. "The cat is well and truly out of the bag now."

"You knew?" Violet advanced around the end of the bed.

Sebastian didn't say anything for a moment, so I said, "Sebastian would *have* to know. He made Alfred's deception possible." I turned to him. "Didn't you?"

Sebastian didn't reply. Instead, he went through the door to the living room and across to the windows. He stared at the view for a moment. Violet and I followed him into the room. Without turning, he said, "Yes, it's true. I did know. Alfred was"—he lifted the playbill—"Clyde Roberts."

"But why?" Violet asked. "Why would you do that—deceive everyone?"

Sebastian dropped the playbill onto the crowded side table, then took out a cigarette and lighter. He lit his cigarette and began walking back and forth in front of the windows. "It was a rag."

"A rag?" Violet's voice was faint, barely above a whisper. She plunked down onto the sofa.

"A joke?" I asked. "This whole thing was a rag?"

Sebastian rubbed his forehead with the heel of the hand that held the cigarette as he paced. "I didn't intend for it to go this far."

He gestured at Violet. "I had no idea—or intention—that it would get so out of hand."

Violet gripped the arm of the sofa. "I want to hear exactly what happened. Tell me all of it, the whole story."

"All right. You deserve that." Sebastian sat down in the chrome chair I'd occupied earlier and hunched forward, resting his elbows on his knees. I slid into the matching chair across from him, but he didn't seem to be aware of my movement. His thoughts seemed to be focused inward. Without lifting his head, he glanced at Violet out of the corner of his eye. "You knew I went to America?"

"Yes, New York."

"New York was the first place I visited. I was with my father, and he had an invitation to visit an old school chum who lived in Chicago. So we went out there and spent a few weeks with him. His son took me to a vaudeville performance." Sebastian tapped the playbill. "Alfred—or Clyde, as he was calling himself—performed. He was the epitome of a dapper but daft English gentleman. He and his partner wore tuxes and interspersed tap dancing with a running commentary of jokes. They brought the house down, and the girls in the audience swooned over him. My friend and I hung around the stage door afterward, trying to meet two of the female dancers who had been in another act. They let us take them out to dinner, and somehow Clyde managed to get himself invited along as well. After dinner, the girls insisted they had to get back to their boardinghouse because they had an early train to catch the next day."

Sebastian drew on the cigarette, blowing the smoke up to the ceiling. "Once the girls left, the conversation shifted back to the performances. I'd been surprised when Clyde spoke with an American accent throughout dinner. I genuinely thought he was a Brit. Turned out, he had an affinity for accents and could pick up anyone's. At dinner he ran through his repertoire—German count, British gentleman, Australian rancher, Irish pub owner, French playboy. My American friend who had brought me to the show said he thought that if Clyde was in England, he could impersonate a British gentleman without raising any eyebrows."

Sebastian leaned back in his chair and examined the end of his cigarette. "That was how it started. A throwaway line at dinner. But it seemed like it could be a great deal of fun. It would require careful planning, but if I could pull it off, it would be spectacular, the rag to end all rags—elaborate and extended."

Of course the idea would appeal to Sebastian. "It would be quite a coup, wouldn't it?" I asked. "Even better than fooling the dean at your college into thinking you were a prize-winning scientist."

Sebastian frowned. "As I said, I never intended for it to go this far. It was supposed to be a joke that would last a few weeks. A delightful little diversion to liven things up. We would fool everyone then reveal the truth."

"Alfred—Clyde, I mean—dropped everything and came with you to England?" I asked.

Sebastian drew on the cigarette and said through his exhale of smoke, "I said I'd finance the whole thing and threw out a number that I'd pay him if he left the vaudeville circuit that night and came back to England to participate in my little—er—show. Alfred said one show was as good as another, and he was getting tired of the vaudeville circuit. I took him to my friend's tailor the next day and outfitted him with enough clothes for the return voyage. We also agreed on a new name. We picked Alfred Eton. We both thought it was a great joke—a royal first name combined with an elite school."

"But what about his family?" Violet asked.

"Alfred was an orphan. He wanted a fresh start in a new country. I told him he could come with me and fulfill the role for a few weeks. Then when the truth was revealed, he could keep the clothes and the 'salary' I'd agreed to pay him. He could set himself up in England."

I said, "So the bits about India, his dead parents, and you being his godfather were all manufactured."

Sebastian stubbed out his cigarette in an ashtray and leaned back in the chair, smoothing his hand over his slicked down hair. "I'm afraid so. A history in India made it plausible that he wouldn't know anyone in England. He needed a connection, someone who could sponsor him in society. The relationship of godfather was distant enough that I might not have been in touch with him for years, but it gave me a reason to know him and introduce him around town." He looked at Violet and pressed his lips together for a moment. "He was only to play the part for a few weeks, and then it would've been over."

I said, "But your creation got away from you."

"Yes, my little Frankenstein came to life and wouldn't follow directions."

"Why didn't you just expose him? Tell everyone the truth?" I asked. "After all, you were in charge of the whole thing. Once you removed your support and financial backing"—I glanced around the apartment—"Alfred's impersonation would collapse."

Sebastian rearranged his suit jacket, which already fell in a perfect line. "A—um—*difficulty* arose."

I leaned forward. "Alfred had something on you," I said as the thought popped into my mind.

Sebastian looked as if he'd experienced a physical pain.

Violet said, "He was blackmailing you too."

Sebastian tensed. "There were others?"

"Alfred had a proclivity for blackmail," I said.

"Nasty habit," Sebastian said. "No wonder he ended up dead." He threw an apologetic look at Violet. "Sorry, my dear. I'm rattled. I had no idea." He straightened his already flawlessly arranged suit jacket again. "How do you know this?"

I looked to Violet. "It's your story."

"Oh, I shouldn't have said anything, should I?" Violet rubbed a hand across her forehead and looked toward the door.

"The word is out now," I said. "You'd better tell Sebastian."

Violet shook her curls back from her face and let out a long sigh. "I suppose I must now. I found a notebook of Alfred's with a list of names—well, actually, they were nicknames—and amounts. But I don't remember anything that could have been related to you, Sebastian. Did he ever ask you for money?"

"No."

Violet looked at me, her brows drawn together.

I said, "Continuing the masquerade as Alfred was more valuable to him than money. He wanted Sebastian's silence."

"Correct," Sebastian said. "He wanted use of the flat and the motor and my credit with shopkeepers."

Violet shifted back to Sebastian. "What hold did he have over you? You don't seem to care at all what people think of you."

Sebastian ran his thumb down the perfect crease in his trousers. "He found a photograph I took of a certain woman." He hesitated, then said, "The wife of an ambassador. It was a bit . . . risqué, or at least some people would consider it improper. He threatened to release it to the newspapers, and I couldn't have that. I may be a scoundrel, but I draw the line at besmirching a lady's reputation."

Violet smoothed the folds of her dress. "I had no idea Alfred was so . . . so . . . selfish. I suppose he thought the whole thing was a great joke, and he was enjoying it too much to give it up."

"I think that's partly true. He did enjoy the trappings." Sebastian glanced around the apartment. "But I believe he sincerely cared for you and didn't want to lose you. I suppose he was afraid if you knew the truth—that he was a penniless orphan from America—you'd want nothing more to do with him."

"That's not true," Violet said, looking down at her lap.

Sebastian and I exchanged a look. I knew those words were more wishful thinking than fact. Appearance mattered to Violet, and I wasn't surprised she hadn't had a clue about the depths of Alfred's personality or his true motives. She simply wasn't interested in things like that. Bright, sparkling fun—that was her main concern, or it always had been. Perhaps her attitude might change after this.

Sebastian cleared his throat. "So I was not the only one Alfred blackmailed?" His tone was halfway between amusement and irritation. "I should have realized if he blackmailed me, he would do it to others."

"Yes, he certainly didn't stop with you," I said, "but I'm afraid we don't have proof of it." I looked toward Violet.

"What?" Violet looked up. "I'm sorry. I missed what you said."

"Proof. We don't have it."

"Oh. Yes." Her shoulders slumped. "My fault," she said to Sebastian. "I burned Alfred's notebook. I wasn't supposed to have it, you see. I panicked, thinking that the police would arrest me if they found I had it."

"Speaking of the police, I believe we should ring Inspector Longly," I said.

Violet gripped the arm of the sofa. "But he'll arrest me."

"I doubt that." I tilted my head toward Sebastian. "We now have another person who can corroborate your story about Alfred's blackmail."

"But what about the cufflink?"

"Circumstantial evidence," I said. "Alfred could have lost it before you went upstairs. Monty saw him wearing them after your argument. How many dances did you dance with other boys?"

"Three or four, I suppose."

"And then you went upstairs with Alfred?"

"Yes."

"See, that's plenty of opportunity—at least ten, maybe twenty minutes during which the cufflink could have fallen off. And if it did fall off during the struggle on the balcony, then that means the murderer picked it up and planted it on your dress later. If you hadn't run away from Archly Manor so quickly, Uncle Leo's solicitor would have arrived. I'm sure he would have pointed out to the police that just because the cuff-link was lodged in your dress, which no one saw until days later—rather odd, don't you think?—it doesn't clinch a case against you."

"But what if they say all that doesn't matter? It *was* Alfred's cufflink. What if they arrest me?"

Sebastian leaned forward, pressed his hands to his knees, and stood up. "Don't be a ninny, Violet. I've hidden the truth about Alfred too long. It must come out. We might as well take control of the situation and make sure *we* are the ones who tell the inspector our story." Sebastian strode across the room toward the telephone.

Violet jumped up and beat him to it. "Then I'm calling Father's solicitor."

CHAPTER TWENTY-ONE

*W*hen Inspector Longly arrived, he surveyed the living room and said, "I see the party has moved to Alfred's flat."

Sebastian said, "Not exactly. Please have a seat." He gestured to the sofa. Violet scooted as far away as she could from the inspector and glanced at Uncle Leo's solicitor, an older gentleman with a toothbrush mustache and reassuring manner, who was seated in the chair Sebastian had occupied earlier. Mr. Tarpliss had had a conversation with Violet before the inspector arrived. After hearing her story, he'd advised her to tell Longly everything.

"Even the bit about the notebook?" Violet had asked.

"Especially that part," Mr. Tarpliss had said. "Don't worry. You shan't have any trouble from the inspector. As your friends have told you, circumstantial evidence does not a case make. I'll tell you if you shouldn't answer one of the inspector's questions, but Longly is a reasonably intelligent chap. Shouldn't be a problem."

Once Longly was seated, Sebastian sat down in a chair he'd dragged in from the bedroom and said, "I suppose I'd better begin."

Longly had taken out his notebook and balanced it on his left knee, but as Sebastian told his story, Longly stopped taking notes after a few moments. The speed of Sebastian's speech made it impossible for Longly to keep up with his left hand, but he listened intently, and I had a feeling he would remember everything Sebastian said.

When Sebastian finished, Longly said, "The details of this item Mr. Eton was holding over you, what were they?"

Sebastian's gaze flicked around the group and then back to Longly. "Perhaps we could go into that at a later time? I'm sure you'll need us to give a more formal statement, correct? I'd be happy to give you the full details then, particularly if you will assure me that, in exchange for my information, you'll prevent it from going any further."

Longly tapped out a fast beat on the notepad with his thumb. "We can go into your story and your request concerning it in more detail later, Mr. Blakely." Longly directed his attention to Violet. "How did you come to be here?"

Violet looked at Mr. Tarpliss, who nodded. She took a breath and launched into her story. Violet's soft-spoken answers were barely audible. I found it hard to believe that this was my feisty cousin who had gotten into trouble so often. She was completely subdued. I wondered how much of it was an act and how much was genuine. She recounted how she had come to be at Alfred's flat and explained that Alfred had given her a key.

Longly had quite a few questions about the notebook Violet had burned. He said, "I'm not pleased you didn't bring this information forward sooner." He glanced at Mr. Tarpliss, and Violet seemed to shrink into a smaller ball against the arm of the sofa. "Nevertheless, it's important we pursue all these leads, no matter how tardy they might be. I'll need you to write down everything you can remember from the notebook."

I opened my handbag. "I can help you there." I took out Violet's list and handed it to Longly. "Violet wrote this down," I said, leaving out the details that she'd written it down the day after Alfred died and that I'd been carrying it around for days.

Longly's gaze ran down the list, and I could've sworn his lips twitched when he read the words *Lady Snooty* and my parenthetical notation of *Lady Pamela* beside it.

He folded the list in half. "This is another thing that we will have to go over in greater detail. I think at this point we should move to a more formal setting to complete these interviews."

~

SEVERAL HOURS LATER, Violet and I were seated in the first-class carriage of the train heading for Nether Woodsmoor. We'd been interviewed separately and had gone over our statements in great detail with the inspector, which had taken hours. When Longly finally thanked us for our time, Violet had looked weak with relief.

I suggested a hearty dinner first, then a train to Parkview. I knew Violet was exhausted and emotionally drained because she didn't protest and followed me meekly to the restaurant then to my lodgings, where I repacked my valise. Violet had been subdued and had hardly spoken during the whole journey to Derbyshire.

I sent a telegram to Parkview Hall and informed them we would be arriving at Upper Benning on the train. I expected Ross to be waiting for us in his chauffeur garb, but when we stepped off the train, it was Gwen who stood on the platform. She threw her arms first around Violet and then me, squeezing tightly as she whispered to me, "Thank you for finding her."

She tucked her arm through Violet's as we walked through the station. Gwen's motor was parked on the street. "Now, tell me what happened. Where did you go? And Olive says you've spoken to Inspector Longly and everything is fine?"

Violet said, "Olive can explain," and went to Gwen's motor.

"Oh," Gwen said, obviously a bit stung by Violet's tepid response.

"She was at Alfred's flat, and the police have our statements.

There's more to tell, but it will have to be later," I said with a significant look at Violet, who was leaning against the door of the motor.

"Of course, we must get you home," Gwen said. "The good news is that Father is completely recovered, and no one else has come down with the flu, so we're all in the clear." Gwen opened the rumble seat, and Violet climbed in the back. I sat down beside Gwen, and I told her what we'd discovered about Alfred as we set off on a twilight drive through the English countryside.

CHAPTER TWENTY-TWO

*A*s soon as we arrived at Parkview, Violet went straight up to her room. Gwen was about to follow her, but I caught her arm. "I need to talk to you."

"Yes, I'm sure there's more to tell." Gwen glanced up the now empty stairs and sighed. "Violet is going to be in her withdrawn mood, and I won't be able to get a thing out of her. Let's go through to the conservatory. No one will be in there right now."

The conservatory ran along the back of the house. High-ceiled and lined with soaring windows, it was a mass of glass and greenery. The sun was below the trees, and the room glowed with a rosy light. Our footsteps clicked across the black and white marble floor as we made our way through the plants. Urns with trailing ivy lined one side of the room, and the floor was a maze of wide-leafed exotic plants. The air was sultry and heavy with the scent of flowers.

I knew that if I let Gwen get started on her questions, it would take forever to answer them all, so I asked, "Why did you go to Alfred's flat?"

Gwen pushed the wide leaves of a banana tree out of the way, and we emerged into a cleared space in the middle of the room with an arrangement of wicker furniture. "What do you mean? I —I didn't go to his flat."

"Oh, Gwen. You're a terrible liar," I said. Any doubts I'd had about the hall porter's memory evaporated at Gwen's attempt to lie. Why would she lie unless she had something to cover up? "Don't even try. I know you went there."

Despite us being alone in the cavernous room, Gwen lowered her voice. "How did you find out? I was so careful."

"I showed the hall porter a picture of you and Violet, thinking that Violet might have visited Alfred at his flat. But the hall porter pointed out that it was you, not Violet, who he'd seen in the building."

Gwen reached up and smoothed a stray hair behind her ear, and I noticed the scratch on her hand was nearly healed. "I didn't want to go, and I knew Mum would be scandalized, so I told Mum I was shopping."

"But why did you go?"

She raised her chin and met my gaze. "I went to buy him off."

"You offered Alfred money in exchange for leaving Violet alone?" I asked. "Gwen, how underhanded of you. I didn't think you had it in you."

She smiled briefly, then looked away. "It was terribly wrong, but I *knew* he wasn't an honorable man. I couldn't prove it. And Mum was dithering about hiring a detective. I decided approaching Alfred on my own would be the easiest way."

"What did you offer?"

"Passage to America, and two hundred pounds once he arrived there."

"Golly. He turned you down?"

"Didn't even hesitate. I was shocked. I was so sure he would jump at the money. It makes sense now, knowing about his little deception with Sebastian."

"He'd already tried his luck in America," I said. "He was doing much better here."

Gwen sighed. "I suppose I should've offered him more. But it was all I could manage out of the estate account without asking Father for more funds. I knew Father wouldn't approve. He's always held that Peter, Violet, and I must work out our problems ourselves. I'm not sorry I did it, though. Of course, I feel horrible for Violet. I know this is a ghastly time for her, and Alfred's death is tragic, but she *will* get over it. She'll be so much better off without him." A maid arrived, said the cook had a question about the menus for the next day, and Gwen went off to handle it.

I sat in the chair for a long time after she left. The room became gloomy as the sun set, and I wondered how far Gwen would go to protect her sister.

THE NEXT MORNING, seated across from Gwen at the breakfast table, I decided my suspicions were completely ridiculous. With the bright sunlight from the window behind her creating a halo of her golden hair, Gwen was the epitome of delicate beauty. I'd known her my whole life. She loved Violet fiercely, but Gwen wouldn't resort to murder—not even to protect her little sister.

But what if it was an accident? The thought whispered through my mind. Perhaps she didn't mean to do it. Had Gwen approached Alfred again? Had she gone upstairs during the party, perhaps to keep an eye on Violet and Alfred during the romantic fireworks, but found Alfred alone on the balcony and made a second attempt to get Alfred out of Violet's life? Perhaps he'd refused again and grown belligerent. Jane and Violet had said that Alfred had been hostile earlier in the evening. What if that anger had spilled over and he threatened Gwen physically—had she really cut her hand on a broken glass? If she and Alfred struggled on the balcony . . .

I gave myself a little mental shake and focused on my breakfast. I tried to push that scenario out of my mind, but it wouldn't go away. Gwen was reading a letter. As soon as she refolded the letter, I decided it was no good—I had to ask.

We were alone in the breakfast room. "Did you ever . . . renew your offer to Alfred?"

"Hmm?" Gwen's attention was still fixed on the letter as she replaced it in the envelope and put it beside her plate.

"Did you try to buy off Alfred again during Sebastian's party?"

Gwen's gaze flew from the letter to me. "No. Why do you ask that?"

"I only wondered . . . did it come up again?"

"No. He was quite firm when he turned it down the first time. I knew it would be useless to try again."

The butler appeared and said there was a telephone call for Violet, but she hadn't come down from her room.

"I'll take it," Gwen said and left the room.

I put down my cutlery, not hungry anymore. After weeks of getting by on dry rolls and watery tea while longing for filling food, part of me couldn't believe I was leaving food on my plate, but suspecting Gwen turned my stomach. Aunt Caroline came in, said good morning, then went to the sideboard.

Gwen returned to the breakfast table and picked up her letter. "That was Sebastian. He's invited us to Archly Manor for a few days. He's having a . . . um . . . gathering to commemorate Alfred's life. A memorial, he called it."

Aunt Caroline turned, her plate in hand. "A memorial? But has there been a funeral?"

"It's to be today at Finchbury Crossing. A private ceremony with only Sebastian and Thea in attendance. Then Alfred will be buried in the churchyard."

"I don't think there's any need for you girls to go," Aunt Caroline said as she turned back to the sideboard. "A memorial instead of a funeral! I like to think of myself as progressive, not bound by tradition, but certain things are *required*. It's ill bred to—to—dispense with them."

"There is going to be a funeral today, Mum. A private ceremony."

Aunt Caroline sniffed. "Not a *proper* funeral. Holding a 'memorial' as if this Alfred weren't a bounder of the first order." The night before, I'd told Aunt Caroline everything we'd discovered about Alfred.

"Such bad manners people have today." Aunt Caroline sat down at the table. "Imagine holding a funeral but not inviting anyone. Ridiculous! As I said, you have no obligation to attend a so-called funeral."

"Memorial." Violet stood in the doorway in a powder blue dressing gown, her curls flattened to her head. "I'm going. I don't care what you say. He was my fiancé."

"Yes, that's true, darling, but you have no obligation to him now," Aunt Caroline said.

"I should be there. I'm going." Violet looked at Gwen. "Are you coming? Or should I arrange for Ross to take me to Archly Manor?"

Gwen, Aunt Caroline, and I exchanged glances, then Gwen said, "I'll take you, and Olive can come along if she'd like. We can leave after lunch."

he remaining papier-mâché figures that had marked the crossroads guiding guests to the estate for the previous week's house party were gone. As silly as I thought the figures were, they had actually been helpful in navigating the deserted country roads. Without the colorful markers pointing the way, we'd taken a wrong turn, which lengthened the drive and had Violet on edge, thinking we wouldn't arrive in time for the dinner, much less tea.

"Ah, we *are* on the right road," I said as the gates of Archly Manor came into view. "And no reporters, which is surprising. I'd have thought they'd have returned to cover the funeral."

Violet twisted around from the front seat. "That's why Sebastian kept the funeral small. He didn't want word to get out and have the place overrun with newspaper men." Violet had spent some time on the telephone with Sebastian before we departed, planning a dinner in Alfred's honor, which was to take place tonight.

Violet had been tense with irritation after the wrong turn and had only spoken in single-syllable responses, but now she seemed to be in the mood to talk, so I asked, "Who else will be at Archly Manor?"

"Lady Pamela is still there. She stayed on after we left. Monty says he'll come, which I suppose means Tug will be there as well since Lady Pamela is. Sebastian said he'll ask Hugh to make up the numbers." Violet wrinkled her nose. "Although, I hope Hugh doesn't cause trouble. You know how irritatingly priggish he is."

Gwen turned the wheel as the road curved through the parkland of Archly Manor's grounds. "I'm sure Sebastian invited him for Muriel."

"Yes, poor thing," Violet said. "I can't imagine what she sees in stuffy old Hugh." After a moment, she added, "And James, of course. He's always at Archly Manor if Sebastian is there."

Our arrival was treated as casually as it had been the first time we arrived. No one came out onto the sweep to greet us, and Babcock informed us the gentlemen were in the old stable block admiring Monty's new motor but should return momentarily.

We were shown to the rooms we had occupied before. After we freshened up, I met Gwen in the upstairs corridor, where she said, "Violet's already gone down." She motioned to the doors to our rooms. "I find this odd, being in the same rooms. It's like the Saturday-to-Monday all over again."

"Yes. There is a sense of déjà vu about it."

"Thank goodness it's only for one night. We'll be gone by lunch tomorrow."

The door across the hall opened. Lady Pamela surged out but stopped short when she saw us. Then she threw out her arms as if she were going to embrace us both at the same time. "*Darlings*, you've returned!" To my relief, she clasped her hands together and pressed them to her chest. She swayed as if she were on the deck of a ship as she said in a confidential tone, "It *is* so hard to stay away from Sebastian's little gatherings. So compelling, you know." Without waiting for a reply, she turned and waltzed down the hall, weaving back and forth across the thick Aubusson carpet.

Eyebrows raised, Gwen said, "Oh my. Did you see her eyes? Is she . . . ?"

"I'm afraid so." Lady Pamela's eyes were dilated again, and

since a happy disposition was not her normal state, only one explanation came to mind. It also clarified why Lady Pamela had stayed on at Archly Manor. I was certain she wouldn't be able to indulge her habits so easily at her father's country home or London townhouse.

"Well. That does explain certain things," Gwen said. "Thank goodness Violet hasn't been drawn into *that*." Gwen gave me another look. "You don't seem surprised."

"No. I've seen Lady Pamela this way before. I think it's—er—typical for her."

Lady Pamela neared the top of the stairs, and Gwen said, "Should we help her down the stairs? If she tries to skip down them, she might actually hurt herself."

"There's Tug, come to escort her down."

We let Lady Pamela and Tug have a few minutes' lead, then Gwen and I went down. Sebastian met us at the foot of the stairs. "Welcome back to Archly Manor. Thank you for bringing Violet," he said to Gwen. He was in his genial host mode, and I could see he was going to act as though we had never had the conversation in Alfred's apartment.

Gwen said, "Thank you for having us. It's a lovely idea to have a little memorial for Alfred."

"Not so small now," Sebastian said as we walked to the drawing room for tea. "Tonight's dinner is limited, but tomorrow may be a crush. The word is out about our little gathering, and I do hate to turn anyone away."

"Violet, Olive, and I will return to Parkview Hall tomorrow. We don't want to impose."

"You can't leave so soon. It's no imposition at all," Sebastian said. "Besides, Violet is going to look through Alfred's belongings tomorrow. She didn't tell you?"

"No, she must have forgotten to mention it to me," Gwen said.

Sebastian said, "I thought there might be some things Violet might want . . . letters, perhaps. She and I fixed it up on the telephone earlier today. I hope you'll both stay. Surely an extra day isn't *too* long at Archly Manor."

Gwen's smile became fixed. "That would be lovely."

"Excellent." Sebastian stepped back to allow Gwen and me to enter the drawing room first. Violet was chatting with James as they looked through gramophone records, while Tug and Lady Pamela hovered at the table with the jigsaw puzzle. Lady Pamela's giggles carried across the room, more evidence she was high. I didn't believe that a jigsaw puzzle could be *that* entertaining, especially to someone like Lady Pamela.

Thea spoke in low tones to Muriel, who was seated on the sofa beside her. Muriel's face was carefully blank, but Thea didn't bother to hide a frown as she looked at Violet. Hugh stood behind Muriel, a pipe in his mouth. With his receding hairline and paunch, he looked as if a parent had accidentally wandered into a room of Bright Young People.

A mechanical smile appeared on Thea's face. "Hello again," she said as Sebastian escorted us across the room. The words were innocuous enough, but there wasn't an ounce of warmth in them.

Sebastian leveled a look at Thea, then said, "Don't mind my sister. She's rather out of sorts today."

Thea flushed, and her hand fluttered up to adjust her long rope of pearls. "The last few days have been a trying time."

"For all of us," Gwen said. Her tone was even, but I sensed an edge of anger underlying the words. I knew she was being protective of Violet.

A servant approached and spoke to Sebastian. "If you'll excuse me," he said to us with a quick bow of his head as he moved away.

Gwen took a few steps away from Thea and Muriel. With her back to them, Gwen blew out a breath through her nose. "As if I would go off and leave Violet alone here." Her gaze moved to Lady Pamela. "Especially now that I know about some of the things that are going on."

"I know how you feel, but one more day won't make a difference," I said. "Even Violet has enough sense not to get involved in Lady Pamela's—um—activities. Besides, looking through Alfred's belongings is an excellent opportunity."

Gwen looked at me blankly for a moment.

"To see if we can find anything else that might implicate someone else in Alfred's murder. Perhaps something that the police overlooked."

"Yes, of course." Gwen gave her head a little shake. "I'm sorry. I'm just so worried about Violet. I want to get her away from here."

"One more day, and we'll be gone."

"I'd better make sure of that. Who knows? Perhaps Violet has made more plans for the day after tomorrow and has forgotten to inform me of them. I'll speak to her." Gwen went to join Violet and James.

Monty appeared at my elbow. He handed me a cup of tea. "The party reassembles. Just as if we were in a novel," he said as we moved to another grouping of chairs. "I expect Longly to arrive at any moment, call us all into the library, then point an accusing finger at someone."

"Who do you think that would be?" I lifted my teacup to my lips.

"No idea. Unlike you, I'm not clever about that sort of thing. I never guess the murderer in novels. My job here is simply to round out the guest list. Of course, now that the word is out about Alfred's dodgy pastime of blackmailing people, it widens the field considerably. Not surprising, really."

"It's common knowledge now?" I asked.

"Yes. Everyone is too well bred to speak of it here, but the news has traveled. I heard about it from my man, who heard it mentioned below stairs. No use trying to keep it under wraps. The servants always know everything."

"Oh, I don't mind if the word is out. I think everyone should know what a cad Alfred was. Perhaps that's wrong of me to say as we're about to have a memorial for him, but he's caused Violet and Gwen quite a bit of pain." I sipped my tea, then asked, "Why did you say you weren't surprised Alfred was a blackmailer?"

"He was a sneak. I went to school with enough of his kind to know one immediately. He tried to blackmail me, you know." He picked up a sandwich.

"You?" I asked, then noticed he was munching noisily through his cucumber sandwich.

He swallowed, then said, "Horses. It's always the horses. I love them dearly. Can't stay away. I overextended myself at the races. Alfred hinted he'd tell my father."

"You don't seem upset about it."

He finished off the sandwich, then picked up another. "Wasn't. I made sure Alfred didn't have a hold on me."

"How?"

"I went to the pater and confessed all." He smiled. "Marvelous to have it all out in the open."

"Smart." I watched him eat his way through the sandwich, surprised that I'd never noticed his rabbit-like chomping. "Did Alfred ever call you by a nickname?"

"He tried. I put a stop to it pretty quickly."

"Was it Muncher, by any chance?"

"See, you *are* the clever one. How did you know?"

"Lucky guess. Did you ever hear him call anyone Songbird?"

Monty stared at his tea a moment, then shook his head. "No, can't say I did."

I didn't want to linger on the subject of nicknames. I didn't want to tell Monty that Alfred had listed the word *Muncher* as a description in his notebook. I surveyed the room. "Well, even if you weren't worried about Alfred's tendency to threaten and demand money, someone here was. No guess as to who it could be?"

"No. You've covered that quite well."

"What do you mean?"

"I've heard you've been industrious in your effort to keep Violet from being arrested."

"There's no threat of arrest," I said. "She didn't do it."

"Yes, I think you're right. But then, I think everyone is innocent."

"I suppose that's the difference between you and me. I think everyone could be guilty."

"Except for your cousins."

"Of course," I said, but guilt pricked at my conscience as I thought about my suspicions of Gwen. I made a mental note to speak to the kitchen staff and see if anyone could confirm Gwen had cut her hand on a broken glass. Despite Gwen's denial that she had approached Alfred again, I couldn't stop those thoughts from whirling around in my mind.

Thea's voice carried across the room. "Completely unacceptable." She picked at a loose thread dangling between two of the pearls on her necklace. "Shoddy workmanship. Not up to standards at all. So disappointing, but then what can you expect of foreign workmanship?" She made a noise as she removed the necklace. "It could break at any moment. It's literally being held together by a thread."

The pearls pooled in her hand, dripping over her fingers in long loops as she held them out to Muriel. "Take these upstairs, then telephone Dixon's and tell them I want them repaired immediately. You can take them in first thing Monday morning. I have an engagement Monday night and want to wear them."

Hugh removed his pipe. "No need for Muriel to go. Ring for a—"

But Muriel had already stood and was cradling the pearls in both hands. "I won't be but a moment," she said to Hugh with a warning look. He clamped his lips around the pipe. Muriel left the room, and Monty said in an undertone, "I'm sure we'll hear about the one hundred—"

"One hundred fifty pearls," Thea said. "That many perfectly matched pearls are difficult to come by, and I can't have the thread fraying. Completely unacceptable. You know my dear husband brought them home from a trip to Singapore. Each one individually hand selected."

"Here it comes," Monty said, his voice low.

Thea said, "It never pays to be cheap," as Monty whispered the words at exactly the same moment. I didn't dare glance at him because I knew I'd laugh, which would be frightfully inappropriate.

I kept my gaze fixed on the rose pattern on the carpet and muttered, "You're terrible."

"One must find amusement where one can at these affairs."

SEBASTIAN LEFT us to our own devices for the rest of the afternoon. Violet retired for a nap, and Gwen curled up in the library with *The Lady*, saying she never had time to read it at home. I didn't want to read or stroll in the gardens, and I knew Lady Pamela wouldn't want my help with the jigsaw puzzle she was pretending to work on, so I went off to look for Sebastian.

I found him in the billiard room, where a game had just broken up. Monty and Tug had left to take Monty's new two-seater for a drive, and Sebastian agreed that it would be a good time to show me his studio. "You'll find it dreadfully dull and tedious," he said as we went upstairs. He didn't stop on the floor with the bedrooms but continued up the next flight of stairs to the top of the house.

"I doubt anything you have an interest in is dull."

He flashed a wide grin, which seemed to stretch the skin of his lean face tight over his skull. "Thank you."

The nursery was at the far end of the hall, and I could hear the piercing voices of Paul and Rose. Sebastian took a key and unlocked the studio door. "I can't have anyone messing about in here. Chemicals, you know."

"I imagine so." The room was large and open with a bare wooden floor. Sunlight flooded through three tall windows, lighting up the space. Tables and chairs of various styles were pushed up against the walls beside rolled carpets and a rack of clothes with a shelf above it stacked with hats, wigs, and shoes. What I supposed must be props were scattered around the tables —mirrors, clocks, vases, and bits of masonry. A wooden swing lay in a corner, the ropes coiled on the floor, while the papier-mâché figures that had guided the way to the Silver and Gold party loomed in a corner like something out of a nightmare about a circus.

Photographs lined the walls and drew my attention. I'd never seen Sebastian's photographs. I'd only heard they were interest- ing, which had a wide range of possible interpretations. I thought Sebastian dabbled in photography, but after seeing several of the photographs, it was clear he had a unique talent. The photographs were surprisingly compelling. The images lining the walls were obviously set pieces, elaborately designed and staged, but they didn't have the stiffness I'd often seen in studio portraits.

In each one, Sebastian seemed to have captured the person- ality of his subject. I inched around the room, surprised to find familiar faces mixed in with the photographs of society hostesses. James, seated at a desk covered with papers, pen poised, stared seriously over his glasses, which had slipped down his nose. Jane, the former housemaid, looked over her shoulder, a cheeky grin on her face. I slowed to study a landscape—the only landscape I'd seen so far—but then I spotted Muriel standing behind a garden statue, nearly hidden by the shadow. "I'm fascinated with these," I said.

Sebastian was moving around the other side of the room, unlocking another door. "Hmm . . . what?"

"You've managed to capture everyone's personality."

He grinned. "I know."

I rolled my eyes. "The correct response is *thank you*."

"I'm never correct. So boring."

His attitude should have been off-putting, but a part of me admired his complete disregard for convention. I turned back to the photos. Hugh stood importantly on a portico of a grand house, his attention fixed on his open pocket watch, a pose that brought his hand to his chest in a position reminiscent of the paintings of Napoleon with his hand tucked into his coat. "Is this Hugh's home?"

"His father's. Hugh will inherit it someday."

"Lucky Muriel," I said but wondered how she would get on as the mistress of a grand estate. I had a hard time picturing her managing the servants.

I moved to the next photo. "Who is—oh, it's Thea." She wore her long strand of pearls, and her hair was the same, but she was so slender I hadn't recognized her immediately.

Sebastian squinted across the room and saw which photograph I was looking at. "Yes, she was my first subject and got tired of posing for me. I learned to photograph people with her as my model. I only convinced her to let me take her picture that day because she'd just received the pearls—her famous one-hundred-fifty-perfectly-matched-pearls," he said. "Thank goodness she wanted to show them off. Otherwise, I don't think I could have convinced her to step in front of the camera."

I strolled, scanning the room and saw several more photographs of Thea, all of them in unique and different poses. I halted in front of an arresting image of Lady Pamela with her arms crossed and leaning on a mirrored surface. Her head was tilted, and her cheek rested on the back of one hand. The mirror created a double image, showing Lady Pamela right side up as well as upside down in the reflection.

The composition of the photograph was unusual, but it wasn't what caught my attention. It was her jewelry. Lady Pamela wore a double-strand pearl bracelet with two square-cut jewels surrounded with small diamonds.

"These stones in this photograph, what were they?"

Sebastian looked up briefly from fiddling with a camera. "Emeralds."

"You're sure?"

"Yes," he said unequivocally.

I stared at the portrait for a long moment, then said, "Do you have a telephone on this floor?"

"No. They're all on the ground floor—under the stairs, in my study, and the butler's pantry. Why?"

"I need to call Inspector Longly."

"How very tedious. Must you?"

"I'm afraid I have to. He must see this picture."

CHAPTER TWENTY-FOUR

J used the telephone in Sebastian's study. After waiting an extremely long time on the line, I was finally connected with Inspector Longly. We exchanged greetings, then I said, "I think you should see a photograph here at Archly Manor. It's a picture of Lady Pamela wearing a pearl bracelet. They could be the strings of pearls that were in Alfred's pocket."

"You can tell that from a photograph?"

"I know it sounds unbelievable, but bear with me for a moment. The bracelet has two square-cut jewels that link the strands of pearls. I can't tell exactly what color the stones are in the photograph, of course, but they're obviously darker stones, not diamonds. Mr. Blakely took the photograph, and he says the stones were emeralds. On the night of the Silver and Gold party, Lady Pamela forgot her handbag. It was on a table near me, and when she came back for it, several things spilled out, including two square-cut emeralds surrounded by smaller diamonds. At the time, I thought they were dress clips, but they look exactly like the stones in the photograph."

"So you think the pearls were detached from these jewels that linked the two strands of the bracelet together?

"Four strands," I said. "They're double strands of pearls. Two strands connect the jewels. Yes, I think the pearls and the jewels were separated."

"Why?"

"Well, the mostly likely possibility is that Lady Pamela cut off the strands of pearls and gave them to Alfred."

"Instead of cash for a blackmail payment?" Inspector Longly asked. I'd expected that he'd sneer at the idea, but his voice was thoughtful. The line was silent for a few moments, then he said, "Is Lady Pamela at Archly Manor?"

"Yes. Sebastian is giving a small dinner party, and she's attending."

"And you returned?"

"The dinner party is in honor of Alfred. Violet was determined to be here, so Gwen and I came with her."

"I'll see you shortly."

~

THE DRESSING BELL had already rung by the time I hung up the telephone. I dressed quickly with Milly's help, changing into a gown of turquoise chiffon with glass beads in a geometric design on the dropped-waist bodice. Gwen had given it to me when she cleared out her wardrobe last season, and I'd hemmed up the skirt so it didn't brush the floor. I rushed downstairs and managed to enter the drawing room shortly before Babcock announced dinner.

Monty, who was near the door when I walked in, cocked an eyebrow. "And what have you been up to?"

"Running late, I'm afraid."

"No, it's more than that. You have an air of excitement fairly shimmering around you."

"I don't know what you mean." I drew a breath to calm my racing heart. "It's only because I had to rush down."

"I trust you'll tell me later. I do want to hear all about it."

We went in to dinner, and it was fairly subdued, at least according to the standards of Archly Manor. Violet wore a black silk dress with floaty chiffon sleeves and a black feather in her hair. Gwen wore a lavender gown with a lace overdress. We drank a toast to Alfred, and the whole thing was rather well done, which surprised me. Except for a few cutting remarks from Lady Pamela, the tone of the evening was one of reminiscing, and no mention was made of the way Alfred had died. I was tense, listening for Longly's arrival, wondering if he would interrupt dinner.

But the pudding was served and the tablecloth was removed without an appearance from Scotland Yard. The men opted to skip their port and cigars and joined the ladies directly in the drawing room. We were discussing whether or not we should play bridge, when Babcock glided into the room, whispered something in Sebastian's ear, and then came to me and murmured, "Inspector Longly has arrived and wishes to speak to you in the reception hall." I excused myself and followed Sebastian out the door.

Inspector Longly's suit looked a bit out of place compared with my opulent gown and Sebastian's tuxedo. Sebastian drew a set of keys out of his pocket as he greeted the inspector. "I understand you need to see a photograph in my studio."

"Yes, let's start there."

I led the way up the stairs with Sebastian, Longly, and a constable trailing behind me. Sebastian unlocked the studio, and I showed Longly the photograph. He examined it with his one arm behind his back, then he stepped closer and traced a finger above the strings of pearls, counting under his breath. "Twenty on each strand," he said to the constable, who made a note. Longly turned to me. "Describe these stones again that you thought were dress clips."

I went over everything, describing how they had fallen out of

Lady Pamela's handbag. "I didn't look at them closely, just scooped them up and put them back, but they were square cut like the ones in the photograph, and they had a surrounding line of small diamonds."

Longly nodded, then said to Sebastian, "Do you have a copy of this photograph?"

Sebastian picked up a folder from a worktable. "I made one this afternoon. I thought you might need it."

Longly glanced inside. "Thank you. You both can return to the drawing room. Mr. Blakely, I need to use your study again."

Sebastian took Longly and the constable to his study while I slipped back into the drawing room and was immediately recruited to play bridge. Sebastian returned shortly after I did and whispered in Lady Pamela's ear. She'd been jittery during dinner, constantly shifting position in her seat, adjusting the flatware of her place setting, or fidgeting with her jewelry. Her eyebrows lowered into a frown, but she followed him from the room, the beads on her pink dress clacking against her long necklaces.

I had a terrible time concentrating on the game and apologized to James when I put my cards down. "I'm sorry, my mind's not on the game."

"It's fine. Happens to everyone," James murmured in his even-tempered way, but he didn't leap at the idea of another game with me as his partner. The evening ended early without Lady Pamela returning to the drawing room.

I went up to my room and rang for Milly. "Did Lady Pamela retire early?" I asked as she unbuttoned the row of small buttons on the back of my dress.

"No, she was with Inspector Longly." Milly put my shoes away. "Apparently, he spoke to her ever so nicely, trying to convince her to talk to him, but she wouldn't say one word more."

"How do you know this?"

A flush stained her cheeks. "George, one of the footmen, was in the hall."

"I see. So what happened?"

"Lady Pamela told the inspector he could wait on her in the morning at Harlan House in London, then she had everything packed and left."

CHAPTER TWENTY-FIVE

*T*he next morning at breakfast, Thea announced, "I've had a telegram from my husband. The children and I are leaving directly to go to Brazil."

I stopped spreading marmalade on my toast. "You're leaving today?"

"Heavens, no. Too much to do today. Tomorrow—although how Mr. Reid imagines I can get everything done today, I don't know. But he's booked passage for us for tomorrow, so it *must* be done. Muriel will have to cancel the interviews of the governess applicants scheduled for next week and send my regrets to Lady Smythe. So disappointing to miss her garden party. I was so looking forward to it."

Gwen set down her teacup. "Will Muriel accompany you?"

"Of course. Travel halfway around the world with two children on my own? Impossible! Oh, and I must contact Monsieur Babin to halt the work on the townhouse until we return."

Sebastian turned from the sideboard. "I'm sure they can carry on without you."

"And leave them unsupervised for six weeks? Unthinkable."

"You let them work now unsupervised."

"But I'm only a few hours away. Should anything come up, I could leave at a moment's notice."

"But you never do," Sebastian said under his breath as he passed behind my chair.

"I heard that, Sebastian," Thea said. "I go up to town often. *Quite* often. It's different if one is out of the country. Unless you'd like for me to refer all of Monsieur Babin's questions to you?" She smiled at him across the starched linen.

"Certainly not!" Sebastian circled his knife in the air. "Go on. Cancel your Monsieur Babin. If I approved the wrong shade of paint, I'd never hear the end of it."

As Thea continued to verbalize her list of things that *must* be accomplished, I excused myself from the table and went to the kitchen. I knew I would disturb the servants' hall by showing up unannounced, but I had to do it. I'd stared at the ceiling for a long time last night and finally decided that no matter how things turned out with Lady Pamela, I had to ask a few questions about Gwen for my own peace of mind.

The cook, Mrs. Finley, shooed away her underlings when I asked to speak to her. "Hello again. Sorry to interrupt."

"That's all right. I can work while we talk if you don't mind."

"Please do. It's about the night of the Silver and Gold party. You were shorthanded?"

Mrs. Finley sprinkled flour across a board, then turned a mound of bread dough out of a bowl and began to knead it, her stubby-fingered hands moving and turning the dough deftly as she added a bit of flour now and then. "Yes. Katie was off to care for her sick mum, Jane was acting uppity, and Mrs. Foster had twisted her ankle. It ballooned up to twice its size, and Doctor Evans said she had to stay off her feet. Even with the girls up from the village, it was hard to get everything done. They're well-meaning but not fully trained, if you know what I mean."

"I understand. My cousin Gwen, Miss Stone, came down to give you a hand?"

Mrs. Finley shaped the dough into loaves. "That she did, and I was much appreciative. She knows how to run a household."

"I know she was glad to help. Gwen is like that."

"Kindhearted, she is."

"But there was a little accident?"

Mrs. Finley put the loaves in pans and wiped her hands on a towel. "It was that foolish girl Mary. One of the girls from the village, come up for the evening. She dropped her tray. Miss Stone went to help pick it up and got a gash on her hand for her trouble. I wrapped her hand in a clean towel, and Miss Stone said not to worry about it. She would get a plaster for it herself."

A delivery arrived, and Mrs. Finley needed to check it. I thanked her for her help and returned upstairs, relieved that my suspicion had amounted to nothing. I also felt a little guilty about it, but my brain was the kind that wouldn't quit once I got on a track. I couldn't put it out of my mind. The little detail would have kept bothering me if I hadn't sorted it out.

THE REST of the morning passed quietly. After lunch, the men went off for a drive in the motors, Thea directed the maids as they packed for her, and Gwen and I helped Violet go through Alfred's things. Gwen hadn't liked the idea of staying at Archly Manor another day, but she was too good-natured to stay upset for long. By the time we were actually sorting Alfred's belongings, Gwen was back to her usual helpful and practical self.

Sebastian had said his man would take care of Alfred's clothes, but Violet had insisted we do it, which gave me an excellent excuse to check every pocket and seam. I'd come up with absolutely nothing so far. I folded a suit jacket then stacked it in a box. I fingered the fine cloth and the well-placed stitches. "Sebastian was certainly not stingy when he outfitted Alfred for his role as a gentleman."

Gwen, who was stacking shoes, said, "Yes, someone in the

village will make good use of all this." She'd already talked to the housekeeper about the distribution of Alfred's belongings. She turned from the wardrobe with a stack of records. "These were behind the clothes. Violet, do you want any of these records?"

Violet sat on the floor surrounded by stacks of half-unfolded papers and a scatter of envelopes, which I'd found on the top shelf of the wardrobe. All the letters were from Violet, and I'd handed them off to her. Violet flipped through the records. "No, there's nothing good—only ballads." She handed them to me, and I put them in the box with the clothes.

Other than the letters, his clothing, and his shaving gear and comb, there was nothing of a personal nature in Alfred's room. It seemed the only bit of his past Alfred had brought with him were the playbills he'd left in the London flat. I couldn't imagine not bringing anything when one went to a new country. For my short move to London, I'd brought photographs and notebooks along with my sewing kit and several books that I absolutely had to have with me.

"So the vultures have come to pick over the leavings." Lady Pamela stood in the doorway, her arms crossed over her chest. "Didn't expect to see me, did you?" She sauntered into the room and stopped squarely in front of me. "I know it was you who told the inspector about my bracelet."

Across the room, Gwen sent me a puzzled look.

Lady Pamela looked over the clothes we'd packed, then picked up the jacket I'd folded. She shook it out. "Alfred always did look nice in this one." She dropped it back into the box.

"What happened with the inspector?" Gwen asked.

Lady Pamela turned and picked up Alfred's comb. "A little . . . misunderstanding." She opened the straight razor and ran her fingertip along the edge of the blade. "Once Inspector Longly spoke with my solicitor, everything was cleared up."

I picked up the jacket she'd dropped and shook it out with a snap. "But the pearls *were* yours. And they were in Alfred's pocket."

She flicked the blade closed and slammed it down on the bureau. "Which has absolutely nothing to do with his death. I gave them to him and that's all." Lady Pamela strolled back to the door. She turned and fixed her gaze on Violet. "Believe me, if I wanted to kill Alfred, I wouldn't do it when he had my jewelry in his pocket. I'd never be such an idiot. I'm sure it won't be long before the true culprit is identified and arrested." Lady Pamela turned away. A few seconds later, a door down the hall slammed.

Violet, her mouth set in a line, stared at the door after Lady Pamela left. "I'd like to throw something at her, but I won't give her the satisfaction of being able to point it out as evidence of my temper."

"What's this about pearls?" Gwen asked me.

"Inspector Longly showed me several strands of pearls that were found in Alfred's pocket. I think they were Lady Pamela's, and she used them to pay off Alfred on the night of the Silver and Gold party."

"But why would she use her pearls?" Violet asked. "She has loads of money."

"Maybe not." I refolded the jacket. "I've heard her father keeps her allowance small."

"He's stingy?" Gwen asked. "I've never heard of Lord Harlan being a miser."

"Perhaps." I explained how I'd seen the photograph in Sebastian's studio. "Lady Pamela must have taken off her bracelet, snipped off the strings of pearls, and given those to Alfred while keeping the emeralds. If she's telling the truth, she simply gave Alfred the pearls and went back to the party. If not, perhaps she decided that she didn't want to face years of blackmail and decided to push him over the balcony."

"But wouldn't she have done that before she gave Alfred the pearls, rather than after?" Violet asked.

I tucked the jacket back into the box and sighed. "Yes, that's the weakness in the argument."

Violet scraped the letters into an untidy pile. "I'm going to put these away. And don't follow me, Gwen. I want to be alone."

After Violet left, Gwen looked at me, her shoulders sagging. "What are we going to do? Violet could live her whole life under the shadow of Alfred's death with everyone whispering she did it. Lady Pamela will see to it rumors are spread around."

"Yes, if only to preserve herself."

THAT NIGHT when I was dressing for dinner, Milly came in to help me, but I'd already changed into another dress that Gwen had given me, a royal blue silk with a skirt that ended in a zigzag of beaded points. Milly picked up a bracelet of Venetian beads and held it out to me along with my gloves, but then she stopped and examined the bracelet. "This thread is about to break. Would you like me to mend it?"

I stared at her. Who else had been talking about mending a necklace . . . ? *Thea.* The night before, she'd complained about her pearls . . .

Like a key turning in a lock, the memory opened up a train of thought.

"Miss? Perhaps your pearls instead?"

"Yes, that's fine." I took them and dropped them over my head.

"Would you like me to strengthen the thread?" Milly asked. "It would be a shame for it to break and lose the beads."

"What? Oh, yes. Please do that."

I pulled on my gloves, my mind racing as I settled them on my fingers. I realized Milly was speaking again. "I'm sorry. What did you say?"

"Will that be all?"

"Yes, thank you."

Milly closed the door as she left, and I stood motionless, my thoughts going around and around. *Five* strands of pearls. There had been five strands of pearls found after Alfred died, four in his pocket and the one I'd found on the terrace. I listened to the foot-falls in the corridor as everyone went down to dinner. If the four strands of pearls in Alfred's pocket belonged to Lady Pamela, then what about the fifth? Was it from Thea's necklace?

I sat down at the dressing table and fingered my pearls. What if Thea hadn't taken the sleeping powder? What if either she or Jane—or both of them—were lying?

If Thea was awake instead of sleeping, she could have been on the balcony struggling with Alfred. Perhaps Alfred had gripped the pearl necklace, and it snapped as he went over the edge. Pearls were strung with knots between each one. A section of Thea's pearls could have snapped off in Alfred's grip as he fell.

When I stepped on the strand of pearls in front of the doors to the ballroom, was Thea upstairs, moving quietly back to her room where she could mend the necklace? Her pearl necklace was long enough that several pearls—even ten or so—wouldn't be noticed. She must have worn a wig to disguise her brunette hair. I wondered if there was a dress-up box in the nursery, or—yes, I had seen wigs in Sebastian's studio.

I was contemplating a quick search of those areas when another thought hit me that brought me to my feet. Thea was leaving Archly Manor tomorrow to go to Brazil. Had her husband really wired for her to come, or was it a good excuse to get out of the country before Longly began to examine all the pearl jewelry at Archly Manor and she became a suspect?

Should I call the inspector? I took a step to the door, then stopped. I couldn't go to him with a hunch. I couldn't telephone him again with another tidbit of information so similar to my last one. Especially since it hadn't gone well with Lady Pamela. I had to make sure. I gave a decisive little nod to my reflection. There was only one way to find out.

I left as late as I possibly could, giving everyone plenty of time to go down to dinner, then peeked out my door. No one was in the hall. I darted out the door and slipped into Thea's room. I

SARA ROSETT

scanned the assorted trunks and hatboxes. It might already be packed—no, her jewelry case sat open on the dressing table.

I locked the door, padded across the room, and carefully removed the long strand of pearls. I found the frayed bit of string Thea had noticed earlier. I perched on the dressing table stool and started on one side of the dangling piece of thread and began counting, touching each pearl as I worked my way around the necklace. As I neared the end, my heart hammered along with my whispers, "One thirty-eight, one thirty-nine, one forty."

I reached the frayed bit and sat still, the pearls warm in my hands. "One hundred forty pearls, not one hundred fifty." A little thrill went through me. I'd been right.

I moved to a lamp, switched it on, and examined the frayed thread. The pearls were individually knotted, and it was easy to see a new bright white thread had been used to repair a break between the pearls. The white thread contrasted sharply with the older, yellowish thread of the rest of the strand.

But why would Thea push Alfred? Her name wasn't in Alfred's notebook . . . unless . . .

I went back to the dressing table and pushed the lid of the jewel box closed. The initials *D.R.* were engraved on an oval plate attached to the lid. Not Thea Reid, but *Dorothea* Reid. The short, two-letter scrawl Violet remembered from Alfred's notebook wasn't an abbreviation for the word *doctor* or a nickname. They were the initials of Dorothea Reid.

My hands went clammy, and I returned the pearls to their position in the jewelry box. I was careful to leave the lid open just as I'd found it. I went to the door and listened for a moment, then remembered the light. I scuttled across the room, switched off the lamp, then slipped out and made my way down to the drawing room.

At the bottom of the stairs, instead of turning left for the drawing room, I turned right and hurried down the hall to Sebastian's study. I closed the door and went to the telephone. It again took a while to be connected to Scotland Yard. I listened to the clicks on the line as the clock on the mantle ticked. I expected the door to open at any moment with someone—Gwen, Violet, or perhaps a servant—tracking me down.

Finally, a male voice came on the line, but it wasn't Longly. "I must speak to Inspector Longly."

"He's on a case," a gravelly voice said. "Message?"

"Have him telephone Olive Belgrave at Archly Manor. It's urgent. I must speak to him tonight." After a few seconds of dead air, I said, "Hello? Are you still there?"

". . . Belgrave . . . Archly . . . Manor," he said, drawing out the syllables. He must have been speaking as he wrote the words.

"It's urgent. Make a note of that as well. I *must* speak to Inspector Longly tonight."

"As I said, he's on a case. May not be in until late."

"Then I need to speak to someone else."

"I suppose I could have the constable telephone when he gets in later."

"Yes. Please do that."

I replaced the ear piece and blew out a breath, but I didn't feel relieved. Once I told Longly what I'd found out, would the outcome be any different than the one involving Lady Pamela? A broken necklace didn't prove Thea's guilt. I was sure if she was confronted with the necklace, Thea would come up with some excuse for it—most likely she'd blame the damage to her necklace on her maid. No, if I wanted to help Violet, I had to do more than point out a frayed thread.

I steadied my breathing. I didn't want to enter the drawing room vibrating with energy as I had the day before. Monty had picked up on my excitement then. I had to be more circumspect. When I entered the drawing room, I paced sedately to where Violet was speaking to James in a corner. "James, I need to speak to Violet for a moment alone. You don't mind, do you?"

"Of course not." He ambled away.

"Violet, I need you to do something tonight at dinner. I think we can flush out the person who killed Alfred."

"What do you mean?"

Babcock entered and announced dinner. "I don't have time to explain it right now. Will you help me?"

"Of course. What do you need?"

I whispered a few sentences in her ear.

"That's all?"

"Yes. That should do it."

"Do what?"

"Set a nice little trap."

"A trap?" Violet asked.

"Not so loud," I said through a smile. "Don't worry, I'm not setting you up as bait."

"Who, then?"

"Me."

CHAPTER TWENTY-SIX

"No greeting for your old pal?"

"Jasper! What are you doing here?" I'd been so lost in my thoughts, I didn't realize someone had fallen into step beside me.

"I was nearby and decided to drop in. I hear there's been an exciting turn of events."

Jasper and I followed Muriel and Hugh into the dining room. "Yes, quite a bit has happened."

"You'll have to tell me after dinner. I'll wait with bated breath." He drifted off to the other side of the dining table.

Violet was seated not far from me. About halfway through dinner, during a lull in conversation, she said to Tug in a clear voice, ". . . nothing to worry about, Olive figured it out—who pushed Alfred, I mean." She shot a triumphant look in Lady Pamela's direction. "It's only a matter of time. She'll contact the inspect—"

"Violet!" I said.

"What? Oh." She glanced around the table, then murmured, "I didn't realize . . ."

Gwen cleared her throat. "Such lovely weather we had today. Where did you go on your drive, Monty?"

Conversation resumed, but it wasn't my imagination—there was a definite tension in the air for the rest of the meal.

AFTER DINNER, Violet insisted that Alfred wouldn't have wanted us to sit around like "sad sacks" and convinced Sebastian to move the gramophone to one of the doors that opened onto the terrace. Sebastian's collection of music included some records he'd brought back from America, and we danced across the terrace to the strains of *Dancing Time*. Aunt Caroline would have disapproved of the evening's entertainment, but I thought Violet was probably right. Excellent food, dancing, and music was exactly the right type of wake for Alfred.

Monty asked me to dance. As he took my hand, he said, "So you've figured it out. And let me guess—you won't give me even a hint?"

"No, I'm sworn to secrecy. I can't tell anyone until I speak to Inspector Longly."

"Probably not a good idea, keeping it to yourself."

"I know what I'm doing."

The music came to an end, and Jasper strolled up to us. "Cutting in on you, old boy," he said to Monty, who still held my hand. Monty didn't let go. "Well, I suppose that depends on what Olive wants, doesn't it?"

I twisted my hand out of Monty's grip. "Don't be a goose, Monty. Of course I'll dance with Jasper. We're all dancing with everyone," I said.

"If that's what you'd like." Monty stalked off.

"Touchy chap," Jasper said as we began to foxtrot.

"I don't know what's gotten into Monty," I said. "He's usually so good natured."

"*I* know," Jasper said.

Several beats of music passed. "Well, what is it?"

"He likes a clear playing field—no competition."

I stared at Jasper for a moment, then looked over his shoulder to where Monty stood, arms crossed as he watched Jasper and me, a frown wrinkling his forehead. "But that's silly. You and I are pals."

"Of course we are." Jasper smiled at me, and a warm sensation fluttered inside me. "Got the wrong end of the stick, doesn't he?"

Was that a hint of flirtation in his tone . . . or was it a challenge? Before I could respond, Jasper continued, "But you can't tell Monty that. Once he's in a mood, there's no talking to him."

Jasper directed our steps to the dim end of the terrace, away from the light glowing from the drawing room. "Now, what are you up to?"

"What do you mean?"

"That scene in the dining room you and Violet staged. What game are you playing at?"

"We're not playing at anything."

Jasper raised one eyebrow. "I don't believe you." He tightened his grip on my hand, and we whirled through a series of tight turns, his gaze locked on mine. "You're not dancing around the terrace without a care in the world—you're up to something. You can't fool me, you know. You're playing in deep waters. I have no doubt you figured out the murderer—that's just the clever sort of thing you'd do. It's the other bit that worries me."

I looked back at Monty. He was still glowering as he watched Jasper and me. For the little plan I'd set into motion with Violet, I needed someone with me for the rest of the evening. I'd thought I would ask Monty, but it didn't look as though he was in the mood to be helpful at the moment.

I returned my attention to Jasper. "Perhaps I am up to something . . . and I could use a little help," I said, realizing I'd rather have Jasper with me anyway. Obviously, Monty's mood blew hot and cold, something I hadn't known before. Jasper could be decidedly flighty about some things—like his clothing—but I knew I could trust him.

"Good," Jasper said. "That'll work out well, because I intend to stick to you like glue for the rest of the evening."

~

"WHEN I SAID I would stick with you for the rest of the evening, I had no idea that you were going to keep me up until dawn."

"It's not dawn," I said. "It's barely two o'clock. Sebastian's parties always go until the wee hours of the morning. Don't tell me you didn't know that." I adjusted the arrangement of pillows in my bed and stepped back for a critical look. "Will it do?"

Jasper stood beside me, his head tilted to one side. "In the dark? Yes. It will fool someone, but only for a moment or two."

"That's all we need." I moved to the main light switch near the door. "You go sit down on the floor over there on the other side of the wardrobe. I'll turn off the light and check if I can see you from this side of the room."

Jasper moved across the room and hunkered down on the far side of the hulking piece of furniture. I switched off the light, and darkness filled the room except for a band of moonlight coming in through the window where I'd pulled back the drapes. The pale shaft of light fell across the bed and showed the dim outline of what looked to be a figure under the blankets. I peered into the blackness around the wardrobe, but I couldn't see any shadows or an outline that resembled a person. "I think it will work."

I moved slowly across the room, hands extended in front of me so that I didn't bump into anything. I navigated around the chairs in front of the fireplace.

"Over here," Jasper said, and I turned a degree, following the sound of his voice.

My extended hand brushed against his fingers. I felt my way up his arm to his shoulder and sat down beside him. "Good idea to move the chairs slightly," I said. "If she has a torch, the wingbacks should shield us from her view, at least from the doorway."

I became aware of the scent of lime, which must have been Jasper's aftershave, as I settled back against the wall.

After a few moments of silence, Jasper asked, "How do you think Thea will do it?"

"She'll want to get me out of the way. Death by misadventure would be the best thing for her. The simplest method would be an overdose of sleeping powders," I said.

"Cold?"

"No. Why?"

"You shivered."

"I did? Well, it's odd to speak about someone plotting one's death."

"I can see how that would give you a bit of a chill. Would you like my jacket?"

"No. I'm fine. Thea's not going to kill me. We just need to catch her attempting it. She'll have exposed herself as the one person who had to silence me—surely the inspector will be able to arrest her then."

"It would be better if your inspector were here."

"Yes, I know, but I couldn't talk to him, and Thea is leaving in the morning. Going to Brazil—or so she says."

"Ah, I begin to see why you're so dead set on this scheme—it's for Violet, isn't it?"

"Yes. She shouldn't have to live in the shadow of Alfred's death."

"Your loyalty is astounding, you know." Jasper shifted position. "Someone might go to all this trouble for themselves, but rarely would someone do it for anyone else."

"Hush—did you hear that?"

Footfalls sounded faintly, grew louder, then continued past the door.

After a moment, Jasper said, "False alarm. Do you ever use sleeping powders?"

"No."

"Hmm. Might be an issue for Thea."

"Yes, but I'm sure Thea plans to tell the investigators I couldn't sleep and asked her for some powders. Tragic I took too many by mistake, that sort of thing."

"I suppose if that doesn't work, her other choice would be suffocation," Jasper said. "It's quiet. She could straighten the cushions and pillows, then pour some of the sleeping powder down your throat afterward and hope the doctor misses any signs of suffocation."

Hearing Jasper lay it out so analytically sent another shiver through me. "Enough about that," I said. "It doesn't matter what method she tries. She won't succeed."

"Quite. Your protector is here."

"You're not my protector. You're my witness."

"That's rather a comedown. Well, think of it however you like." His voice became serious. "You're quite sure it's Thea who will arrive?"

"Yes, why?"

"Because I don't fancy a bout of fisticuffs in the dark with some hefty man. Don't want to pull my punches then find out it's actually a man and I should have gone all out."

"It can't be a man. It was a blonde woman in a dress on the balcony who pushed Alfred."

"So a man couldn't wear a dress and a wig?" Jasper asked. "Sebastian does have a thing for costumes, you know."

"Yes, I know that, but only women were on this floor when Alfred was pushed," I said, my words coming slowly.

"You don't sound so sure of that."

"I'm only wondering where Sebastian was when Alfred died." The footmen had sworn no one else had gone upstairs, but they'd lie for Sebastian if he told them to . . . and he did have the rack of costumes in his studio. I rubbed my forehead. "Now you have me doubting myself." I shook my head and shifted so that I was sitting straighter against the wall. "But then how would Thea's pearls come to be on the terrace and her necklace shortened and mended? And I don't think she would recruit anyone to do this for her. It will be Thea," I said and told him about the pearls and how I figured out it was Thea who'd pitched Alfred over the balcony.

"Well, I can't fault your logic there, except for the fact that you can't figure out *why* Alfred was blackmailing her."

"Yes, it would make a much more reliable argument for Inspector Longly."

I felt Jasper's shoulder shrug against mine. "Who knows? Perhaps something to do with her husband's frequent extended overseas trips? Maybe he's not the upstanding businessman he wants everyone to believe he is. I've heard a murmur or two about him and his amazing success in business—questionable practices. I thought it was sour grapes, but maybe there's a bit of truth there."

We fell silent after that, except for Jasper's occasional complaint he couldn't feel his legs. Every time I heard footfalls in the corridor, I went rigid. My heartbeat sped up. Jasper leaned his head against the wardrobe, and I could tell from his breathing he'd fallen asleep.

By three o'clock, the household had settled down, and the only noises were the quarter hour chimes from the little clock on the mantelpiece and the occasional creak and groan of the house as it settled. I was considering putting my head on Jasper's shoulder and taking a short nap when I heard the click of the door latch releasing.

I gripped Jasper's arm with one hand and reached out to cover his mouth with my fingers, expecting him to make some sort of noise, but he came fully awake the moment I squeezed his arm and didn't make a sound. I used my grip on his arm to balance as I shifted so I was crouched, ready to spring up.

As the door swung open, the shadow of a figure stretched across the carpet to the foot of the bed.

"It's a child," I said to Jasper as I stood. I caught the back of the chair as the blood rushed tingling into my legs and feet. "Paul? Is that you?"

"Miss . . . Belgrave?" He scrubbed his hand across his hair and blinked as he came a few steps into the room. "Where's Muriel? I had a nightmare and want her to sing to me. She does that sometimes, and it helps me get back to sleep."

I went across the room to him. He was in his pajamas and had a bleary-eyed look about him. In the light from the hallway, he spotted Jasper, who'd stood up and moved toward us. "What's he doing?"

"A game," I said quickly. "We're playing a game."

"Topping!" He came fully awake. "I want to join."

"I'm afraid we can't do that. You should be back in bed. It's late." I put my hand on his shoulder to turn him to the door. "Let's go look for Muriel. I'm sure she's upstairs."

"But she's not. She's not in her room. I looked, and she wasn't there. I wanted her to sing for me because it helps me go to sleep," he repeated.

"That's nice of her. You must be very special. Mr. Eton tried to get her to sing once, and she wouldn't do it."

Paul nodded. "She only sings in the nursery. Mr. Eton used to ask her to sing. It makes her mad, and when he called her his songbird, that made her even madder, so I never call her that."

I'd been inching Paul to the door, but I stopped and dropped down onto my knees so my face was the same level as his. I put both hands on his shoulders. "Songbird? Are you sure that's what Mr. Eton called her?"

"Yes, not often, just every once in a while. It made her so angry, so I never do it."

I went cold all over. Little details—gramophone records and a few words casually spoken—hadn't seemed important, but now they slotted into place and created a picture that set my heart thumping. I stood up. "I was wrong." A band tightened around my chest, choking off my breath and my words. "I was wrong—so wrong."

CHAPTER TWENTY-SEVEN

ighting to draw in a breath, I dashed out the door and down the corridor to Thea's room. I threw the door back against the wall.

Muriel had changed out of her evening gown and now wore a day dress, a hat, and gloves. She stood at Thea's bed, a valise on the floor beside her feet. With her arm wrapped around Thea's shoulders, she held a glass to Thea's lips. The bang of the door against the wall startled Muriel, but Thea only tilted her head slightly and seemed to struggle to lift her eyelids.

I raced across the room, trying to ignore the constriction in my chest, and knocked the tumbler from Muriel's grasp.

She jerked her arm out from under Thea's shoulders. Thea's upper body flopped onto the pillows as Muriel spun away from the bed, her long beaded necklace whirling through the air. She gave my shoulder a hard shove as she turned.

I stumbled backward a few steps, caught my balance, then lunged for Muriel, who was charging for the door. She had a head start on me, but I grabbed the long necklace that was bouncing against her shoulder blades and yanked.

She jerked backward, hands at her throat. The necklace snapped and beads rained down, plinking onto the furniture and floor. Then Jasper was there, blocking Muriel's path to the door. He grabbed one of her wrists and twisted it behind her back, immobilizing her. Muriel writhed against Jasper's hold, but he captured her other wrist and imprisoned it behind her back. She jerked from side to side, panting.

He raised an eyebrow at me. "Shocking lack of manners."

My legs felt like pudding, but I moved to the bed and checked Thea. She was breathing. Some of the pressure on my chest eased, but it was still an effort to force out her name. "Thea?"

Her eyelids fluttered.

I pushed away from the bed and inhaled a raspy breath. "I think she'll be . . . okay. I'll get Sebastian . . . to call . . . a doctor." Muriel was still lunging and fighting against Jasper's hold, but her strength seemed to be diminishing. Her movements were getting smaller, and she was panting harder.

Jasper hitched one of Muriel's arms higher, which subdued her. Jasper said, "Run along. then. We'll wait for you here."

SEBASTIAN CLOSED THEA'S DOOR, leaving Dr. Evans with her, and stepped into the hall with Jasper and me.

The doctor and the police had been summoned, and Muriel was locked in an empty room on the top floor with a hefty footman standing guard outside until the police arrived. Paul, who'd run into Thea's bedroom with Jasper, hadn't seemed traumatized, and Mrs. Foster had been summoned. She'd called for Milly, who had taken Paul back to bed.

Sebastian released the door handle of Thea's room and ran his hand over his bony face. "You'll have to forgive me," he said to Jasper and me. "I'm not completely awake yet. *Muriel* killed Alfred? Why?"

"Muriel was the songbird. She has to be," I said.

"I'm sorry?" Sebastian said.

"Alfred was blackmailing Muriel. He used nicknames when he listed his blackmail targets in the notebook Violet found. The word *Songbird* was on the list, but I couldn't figure out who it could be. Not everyone on the list paid Alfred," I said, thinking of Monty, "so I assumed the person who Alfred called Songbird had refused to pay, and Alfred had let it go. It appears I was wrong—so wrong."

"But why?" Sebastian asked. "What reason would Alfred have to blackmail Muriel? She's so . . . bland."

"I think Alfred and Muriel must have known each other in America."

Jasper swiveled toward me. "Why would you think that? Has Muriel ever been across the pond?"

"I believe she has, at least from her vocabulary." I turned to Sebastian. "I lived in the States for a while, and Americans refer to the post as *mail* and instead of the word *rubbish*, they use the word *trash*. Muriel used both of those American terms. I noticed Muriel said she put Thea's letters in the mail that first day at the picnic, which made me think we might have that in common, a visit to the States. But when I asked her at dinner, she said she'd never traveled to the United States. And we know Alfred was in America too."

Jasper said, "It's a rather large country, though."

"But Alfred teased her—or perhaps taunted is a better word—at dinner before the Silver and Gold party. Remember?" I said, walking down the hall to Alfred's room. Speaking over my shoulder to the men following me, I said, "Alfred asked if Muriel would sing for us, and she said she couldn't carry a tune. There was an undercurrent between them. If she was the Songbird in Alfred's notebook, what better way to hide that talent than to pretend she couldn't carry a tune?"

Alfred's room was still empty, and the door was open. I clicked on the light. The boxes we'd filled with Alfred's belongings sat in a row by the door. "Thank goodness they're still here." I pulled out the records and flipped through them. "Yes, here it is.

Alfred knew she could sing because he'd heard her when she performed in vaudeville."

I separated one record from the others and read the label, "Muriel Webb, the Songbird Serenader, performing your favorite vaudeville ballads." I handed the record to Jasper. "I bet among those playbills Alfred had in his flat is at least one with Muriel on it along with the Dapper British Gents." I shook my head, angry with myself. "I should have looked at these more carefully."

"How could you know they were important?" Sebastian asked.

"Alfred doesn't have a gramophone in here, and he didn't have one in his flat. Why would he have kept these records hidden away in his wardrobe? Most people keep their records near the gramophone. I should have realized that these were important, but it didn't come together until Paul said Alfred called Muriel a songbird."

Sebastian stuffed his hands deep into the pockets of his dressing gown. "But then why did Muriel try to kill my sister?"

"Remember Violet's comment at dinner about me knowing who killed Alfred?" I tightened my grip on the record. "I thought it would smoke out the killer and make them come after me." I swallowed. "I was foolish. I thought it was Thea who'd killed Alfred, but it was really Muriel. She must have dressed in Thea's clothes, and I imagine she wore a wig. When Violet made the statement at dinner, Muriel must have decided to kill Thea. She could set it up so Thea would take the blame for Alfred's death. I'm sure we'll find a 'suicide note' Muriel prepared, which has Thea confessing to killing Alfred. And I would have fallen right in with it, fool that I was."

Jasper touched my arm. He was about to say something, but Dr. Evans tapped on the open door to Alfred's room. "Good news. Thea will awaken later, perhaps with a slight headache, but otherwise no worse."

Sebastian let out a shaky breath. "Thank you, doctor."

Despite all the carping between Thea and Sebastian, there was an affection between them—a prickly sort of affection, but affection nonetheless.

"I'll be by later tomorrow—er—today to check on her again," Dr. Evans said. He and Sebastian shook hands, then Dr. Evans said, "No need to ring for anyone. I'll show myself out. I'm sure you want to see your sister." He left, and the three of us went into Thea's room. Sebastian went directly to the bedside, where Thea lay unmoving.

I went to the writing desk and studied a piece of paper tucked under the corner of the jewelry box. Jasper looked over my shoulder and read the note aloud, "I'm sorry. I didn't mean to do it. Please forgive me." It was signed with Thea's name.

Sebastian came to stand on my other side. "It looks remarkably like Thea's writing."

"Muriel was Thea's secretary," I said. "She'd have plenty of correspondence to copy from. No, better not touch it."

Sebastian retracted his hand. "Of course, you're right. The police will want to see it exactly as it is."

"Yes, as well as this," Jasper said.

I hadn't heard him move away, but now he was across the room beside the bed, hunched over the valise that had been beside Muriel's feet when I had entered Thea's room earlier. "Someone must have kicked it during the scuffle," Jasper said. The valise lay on its side, clothes and shoes spilling out of it. "Look there, at the bottom." Jasper pointed to a glimpse of flaxen strands peeking out between a tangle of fabric.

"I recognize that wig," Sebastian said. "It's from my studio. She must have slipped in one day when I was in the darkroom and taken it."

"But how did she do it?" Jasper asked. "Wasn't she in the nursery watching the children during the fireworks?"

"No, she left." The three of us turned toward the piping voice. Paul peeked around a chair near the door.

I stretched out a hand. "Obviously, you didn't go back to bed. How long have you been listening?"

"A while. I came to check on Mum."

"She's fine. Just asleep. Come see for yourself," Sebastian said.

Paul crossed the room and leaned on the edge of the bed for a few seconds. "When will she wake up?"

"Later today," Sebastian said. "Now, what's this about Muriel leaving the nursery on the night of the fireworks?"

Paul twisted the button on his pajama shirt. "After Jane came up with a treat from Cook—she'd promised to send up punch and cakes for me and Rose—Muriel said Mum had changed her mind, and we couldn't watch the fireworks. I was going to sneak out of bed, but I got so sleepy I couldn't keep my eyes open no matter how hard I tried. I drifted off but woke up later. That's when I heard the pops of the fireworks."

"And you were determined to see them, weren't you?" Jasper asked. Paul swallowed, and Jasper said, "You snuck out of bed? I would have done exactly the same."

Paul glanced at Sebastian, who gave him a nod. "Yes," Paul said. "I was trying so hard to be quiet, but then I saw Muriel's door was open and *she* wasn't in bed. It wasn't fair she'd get to see them when we couldn't."

I crouched down, put a hand on his shoulder, and asked in a soft voice, "Then why did you say Muriel was in the nursery when I asked you?"

"Because she was—at first. When she put Rose and me to bed, she stayed up a while. I know because I checked. Every time I looked out, she was out there. It was only later that she left. You didn't ask if she'd been there the *whole* time, just if she was there."

I brushed the hair off his forehead where it was falling in his eyes. "Yes, you're absolutely right. Don't worry. You're not in trouble." I stood and sighed, exchanging a glance with Jasper. "This could have all been avoided if I'd asked the right question."

The door thumped against the wall. "Now see here, what's all this?"

Hugh stood in the doorway, his dressing gown wrapped around his tubby figure. What little hair he had stood straight up on his head. He held an unfolded letter and an envelope, which he waved around. "What's all this commotion? I'm a light sleeper at the best of times, but how's a man supposed to rest with all this noise?"

Sebastian ruffled Paul's hair, then turned to Hugh. "Ah—Hugh, old chap . . ." Sebastian's glance pinged between Jasper and me. "We have some—er—difficult news."

"Can't it wait until later? It's four in the morning. Shoving notes under doors and tramping in the corridors. Outrageous behavior. It wouldn't be tolerated at Stratham House."

"I'm sorry we woke you," I said. "Did Muriel leave you a note?"

"Yes—how did you know?"

"And she said she'd been called away," I said. "A sick relative of some sort, I expect?"

Hugh nodded. "Her aunt in Yorkshire."

I looked at Sebastian. "I'll take Paul back to bed," I said. Sebastian sighed, clearly not pleased to be the host at this particular moment. He walked across the room and clapped a hand on Hugh's shoulder. "Come down to the study, old boy. You're going to need a drink."

It was nearly noon the next day before things calmed down at Archly Manor. The local police arrived, followed by Scotland Yard. Thea awakened but kept to her room.

I sat across the desk from Inspector Longly in Sebastian's study. Jasper sat in the chair next to me, and Sebastian hovered in the back of the room by the bookshelves.

Inspector Longly had been questioning Jasper, having him tell every detail of the evening from his perspective. "And then I held tight to Muriel until we had her locked up," Jasper said. "I understand the local police chaps carted her off. Is she still about?"

Longly looked up from his scrawl of notes. "She's been transferred to London," he said, then moved his gaze to me. "She'll be charged with Alfred's murder as well as attempted murder."

The corkscrew of worry and tension inside of me unwound a few degrees. "That's wonderful news for Violet."

Longly put down his pencil. "Yes, but it could have gone so differently."

A white-hot rush of guilt raced through me. The more time I'd had to think about the events of the night, the more I regretted them. I sat forward and gripped the edge of the hefty desk. "I know, and I'm so sorry—when I think of what could have happened, I—well, I feel physically ill."

A tightness squeezed my lungs, and I closed my eyes for a moment to focus on drawing in a breath. "I never imaged it could be Muriel—" *Breathe. Take a slow breath. In. Out.* "Or that she'd be so desperate as to kill Thea."

The image of Paul, his eyes blurry with sleep, came to me, and a knife-sharp pain pierced me at the thought of how close he and Rose had come to being motherless. I knew how ghastly it was to not have a mother. The thought that I might have actually caused another child to be in that position . . .

Longly's words registered, and I dragged my thoughts back to the study. ". . . couldn't have waited until I arrived?"

"Setting a little trap seemed the best thing to do. I was so sure that Thea had pushed Alfred, and she was scheduled to leave the country today." Jasper gave me a small encouraging smile. I pulled in another breath, and it came easier this time. "Even if you had arrived before Thea left and talked to her, all she had to do was deny everything. There was no way to prove she'd actually done it. Even the piece of her necklace I found on the terrace wasn't proof she'd killed Alfred. All she had to say was her necklace broke sometime during the evening, and it had been mended."

Longly frowned at me. "Nevertheless, you shouldn't have interfered. I won't say anything else because I can see you're punishing yourself quite enough. And you shouldn't have interfered either, Mr. Rimington. It's always best to leave these matters to the police." He pulled his notebook toward him and focused on it. "I have everything I need at the moment, but I'll need to speak to you both later. You're free to go now."

Jasper held the door for me. As we walked down the hallway, I said, "I feel about the size of an ant."

"Nonsense," Jasper said. "The dutiful inspector had to give us a good talking-to. Probably in the regulations. Don't let him worry you. You caught your man—er, woman, I mean. That's the main thing."

"With your help," I said. "I don't want to think about what could have happened if you hadn't been there with me at the end. You were exactly right, you know. I move too quickly sometimes. It wouldn't hurt to slow down."

He grinned. "Only occasionally."

Gwen emerged from the drawing room. "There you are. We've been waiting for you." She took my arm and propelled me to a sofa where she plunked us down side by side. Violet and James were already sitting in chairs next to the sofa, and Monty folded the newspaper he held and strolled across the room. Tug sat slumped in a chair away from everyone else, sipping a drink.

Gwen said, "We want you to tell us everything that's happened. We can't get a word out of that inspector—infuriating man. Was it really Muriel who killed Alfred? Is it true?"

"Yes, it was Muriel," I said. "I thought it was Thea, but I was completely wrong." Funny how the more I said it, the easier it got. I explained about Thea's pearls, then said, "But it was Muriel. Alfred had a hold over her. She was Songbird."

Violet's eyes widened. "Alfred was blackmailing Muriel?"

"Yes, she and Alfred were on the same vaudeville circuit. She was the Songbird Serenader." Longly had unbent enough to confirm that his men in London had examined the playbills found in Alfred's flat. Both Muriel and Alfred were listed on several of the playbills.

"But Muriel's British. How did she end up in vaudeville?" Monty asked.

Longly had also given me what background they'd been able to find on Muriel. "Remember when Thea told us Muriel went to live with an aunt after her parents died? Well, that aunt was in America."

Violet said, "And Thea said Muriel and her relative didn't get along."

"That's right," I said. "After a year, Muriel ran away and used her singing to survive on the vaudeville circuit. Later, just like Alfred, she reinvented herself, applying for a position as a governess for a British family with five children traveling from America to London. After working for the Canniford family for a year, she replied to an advertisement and became Thea's secretary and governess. It was because of her relationship with Hugh that Alfred was able to use her past to blackmail her. Thea wouldn't have been thrilled to find out she was employing a former vaudeville performer, but Hugh's family . . ."

"So that's why Hugh departed so suddenly," Violet said as Sebastian came into the room.

"Hugh's gone?" I asked.

Sebastian nodded. "He left moments after the police said he could leave."

"As did Lady Pamela," Monty said. "Although, she seemed much more reluctant to leave."

"Lady Pamela's gone as well?" I'd missed more than I thought while Jasper and I were closeted with Longly. Lady Pamela's departure explained Tug's morose air. He hadn't moved from his chair and seemed to be only interested in the drink in his hand.

Monty tucked his newspaper under his arm. "Lord Harlan sent a dragon of a woman—an aunt, I believe—to collect Lady Pamela. They're off for an extended stay at some health resort."

Gwen and I exchanged a glance. I could tell that Gwen thought the same thing I did—Lady Pamela wasn't on her way to a spa.

Violet said, "I bet Lord Harlan's sent her to one of those exclusive hospitals for a drug cure."

Gwen and I stared at Violet. Gwen asked, "What?"

Violet raised her eyebrows. "You thought I didn't know?" She waved a hand dismissively. "Everyone knows—or suspected. Isn't that right?" Violet looked from James to Monty to Sebastian. "See? They know too. I don't know how someone could miss it, actually." She shifted toward me. "Now, Olive, let's get back to Muriel and Hugh. If his family found out about Muriel being a performer, they'd be horrified. Absolutely horrified. They're the highest of sticklers."

James said, "And I understand Hugh intends to run for Parliament."

Violet shook her head. "They'd *never* accept Muriel if they knew the truth. And can you imagine if it came out later and the gossip sheets got ahold of it?"

"That's precisely why Alfred blackmailed her," I said. "And why Muriel pushed him over the edge of the balcony. She didn't want him continually threatening to expose her. Hugh had proposed, and she was set to move on to a new life."

"But wasn't she in the nursery?" Gwen looked to me. "She went up after dinner."

"Muriel was in the nursery but not during the whole evening. Paul said he got sleepy and missed the fireworks. I think Muriel gave both the children some of the sleeping powder. Paul said Jane brought a special treat of punch and cakes Cook had sent up. Jane must have mentioned to Muriel that Thea had taken a sleeping powder."

"Why would they discuss Thea?" Monty asked.

"It wouldn't be unusual for Jane to mention something like that to Muriel," Gwen said. "After all, Muriel was on duty as both a governess and a secretary. Jane was probably letting Muriel know Thea wouldn't need her again that night."

"But how did Muriel do it?" Violet asked.

"After she put the children to bed, Muriel snuck down from

the nursery and changed into the gown Thea had worn that night, including the pearls. Muriel wore a blonde wig from Sebastian's studio to disguise herself. If anyone did see her, they'd assume it was Thea. Of course, I didn't see any details of who was on the balcony, but I suspected Thea because of the pearls."

"But you did figure it out eventually," Violet said. She hopped up from her chair and gave me a quick hug. "I don't know how to thank you."

"Just be careful who you get engaged to next time."

"Oh, I will. I'll probably become an old maid after this." she said, but her gaze strayed to James, who flushed up to the rims of his glasses.

TWO WEEKS LATER, I left the tube station and strode down the pavement, comfortable in the knowledge my rent was paid and I had funds in the bank. After Muriel was arrested, I'd returned to Parkview Hall with Gwen and Violet, where I'd borrowed Uncle Leo's secretary's typewriter and pecked out a report for Aunt Caroline with all the details of the incident at Archly Manor— well, almost all the details. I'd glossed over a few things, like my misplaced suspicions of Gwen. But on the whole, it was a thorough précis, complete with a detailed accounting of every penny spent.

Aunt Caroline had skimmed it and said, "Of course we'll cover your expenses, plus an extra fifty pounds above what we agreed on, I think."

It was an astronomical amount. When I protested, Aunt Caroline shook her head. "You saved Violet and proved Alfred was a wastrel. I'll not have any argument. I always pay my bills promptly," she'd said as she held out the paper to Gwen, who'd actually counted out the notes and pressed them into my hand.

The call of a newspaper boy drew me to the corner. I bought a newspaper and opened it to the Positions Wanted section.

Someone jostled my elbow, and I moved to the edge of the pavement. In the shadow of the building, I skimmed the columns until I found my ad.

Do you have questions but can't use conventional methods to find answers? Do you have problems? Discreet, confidential solutions obtained. Perplexing problems and delicate situations our speciality.

I closed the paper with a swell of satisfaction. I couldn't wait to see who replied.

THE END

Sign up for Sara's Notes and News at SaraRosett.com/signup to get exclusive updates, members-only giveaways, and new release notifications.

THE STORY BEHIND THE STORY

The idea for the High Society Lady Detective series came when I was writing a book in the *Murder on Location* series, which is set in modern times in the small Derbyshire village of Nether Woodsmoor. I was writing about the stately home, Parkview Hall, and a stray thought flitted through my brain. *What was Parkview Hall like in the 1920s? Who lived there?* The idea intrigued me, but I had a book to write. I put my nose back to the grindstone and finished off the book I was working on, but the idea of a historical series set in and around the world of Nether Woodsmoor stayed in the back of my mind. Once the modern book was finished, I dived into research and plotting.

I decided *Murder at Archly Manor* would be a more interesting story if my main character, Olive, was a bit of an outsider struggling to find her place in the world. Olive is related to the Stones of Parkview Hall but doesn't have their social standing—or their bank account—which, while not an ideal situation in real life, is an excellent starting point for a novel!

I love Golden Age mystery fiction as well as historical mystery novels, especially those set in the 1920s, so writing *Murder at Archly Manor* was one of the most enjoyable writing experiences I've had. The clothes! The slang! The music! In short, I loved every minute I spent researching. But because I love this type of mystery, it was also one of the hardest books to write.

I spent a lot of my time searching out details about life in 1923. What kind of stockings did young women wear? (Silk or rayon in light colors.) What was a hall porter? (A doorman on duty at the main entrance of a building of flats.) When was the sentence, "The quick brown fox jumped over the lazy dog," first used in type-writing manuals? (1890.) Did people use the term "sour grapes" in 1923? (Yes, it originated with Aesop's fables in ancient Greece.) Could someone go to the library in the British Museum and look at maps in 1923? (Yes.) When was the first telephone box intro-duced in London? (1920.) Was the term "country house weekend" used at the time? (No. The term "country house weekend" didn't come into the vernacular until later. In the early 1920s, people called their short getaways "Saturdays-to-Mondays.")

Besides researching the details of daily life, my research on the time period gave me a jumping off point for some of my charac-ters. The idea for making the owner of Archly Manor a society photographer came after I read about Cecil Beaton, who was one of the Bright Young People. Beaton attended Cambridge and made a name for himself with his photography. His sisters were his models, and his iconic portraits of the society set from the twenties capture the energy and angst of the time.

When I was working on the rough draft of this book, I searched for images of women from the early twenties for inspira-tion and discovered the silent film actress Colleen Moore. With her energy, her humor, her up-beat personality, and her work ethic, she captured the essence of Olive Belgrave. I spent a fun evening watching YouTube clips of Colleen Moore. Sadly, most of her silent movies are lost, including *Flaming Youth*, which popular-ized the term *flapper*, but snippets of her movies remain as well as still photography with some gorgeous costumes. Check out my Pinterest board about Murder at Archly Manor for more fashion, character inspiration, and other tidbits from the 1920s.

Much of my research was spent reading fiction—it was hard

work, but someone had to do it!—published in the early 1920s, including *The Secret Adversary, The Mysterious Affair at Styles, The Murder on the Links,* and *The Man in the Brown Suit,* all by Agatha Christie. Other titles from my 1920s reading list: *Whose Body?* by Dorothy L. Sayers and *The Astonishing Adventure of Jane Smith* by Patricia Wentworth. I also read Georgette Heyer's first detective novel, *Footsteps in the Dark,* although it was published later, in 1932. *Highland Fling* by Nancy Mitford isn't a mystery, but it depicts the lifestyle of the Bright Young People and captures the mood and dialogue of the times.

Nonfiction books helped round out my research, including *Long Weekend: Life in the English Country House, 1918-1939* by Adrian Tinniswood, *The Golden Age of Murder* by Martin Edwards, and *Bright Young People: The Rise and Fall of a Generation, 1918-1940* by D. J. Taylor.

I hope you enjoyed Olive's first case. She'll be back in her second adventure, *Murder at Blackburn Hall.* If you'd like to keep up with me and my books, please sign up for my newsletter. I'd love to stay in touch!

ABOUT THE AUTHOR

USA Today bestselling author Sara Rosett writes fun mysteries. Her books are light-hearted escapes for readers who enjoy interesting settings, quirky characters, and puzzling mysteries. *Publishers Weekly* called Sara's books, "satisfying," "well-executed," and "sparkling."

Sara loves to get new stamps in her passport and considers dark chocolate a daily requirement. Find out more at SaraRosett.com.

Connect with Sara
www.SaraRosett.com

Moving is Murder
Staying Home is a Killer
Getting Away is Deadly
Magnolias, Moonlight, and Murder
Mint Juleps, Mayhem, and Murder
Mimosas, Mischief, and Murder
Mistletoe, Merriment and Murder
Milkshakes, Mermaids, and Murder
Marriage, Monsters-in-law, and Murder
Mother's Day, Muffins, and Murder